He brings me c  touching. Rubbing says, "Do you understand what I'm saying?"

"Yes, I do." But my mind is growing cloudier, thrown off kilter by his nearness—the inexplicable animal magnetism that draws me to him or maybe it's my own sleep deprivation that has me lifting my arms, while my fingers seek out the soft hair at the nape of his neck to caress. I softly moan as our mouths come together and our tongues join. A longing sparks inside of me, making me want more as my body presses against his, but he takes a deep breath and pulls away.

"I didn't come here to seduce you." His voice is firm as he creates distance between us.

"I didn't think you did." I shake my head. "I'm the one that kissed you. Sorry, if that's not what you wanted." Now I feel embarrassed. No, that's too mild a term. Mortified is more like it.

"It's what I want…and even more," he says gruffly, passion glowing brightly in his eyes as he reaches out and pulls me to him.

Orange Blossoms-
Love Blooms

by

Dalia Dupris

California Hearts

Orange Blossoms-Love Blooms

Cover Art by *Abigail Owen*

The Wild Rose Press, Inc.
PO Box 708
Adams Basin, NY 14410-0708
Visit us at www.thewildrosepress.com

Publishing History
First Mainstream General Rose Edition, 2020
Print ISBN 978-1-5092-3146-1
Digital ISBN 978-1-5092-3147-8

California Hearts
Published in the United States of America

Dedication

For my husband, George, and daughter, Tatiana,
for their unconditional love and support.

Acknowledgements

Thank you to the loyal readers of my first manuscript drafts: Dana Jackson, Yolanda Johnson, Regina Golden, Denise Knight, Gina Tucker, and Priscilla Cruz. Your enthusiastic feedback meant the world to me. The honest critiques of my fearless fellow writers, L'Tanya Leone and Patty Cooper, helped me to craft a better story. It meant a lot to me that Maria Coleman, my recently departed friend, always saw me as a writer. I'm grateful to Marlene Ochetti's encouragement of my artistic endeavors. Judi Fennel, your feedback is invaluable and has made me a stronger writer. I am thankful to the organizers of the California Dreamin' Conference for the opportunity to meet my wonderful Editor, Ally Robertson of The Wild Rose Press. Her belief in my stories made my publication dreams a reality. I am appreciative of my encouraging friends and caring family of five siblings: Betty Spillman, Dewayne Jackson, Donald Jackson, Tony Jackson, and Dana Jackson. If Clay were still alive, I know he'd be excited too. I am especially indebted to my husband, George, and my daughter, Tatiana, for their patience and support of the countless hours I spend behind closed doors crafting imaginary scenarios, instead of hanging out with them in the real world. Love makes all things possible.

Chapter 1
Round One

The doorbell chime echoes throughout the house, signaling that it's show time. No more rehearsing in front of the mirror. This is it—the real deal, the day of reckoning I've been anxiously anticipating for the last forty-eight hours. This has to be what it feels like when the bell has rung and the boxer hovers in a corner, restlessly pacing, prepped and prepared to enter the ring, hoping for a win, secretly praying that he won't be the one knocked out cold on the floor, disoriented and defeated.

Holding my arms close to my body, I ball my hands into tight fists, keep my left hand in front of my face, positioned to block an opponent's oncoming blows, while my right fist jabs at an invisible enemy. I need to get a grip and stop imagining myself as some kind of Muhammad Ali. Even though Ol' Man Cole is fifteen minutes early, it's not smart to keep him waiting. I got this.

I shake out my hands, scrutinize my face, decide to add one final stroke of mascara, a dash of lipstick and I'm *almost* ready to head downstairs, but first I smooth down my bangs, which perfectly conceal the Z-shaped scar that juts out above my left eyebrow like a miniature lightning bolt.

Walking down the stairs, I straighten my shoulders,

take a deep, calming breath, and shake off any doubt that the elderly banker will be anything less than impressed with the ingenuity of my plan. I pause to peer through the peephole, casting a quick glance at the one person on the planet who has the power to crush my family's destiny. Do I resent the fact that a complete stranger who knows absolutely nothing about Hartland Orchards has an input in how we conduct our family business? Not much, but sort of a lot.

What? Incredulous, I shake my head and blink a couple of times, not believing what—or should I say *who*—is standing on my porch. What the heck is *he* doing here?

Staring back at me with a huge grin across his smooth brown face is not the paunchy, old, bald banker I'm expecting, instead it's the last person I want to see now—or ever really. Will Jared Chandler ever disappear from my life? Highly unlikely since he's our family attorney.

I stand motionless and silent in front of the door as I try to come up with a good way to get rid of him as quickly as possible. Subtle hints are lost on him. Even telling him outright that I no longer want to date him failed to penetrate his over-developed ego.

"Elaine, are you going to open the door?" The irritation in his voice is so like him.

He's been standing there for less than one minute and his voice is already laced with impatience. Well, he can stay out there and wait a while longer. If I don't move or respond, maybe he'll do an about-face and leave. Who am I kidding? He's so obstinate that he wouldn't have any problem waiting me out all morning.

How does he know it's me on the other side of the

door? Undoubtedly, he remembers that my sister Morgan leaves for her teaching job by seven. These darn high heels and their loud clicking-clacking sound reverberating against the wooden floors are a dead give-away; obviously, it isn't my father or uncle delaying his entrance. Now, if I had stuck to my usual jeans and sneakers, he wouldn't have heard me.

"Jared, this is not a good time." I'm so over dealing with Jared's unrequited love, especially when so much is resting on this morning's proceeding exactly as I've planned it. "Can you come back later?"

"No, I can't." Clearing his throat, he raps against the door one more time. "I would appreciate it if you wouldn't play these silly games."

"I'm only requesting that you come back later." I don't have time for this. I want to rehearse one more time before Ol' Man Cole arrives at the ranch. Of course, I won't call him that to his face. I've never met the man, but anyone who is a senior banker and has the ultimate decision-making authority to extend our delinquent loan has got to be elderly. A younger man wouldn't have the necessary years of experience to be able to say yes or no to my request.

Reaching into my pocket, I pull out the crumpled sheet of lined note paper containing the outline I created two days ago, which is when my father first informed me that the senior banker had business down the road from us. He had somehow convinced Ol' Man Cole to stop by the ranch. After all, I'm under no pressure. It's only my family's forty-year-old orange groves that are at stake.

"Elaine, I'm still here." He mumbles something undecipherable under his breath. Actually, it *is* decipherable—it's a bunch of swear words. "I'm not leaving until you let me in."

"Okay, fine." I shove the paper back into my pocket and glance at my watch. The sooner I open the door, the sooner he'll leave. I hope.

I've already meticulously planned exactly how the morning *should* progress. I'll greet the banker at the door with a confident smile and a firm handshake before we make our way to the office. After offering him a cup of coffee or tea, I'll thoroughly describe my short- and long-term profit projections. Last will be the tour of the groves before we'll proceed to the *one* area where the fruit are most ripe before continuing on to the newly developed trees that are guaranteed to have our profits soaring. There's no way the banker won't be impressed.

"Hello, Jared." Sighing, I don't open the door completely, but wide enough to see his green eyes, wavy brown hair, khaki slacks, and matching polo shirt. We dated for over five months and I know how much attention he puts into his appearance. Today is no exception. He always looks well put together—at least on the outside. It's the inside that's a mess.

"I was hoping I'd see you." His thin lips tilt to one side in a familiar smirk.

"Well, the odds are that you would find me here since this is my home." *Breathe evenly. It's broad daylight. My father is upstairs, and Uncle Robert is here, too. Every morning he arrives by six thirty, come rain or shine. Jared wouldn't dare try anything with them around, would he?* "Why are you here?"

"I've missed you." He reaches out toward my cheek.

Startled, I step back, stumbling in my haste to avoid his touch. "Don't do that." I clear my throat, grasp the door, and block his entrance.

He chuckles. Perfectly white, veneered teeth complete his smug grin, which I *used* to think, was attractive.

"We meant something to each other. You think I'd forget that? My feelings for *you* haven't changed." He pauses and takes his time perusing every inch of my body with those calculating eyes. "Girl, you *still* look good. You know that, right?"

"Jared, I repeat, why are you here?" My voice is steady, masking any evidence of the underlying tension that causes a trail of sweat to trickle down my back. "I'm in a meeting."

He throws back his head and laughs. "I like you like this—all feisty. It's becoming." He licks his lips. "I like it a whole lot. It turns me on." His voice deepens as he leans forward, closing the distance between us.

"You can keep those thoughts to yourself." My eyes meet his. "I meant every word I said when I broke it off."

I'll never forget how angry he had become when he finally understood that I wasn't being coy or playing games when I ended our relationship. When he'd hit me, I was stunned and angry. I had held my hand to my face and tried to block out the sudden images of my mother that had flashed before my eyes. He had rambled on about how I should be grateful that he had chosen me to be the future Mrs. Jared Chandler. My mother or Jared… I am a woman now, not a child, and I'm not putting up with anyone's crap.

In an effort to distance myself from this

unpredictable person, I press my shoulder against the door to close it, but it's as if he's read my mind as he shoves his foot inside the house and suddenly grabs my wrist, squeezing it so tightly that I feel my pulse throbbing. *Remember to count, one thousand, two thousand, three thousand. Breathe deeply. If fear takes over, he wins.*

"You are mine," he says evenly, taking another step forward, so that our noses almost touch. I see the faint scattering of freckles on his cheeks and the muscle twitching along his angular jaw.

"This is the twenty-first century," an unfamiliar, authoritative voice says.

My head jerks up to take in the sight of a tall man with strong features and a dark suit step onto the porch. He couldn't possibly be Ol' Man Cole, could he? I suppose it's possible, even though I've grossly miscalculated his age and overall appearance by a long shot. Whoever he is, his timing is impeccable. Taller by a good four inches, he hovers over Jared, his voice deep, steady, and menacing. "Slavery is over. One human being cannot own another." His nostrils flare slightly as he folds his arms across his broad chest.

"Let go." I struggle to twist my arm free of Jared's hold, not wanting to be *that* woman—the one who stands by mutely, not doing anything to help herself. Sadly, we've all seen that movie and can't believe how she's so useless, seemingly unable to lift a finger, even if her life depended on it, and it usually does.

Jared's steely grip tightens, causing me to wince as a wave of nausea unfurls in my stomach. I'm trying not to throw up. Not today. Not now. But at least I tried something. However, beads of sweat are popping up on my forehead. It's better than vomiting. It's all relative.

"I don't know who you are, but this"—Jared holds up my arm as if it's a trophy—"is none of your business." His face flushes red with rage as he calculatingly eyes the interloper.

"Let her go." There's an undeniable threat interwoven into those three simple words.

He steps toward Jared, clearly not intimidated. He's big—not just tall—with muscular forearms and eyes dark as onyx.

"Elaine, I've got the table set up." My father enters the foyer, and Jared quickly releases his grasp, dropping my arm like so much discarded rubbish. A crease mars my father's brow as his eyes dart from one man to the other before lingering on me. "What's going on here?"

"Good morning, Mr. Hart." Jared smiles and shakes my father's hand as if nothing out of the ordinary has happened. "It's good to see you again. I have an appointment with your brother." He raises a hand in the direction of the house. "Is he in, sir?" His voice is as sweet as syrup.

My father doesn't answer. His gaze never leaves my wrist, which I've been unconsciously rubbing.

"You okay?" Confusion and something unrecognizable clouds his eyes. He looks at me, waiting for answers.

I blink, unable to speak, before I hastily put my hands behind my back. Silence permeates the air and circles around us like a cumulus cloud, filled with all the potential of a coming storm. Seconds feel like minutes as I struggle to think of an acceptable reply that won't escalate an already tense situation. All the things I shouldn't say pop up, those unbidden thoughts that do not need to see the light of day. Do not say *Jared is violent. He wouldn't let go of my arm. He reminds me of my mother. Walk on thin ice around that one.* I absorb the concern in my father's kind eyes. I affectionately pat his hand and see the veins that appear more pronounced each week.

"Yes." The word comes out in an unexpected whisper that even *I* can barely hear. Clearing my throat, I remember being in a high school play where the teacher was adamant that we had to project so the people sitting in the back row of the auditorium would be able to hear us. I use that voice now—strong, confident and clear. "I'm good, Dad."

"Jared, go on back to the office. I think Robert is still in there." His words are directed at Jared, but his eyes never leave my face.

"Sure thing, sir." Still grinning, he nods at my father. "And I want to say that you are looking well rested this morning." He winks at me before disappearing into the house.

My father continues to look at me with concern. All I have to do is say something, but, honestly, what version of the truth would be okay? Tell him that Jared was squeezing my wrist so tightly that I felt the blood pounding through my veins, that I was on the verge of fainting or that my heart was beating so hard that I was afraid it would pop out of my chest?

"I had just opened the door for Jared when..." Flustered, I look up into the stern face of this man, whose timing couldn't be more perfect. "I'm sorry. I didn't get your name."

"This is David Cole. From the bank." My father tilts his head toward the tall, imposing figure blocking our doorway. "I've told you about my daughter."

"Nice to meet you, Ms. Hart." His voice no longer contains a hint of menace. He looks at me curiously, or is it an expression of concern? "Your father speaks very highly of you."

"Please, call me Elaine." Although I'm grateful for his intervention, I'm also embarrassed that he witnessed my ex boyfriend's rough handling of me.

I take a moment to collect my thoughts from the places they scattered when I saw Jared standing on the porch. When we first began dating, I didn't know that his confidence was really a case of arrogance and cockiness that bordered on narcissism. Had only five minutes elapsed since I opened the front door?

How much of my conversation with Jared had David Cole overheard? Hopefully, not much. Because *this* is not the first impression I was hoping to make with the man who has the power to take over our land. I need to show him that I'm not some damsel in distress, that whatever he saw or heard a few minutes ago is not relevant to my handling of Hartland.

"Okay, Elaine."

He holds out a hand. My fingers disappear in his large, firm grip. For a minute, I think his hands are sweaty, until it dawns on me that *my* hands are damp, not his. Could this be any more awkward? I attempt to inconspicuously wipe my hands on my skirt.

Mr. Cole's eyes shift downward, and he looks at me with a hint of a smile. "Then you have to call me by my first name which is David."

"Now that introductions are out of the way, let's get down to business," my father says firmly.

****

We follow behind my father as he heads to the office down the hall toward the back of the house. Later, *if* he does ask me again about Jared, I'll come up with something that sounds plausible. But, for now, I'm relieved that we're moving on to something else.

"Excuse me. I have to take care of something before I join you."

Slipping into the kitchen before my father can respond, I head straight to the cabinet and remove four hand-blown crystal glasses. These are just a few of the precious items my mother left behind in her haste to discard her old life and embrace her new adventures. I need to stop stalling and head back into the home office to start this meeting with David Cole. Were my assumptions ever wrong—old, paunchy, bald... not one of those words does him justice. The man looks like he just sauntered off the pages of *GQ* magazine.

My goal was to impress David with my knowledge of the groves and my strategy to tackle the challenges of the drought, not to have him wonder if I was more adept at handling the orchards than I am at handling my man, or rather my ex, to be more exact. Thank God Jared is no longer part of my life, except that, of course, he is. It's not easy to get rid of a man who is your family's attorney. It makes sense that people don't mix work and pleasure. I've learned my lesson and won't be making the same mistake twice.

Flushed, I make my way to the sink, turn the faucet on, and splash cold water on my cheeks, carefully avoiding getting my bangs wet. No need to have my hair look as frazzled as I'm feeling.

"Are you all right?"

Standing in the entrance to the kitchen is David,

looking perplexed, probably by the sight of my water-drenched face. Obviously, he entered the room while the water was running, and I was bent over the sink.

"I'm fine."

I can only imagine what he's thinking. As for me, I'm wondering if it's possible for this day to get any worse. No. I can't think like that. I'm going to turn it around, but, right now, cold water is trickling down my face and onto the front of my blouse. I grab a paper towel and blot my cheeks and chest.

"I'm just a little warm." I glance down to find my wet green silk top is molded to my breasts. Great. Maybe when I look back at him, he'll see that I need some privacy and give me a moment.

Nope. It's not that kind of morning when things go exactly as planned or even *slightly* as planned. Glancing up, I see that he's now entered the room and is walking toward me. I fight the urge to step back, away from his now obvious concern and his masculine scent. But not wanting to appear both crazy and rude, I don't move.

"That was—intense back there." His voice is low, as if he wants to make sure that no one else can hear us.

"It was." I came here to compose myself, but the sound of his deep voice is not helping. Instead, I feel more vulnerable, as if he can see right through me and knows how scared I was for a few minutes. "My dad is probably wondering where you are."

"I told him I wanted a drink of water. He directed me here." He pierces me with eyes so dark they look black.

"Oh." I walk over to the trashcan, creating some distance between us to discard the crumpled wet towels. "I appreciate your help. I'm good now. There's coffee and tea in the office, but I was going to bring in some lemonade, and we can get started with our meeting." Taking the pitcher of lemonade from the refrigerator, I hold it in front of me, hoping that it's covering at least part of my wet blouse. "Or did you just want water?"

"Lemonade sounds good." He looks searchingly at me. "Did you want to reschedule?"

"No." I blurt out the word more abruptly than I intended. "Thank you, though. I know you squeezed us into your schedule. Give me a few minutes, and I'll join you in the office."

I control the urge to turn him around and shove him out the door. What I wouldn't give for a chance to push a magical DELETE button and do the last thirty minutes over. But it's too late. David Cole saw something that no one else in my family has seen: the dark side of Jared and how scary it can be. Time for me to go in there and be tough; show him that I'm no victim waiting to be rescued.

After he's finally left the room, I fill the glasses with chunks of ice and the lemonade before placing them on a tray. Closing my eyes, I recite a chant I learned in one of my many abandoned yoga classes, *gah-rang-gah*. After repeating it three more times, I feel slightly more composed. I don't know if those words mean something in another language, but they help just the same. Morgan, my twenty-four-year-old sister, thinks that if I saw a therapist, the nightmares would disappear, but I don't need to talk to a professional. I calmed myself down quite nicely.

I grimace at the reflection staring back at me in the gilded oval mirror hanging outside the office door. Usually, I don't bother with makeup, but today I put forth an effort, hoping that maybe it would provide me with a boost of courage and poise, since I'm uncomfortable with even the *thought* of making a presentation. The peach lip-gloss and coral blush have faded, as has the carefully applied eye shadow that is now nonexistent. What did I expect after dousing myself with water? Not that it matters anyway. It's not my looks that matter; it's what I have to say. Still, it wouldn't hurt if I didn't look as wilted as I feel. I rehearse what I hope appears to be a poised, confident smile before walking into the room.

Before I finish setting the tray down, my Uncle Robert bursts into the room and quickly thrusts his hand out to David.

"Robert Hart here," he says while taking his usual seat across from my father at the opposite end of the table. "Hope I didn't miss anything. Our attorney just needed to drop off some paperwork."

"Mr. Cole met Jared earlier." Dad sets a stack of folders on the table.

"Please call me David." He casts a sideways glance in my direction before he turns his chair to face my uncle. "I met him at the door." His deep voice is even and doesn't reveal any of the tension-filled scene that just played out between him and Jared.

"Excellent. Excellent. Glad you met him. Jared's a damn fine attorney. I brought him in to help with our legal affairs." Uncle Robert leans back in his chair and folds his hands over his protruding belly. "We've got the situation under control. Just a little behind in our payments. Nothing major. It's happened before. We always manage to dig our way out. Twenty-five acres, forty years, we know what we're doing." Focusing on

David, he leans forward. "No need for you to come all the way out here."

"I asked him to come." My father clears his throat and turns to David. "I appreciate you taking the time out of your busy schedule to meet with us. When I learned that you had a meeting that wasn't far from here, I suggested you come by to talk to Elaine and see the orchards for yourself. She has a plan that I'm sure you'd be interested in hearing."

"Humph, I'm not so sure about that." Uncle Robert scowls. "My baby brother here"—he thrusts a finger toward my father—"trusts Elaine to come up with a solution. I keep telling him that we've got this under control."

"My uncle has more traditional views. However, the strategy I'm proposing is—" Before I can finish my sentence, Uncle Robert interrupts.

"Ten goddamn acres to experiment with is too much for my liking." He swivels around in his chair so that his back faces me. "I don't care what *anyone* says, no school can teach you how to run a farm. Sometimes all you end up with is an educated fool. Hell, people were farming from the beginning of time. Pops sure as hell didn't tell us to get school learnin' to do what our people been doin' for decades." The ends of his words disappear as his temper rises. He pounds a beefy fist on the desk. "You plant the damn trees in the ground and get on with it. End of story."

So much for Uncle Robert being able to control his temper and displaying a modicum of professionalism to the one man who controls our family legacy. Nope, that would be asking *way* too much of him.

"Robert is passionate about doing things the same

way we always have." My father smiles, seemingly unperturbed by his sibling's angry outburst. "It's his belief that things will work themselves out."

That's my father, forever the peacekeeper in the family. Whether it was Morgan and I fighting as kids or his brother getting all worked up, he always aims to resolve things amicably.

"I have a different take on the situation which is what I'd like to share with you." I pointedly turn toward my uncle, hoping that my piercing glare will quiet him so I can continue with my presentation. "My uncle is referring to a time when farmers didn't have concerns about global warming. People may try to dispute its validity, but to those working with natural resources, we know that we've had less rain and the fruit yield is low. It is *not* a coincidence."

"Oh hell, spare me that malarkey." Uncle Robert abruptly stands, almost knocking over his chair. "Global warming, my ass."

"Robert, watch your language." Dad eyes David apologetically.

"Elaine is right. We never had this long of a dry spell. Call it what you want, but it's real. At least she came up with a plan to tackle it which is a lot more than either of us did." He purses his lips, looking distracted. "Times change. We have to try something else."

"Are we really going to consider her plan?" Uncle Robert's disgust is evident as he asks the question to no one in particular.

"I'd like to at least hear it since I'm here."

Do I notice a hint of impatience in David's tone? I can't say that I blame him. Uncle Robert can challenge anyone's patience. I remember that my father said the banker was on a tight schedule and just barely able to squeeze us in his busy calendar.

"Suit yourself." Uncle Robert shakes his head. "I've already heard Elaine's idea, and you know how I feel about it. David, sad to say your trip here was a waste of time. Give us a little time, and oranges will be falling off of those trees. Mark my words."

Even though my father and uncle are two years apart and both have speckled black-and-silver hair and brown eyes rimmed with a trace of blue, the similarities stop there. My father is as easy-going as my uncle is cantankerous. Now that he has left the room, the meeting can finally begin.

The problem is that between me expecting Ol' Man Cole and, instead, being greeted by one of the best-looking men I've ever seen, Jared painfully grabbing my wrists, and Uncle Robert's outrageous outburst, I'm feeling less confident by the minute. I barely slept last night and not from the nightmares about my mother's treatment of me as a child, but because I was dreading this presentation. I'm sure that rich, gorgeous David Cole, with his dark brown skin and perfect haircut is thinking that I'm a mess. I quickly touch my still damp, crumpled blouse and remember my streaked eye makeup while admiring David's impeccable dark navy suit, crisp white shirt and red tie. On top of it all, he was probably just being polite, saying that he wanted to hear my recovery plan when the truth is he's probably thinking that if it isn't good enough for my uncle to get behind it, why should he?

"Elaine?" The optimism in my father's voice is not contagious.

Nope, I'm not feeling it. But I will do anything for

Hartland Orchards. While I accept responsibility for the past events that shattered my family, I will not be the reason for my family's future legacy being destroyed.

"Why don't you share your brilliant strategy?" Clearly, my father is my biggest fan. But will David be impressed, or will he focus on the glimpse he had of what went down with Jared? I can't allow myself to get distracted wondering if he thinks I'm not equipped to handle the crops any better than I could handle a hostile man.

"I don't know if it's brilliant, but I'm confident that it *will* make up for the deficits reflected in our profit margins."

There's something about him that exudes an air of confidence and authority. I'm not thrown off by his good looks as much as I am by his distracted expression. When we were standing in the kitchen, it was like he was another person, but now he seems preoccupied. Who can figure out men?

"As you know, the drought has negatively impacted our citrus production. Unfortunately, the *quality* of the fruit has also been undermined by the lack of rain."

"Your father has shared many of his concerns with me." David impatiently taps his long fingers against the table and stifles a yawn. Gone is the gentleness I observed in the kitchen. "Though I recently relocated from Northern California, I'm aware of the weather conditions in Southern California *and* how they have created a challenging economic situation for our clients here. While I can empathize with your plight, I have to look at the bottom line."

"Of course," My father's voice brims with pride.

"Hartland Ranch is a family-owned business that has been profitable for over forty years."

"Until now," David adds matter-of-factly, his expression one of barely disguised boredom.

I admit he did a great job of putting Jared in place, and I'm grateful, but, right now, as we talk about the business, he appears disinterested. Has he already written us off as a loss? God, I hope not.

When he opens a black leather portfolio and pulls out a legal-size manila folder, I cringe, knowing now that his only concern is the bottom line. Can I honestly blame him? Banks are in the business of making money.

"These figures reflect the last three years you've been doing business with us."

Except for the grandfather clock loudly ticking off each minute, there's complete silence as my father and I review the lined ledger sheets. Hartland Ranch is spelled out in bold black letters at the top of the paper, but it's the bright red numbers at the bottom of the page that capture my attention. I've crunched these numbers myself, not once, but countless times, unrealistically hoping that, at some point, a new outcome would emerge. But this is different, seeing them impersonally presented by an impartial stranger has me squirming in my seat. Okay, so maybe he's not impartial since he represents the bank that holds the loan.

"As you know, you are behind in your payment for the *third* time in the last fiscal year." Before selecting a pen and circling the deficit ledger balance, his dark eyes scrutinize my father's face. "We are concerned—"

"Of course, you are," my father interrupts. Sitting up straighter, he continues, "I would feel the same way, if I were in your shoes." He tilts his head toward me. "Elaine has created a foolproof strategy that will enable us to bring our delinquent account up to date. We'll be staying in the black in the future." He rises from his chair, stands behind me, reassuringly resting his calloused hands on my shoulders. "Our resident expert can take you to see the orchards for yourself."

"You sound confident," David says evenly.

He looks confused as he glances over my father's shoulder, his eyes pausing at the blurry photographs I took of the orchards when I was in sixth grade. The pictures show what the groves look like during each season, from winter's first frost through the lushness of a full harvest, when the trees overflow with ripe oranges. My father insisted on hanging the prints, although they are clearly not display-worthy. David squints, apparently trying to get the pictures into better focus.

"I am. Elaine's strategy is fail-proof. As a matter of fact, I'm not needed here." He folds his arms, signaling an end to his participation in the conversation. "I'm going to leave the two of you alone, so she can fill you in on the relevant details." He extends a hand to David. "Again, thanks for squeezing us into your schedule."

"No problem. Elaine has my full attention." David glances one last time at the photographs, shakes his head, then turns his chair toward me.

Not expecting the intensity of his gaze, I avert my eyes and look down at his folded hands, noticing that he isn't wearing any rings or any other jewelry. My thoughts involuntarily turn to Jared. Now, there is a man who never leaves the house without a gold chain dangling from his neck and his Harvard class ring boldly displayed on his finger.

Refocusing, I walk over to the whiteboard, scan my legal pad and start writing out my calculations. Finally, I'm feeling more in control of the direction the conversation has taken. When I'm done, half of the board is covered with data on the avocado industry.

"You may be wondering why I've provided you with a plethora of information on avocados."

"You've got me there. That is a *plethora* of information."

His deep voice sounds mocking as he sets down his pen and leans back in his chair. The no nonsense tone he used with Jared was impressive, but I don't really like it when he's using it with me.

"I can use a different word if you prefer." Darn, why did I use *that* word? When I'm anxious, out pops the uncommon word. I know my plan will save Hartland. His appearance isn't affecting me. Oh, he's good to look at, in the way one might admire a well-sculpted piece of marble, the strong lines of his nose, the firm mouth and dark eyes that give no clue as to what he's thinking. But all the warm concern from earlier has disappeared. I guess I'm now meeting the businessman who's all about the numbers. I sit back down and slide him a bound copy of the data I've been compiling for the last year. "It means a *lot*."

"I *know* what the word means." His lips tighten into a grimace as his eyes pierce me with a lacerating look.

"Of course, I didn't mean to imply that you didn't." The words come tumbling out in an apologetic mumble. *Way to go, Elaine*. He scans the report so quickly that I wonder if he even read one word.

"What does any of this *plethora of information* have to do with oranges?" He holds up the report like it's a wasted use of paper.

Okay, that may be a slight exaggeration, but he *does* hold it up like it's unimportant, shaking my carefully typed and printed pages so the edges flutter in the air.

"I'm getting to that." I say. "There is other—"

"I don't have much time," he interrupts while picking up his cell phone and intently focusing on the black screen as if it had just rung—which it didn't. "I'd like to stick with the groves." He clears his throat.

"Fine." Talk about rude. I could say something about his phone etiquette, but I won't. I need him. Or rather, Hartland needs the bank to not seize our property. Also, I haven't shared the most exciting part of the presentation; the part where I explain how the new avocado groves are going to propel us out of the darkness of this financial hole and back into the light of prosperity. But since I can't get his full attention, maybe I need to show him. After all, my father has met with David several times and no doubt experienced the same frustration I'm feeling, which is why he invited him here to see the orchards, not to listen to more dry facts and data. He knows this man better than I do and obviously realized that he would respond better to seeing versus hearing what we are doing.

"Why don't we head to the orchards? My father wanted you to see the groves in any case."

"That's not necessary."

He takes another glance at his phone, which is still not ringing, nor do I see a text pop up on the screen. His voice is deep and stern, clearly the voice of a man who is used to dishing out orders.

"Are you expecting a call?" I ask. I'm tempted to add, *because, if not, you should stop glancing at your phone*. It's called basic business protocol and good manners.

He cocks his head to the side and raises his eyebrows in surprise before shoving the phone into his pocket. "My schedule is tight. I need to head back to my office."

As the boss of a mostly male crew, I've learned to stand my ground and not be rushed. "I promise, this won't take long." Seconds later, I'm out of my chair and halfway out the door, pausing to glance back to see if he's following me.

Chapter 2
Betsy & the Fortune Cookie

The moist remnants of the morning fog have cleared and what remains is the beginning of an unusually warm fall day. I shield my eyes from the penetrating sun before reaching into the oversized, leather handbag that I took from the coat rack near the back door. I reach in and pull out my dark sunglasses while maintaining a steady pace toward my car. Adrenaline surges through me and propels me to increase my already fast pace, but David's not far behind. I clearly hear his discontented muttering as he catches up with me as I reach the driver's side door of my gray SUV.

"Hey, slow up." A frown creases his brow as he looks from me to my car.

"I know you're busy." I press the key fob which beeps three times before a click signals that the door is unlocked.

He could have allowed me to finish my presentation or at least get to the most important part. Men with the kind of power he has don't have to listen to people like me. They can't begin to understand the sacrifices we make to be able to barely hold onto what we have. It's all so easy for him. He's got nothing to lose.

I bite my bottom lip and push down the frustration

that I don't want to escape. My father is out working in the orchards every day, sometimes from sunrise to sunset as David is sitting somewhere in an air-conditioned bank, deciding people's fate. It doesn't seem fair that he has so much power and we have so little. He could at least pretend to care.

As I open the door, he places a firm hand on my forearm, and I stop dead in my tracks. "What are you doing?" If his expression is any indication, he's irritated, but not more than I am.

"I know you have a limited amount of time, so let's head to the orchards." His hand stays on my arm.

I pull away.

He clears his throat before taking a step back and creating more space between us. "Uh, right."

I open the car door. "Hop in." I toss my purse in the back seat then open the passenger door when he doesn't.

He stands there like a statue, looking insulted, as if I've asked him to do something insane like strip naked and run through the woods. The unexpected visual relieves some of the irritation and tension I'm feeling. Something about him is unnerving and it's probably related to the power he has to decide our fate. Somewhere in the recesses of my mind, I know I'm being unfair, but I shove the thought down as quickly as it pops up.

"I promise you this won't take long." I return his agitated stare with one of my own. For a moment, neither of us says a word or moves. The car is hot inside and I roll down the windows while waiting for him to step inside. What does he think—that I'm going to kidnap him?

"That's not the problem." Slowly, he makes his way around my vehicle, studying it intently, as if he's a potential buyer. "I'd feel more comfortable if I drove."

Most alpha males would. Oh, so now I get it. He's looking at my car with clear disdain. He probably drives some fancy new car, fresh off the lot. I'd bet money on it. It's probably black to match his eyes. I can't deny that my car is old. Heck, it was seven years old when I bought it and that was eight years ago. I never cared much for status symbols or fancy cars. I don't keep up with the various makes and models, but it has been weeks since I washed the faded exterior. I look at my bargain seat covers and can't say the interior looks any better. Morgan's tracing of the words *Clean Me* on the back window isn't helping either. How was I to know that I'd be driving him around in *my* car? I can't swear that it would have made any difference. Dust accumulates daily and washing it weekly is not a good use of water. Still, I thought my father would have driven us to the groves, not me.

"Don't be deceived by appearances." As I say the words, I know I'm being a complete hypocrite. After all, I had such a stereotypical view of what I expected him to look like, and he in no way matches that image. Nope, this is not the Ol' Man Cole I was expecting.

I pat the front passenger seat. "Can you get in already? You're the one who said you were in a hurry. Betsy has never let me down. This will be quick." I run my hand across the passenger seat, feel the chocolate chip cookie crumbs beneath my fingertips, then attempt to inconspicuously brush them to the floor. "I'll show you the orchards that are closest to the house."

"Betsy?" Shaking his head, he reluctantly gets in.

His long legs fold together like an accordion as he reaches under the seat and locates the lever to push it back to give himself more room. "That's better. I hope I don't live to regret this." He grasps the seat belt, securing it diagonally across his broad shoulders, before snapping the metal fasteners together.

It takes twenty minutes for me to pull up beside the rows of orange trees that span as far as the eye can see. I put on the emergency brake, eagerly hop out of the car, and feel more centered now that the familiar scents and scenes of my best childhood memories surround me. How I looked forward to summer vacations when I could be out here each day with my father, checking the orchards, while Morgan occupied herself inside. Some early fruit are already making their colorful appearance, hanging from the center of fragrant white blossoms.

"Is this it?" He's out of the car now, tentatively walking between the rows of trees. "I thought there would be more and that the oranges would be bigger."

"Of course, there are more trees. But in consideration of your time restraints, I've brought you to the beginning of the groves, not the end. This isn't a factory." An edginess creeps into my voice. "Fruit takes time to ripen… when things happen naturally." I touch one of the small oranges. "Everyone is in such a rush these days. That's why there are so many genetically modified products on the market."

"I'm assuming that's not the case here." He frowns. "Because these oranges are small."

"Is that a problem for you? Because we will not compromise on quality so that our fruit can be prematurely hauled off to the market to satisfy consumers who may have forgotten what real fruit tastes like just so people can make more money."

"Ms. Hart—Elaine, I was not *implying* that your produce was genetically modified. I can look at it and see that that is not the case, otherwise, we wouldn't be talking about the size of your small fruit."

"Oh, weren't you?"

I hop back into the car, eager to end this farce of a meeting. We are proud that we don't use artificial colors or chemicals to make the fruit appear more marketable. So why does he make it sound like our organic fruit is inferior? I doubt that David had any intentions of actually listening to my solution for the groves. Looking relieved to end the conversation, he climbs back into the car. As I press my foot on the accelerator, Betsy decides to start shaking. The body of the car rumbles, causing us to visibly bounce in our seats. This is not a good time for her to reveal her quirks.

"I may not know much about oranges, but I do know when it's time to replace an old jalopy with a new vehicle." He emits a grunt as he notices the brightly lit *Check Engine* light flashing on the dashboard.

What nerve. I pat the dashboard. "Betsy is *not* a jalopy and she is fine. That light doesn't mean anything... or so I've been told." I have to raise my voice in order to be heard above the rumbling of the engine. "I don't know who, but I do recall *someone* telling me that those lights come on all the time and I shouldn't worry about it."

"I'm going to guess that the person *wasn't* a mechanic. It means something." He shakes his head and rolls his eyes upward. "It means that your engine should be checked—as soon as possible."

"There's nothing wrong with the engine." Firmly gripping the shaking steering wheel, I add, "All cars have—"

"I can't wait to hear this," he says, snorting and folding his arms. He turns in his seat and eyes me calmly.

"—their idiosyncrasies." It would have been nice if Betsy hadn't decided to act up now. I know I need a new car, probably sooner than later. But that's not really any of *his* business.

"Oh, so that's what you call it—idiosyncrasies. You do like your fancy words, don't you?" He throws back his head and snorts again.

"What… what are you talking about?" I give him a quick side-glance.

"What did you say earlier—*plethora*? And now *idiosyncrasies*?" His laugh is as deep as his voice. He taps the blinking light on the dashboard. "Can you speak plainly? Call it what it is. That check engine light is for your safety… and mine too at this point."

"Well, you needn't be concerned. It's not necessary."

Before I can finish my sentence, Betsy lurches forward over a rock or possibly a pothole, and I decide it's a good time to abandon any further attempts at having a civil conversation.

David must agree with me, because, besides one more snort, he is silent all the way back to the ranch.

****

My heart sinks as I see my father looking content as he stands on the porch, jubilantly waving his arms in the air. Betsy continues to shake and rattle as I slowly pull up in front of him. Joy is etched in every line of his face, crinkles bracketing his eyes, vertical lines framing the upward turned corners of his mouth. He wears the expression of victory—of a man whose confidence in his daughter's ability to get an extension for their delinquent loan is unwavering.

"Everything go well?"

"Great." I avoid eye contact as guilt has me looking everywhere but directly at him.

David jumps out of Betsy as if he's afraid the car might explode at any moment. Which I *kind* of understand since the truth is, I wasn't certain that she was going to get us back to the house. Not that I would ever admit that to him.

"Elaine—" he begins, pointing a finger in my direction and looking at me with distrust, as if I had intentionally planned for my car to have problems. He abruptly pauses, as if he's not sure of what he wants to say. Instead, he does a quick pivot in the direction of my father. "Yes, sir. I learned everything I need to know. You'll be hearing from me." His strides are long as he rushes to the safety of his predictable, or should I say, *reliable* shiny, new car.

And I was right; his Mercedes is as black as his hard eyes.

Long after the dust from his car has disappeared from view, I'm still standing, chewing on my bottom lip, gazing at the now deserted road and knowing that the meeting didn't go the way my father would have wanted or expected. I don't know exactly when things began to go downhill, but I know I've got to make it right.

****

"You're sure Uncle Robert won't be joining us?"

Morgan sets several white cartons of Chinese food on the table. "He's missing out on some delicious food. Not that I'm complaining. His not being here leaves more for us." She rubs her hands together before placing chopsticks, plastic forks, soy sauce, and packets of hot mustard on the round, maple wood dining room table. "Don't think I haven't noticed his pattern of disappearing."

"He's taking care of business," Dad says, bowing his head and closing his eyes. "I'll bless the food. Thank you, Lord, for this food and the two best daughters in the world."

There it is, the same prayer he's been reciting since I was a little girl. Even after all these years, my chest swells with warmth at these words, especially knowing how much I disappointed him today. I'm disappointed in myself, too. After all, David had come to my rescue when Jared had stepped out of line. Plus, he *had* made time to come here today.

I run my fingers through my hair, thinking about how I've got some apologizing to do. I already spoke to my father, who's now looking to me to turn the situation around. I scoot my chair close to his, lean over and give him a quick kiss on his weathered cheek.

"So, I'm to believe that it's coincidental that Uncle Robert is *always* busy on Wednesday evenings, which happens to be my day to prepare, or, in my case, pick up dinner." Morgan looks unperturbed.

My dad winks at me. "I like sharing a meal alone with my two favorite children."

"You mean your *only* two children," Morgan chimes in before adding more food to her plate.

Dad's eyes seek out mine, but I can't meet his

gaze. I choke on my eggroll as my throat constricts and troubling memories surface.

"Here, take a sip," Morgan orders, as she hands me a mug filled with green tea. "No need to wolf down your food," she says while patting my back. "There's plenty here for everyone."

"You okay?" my father asks with genuine concern.

I silently nod while sipping the hot tea, thankful that the warm drink is thawing the chill that passed over me at my father's look. Morgan's innocent comment throws me off kilter because I know what happened the year before she was born. How there were three children and now there are only two. How lucky Morgan is to be able to live in the present and have no knowledge of the distant past.

"I'm good," I say, attempting to sound jovial. "You know the saying, I bit off more than I can chew." Quickly changing the subject, I ask, "How was school today?"

"Same as usual. Some of the students groaned when I presented them each with a book, but most of them were happy. There's one girl, remember I told you about her? Her name is Trisha. She was happy to get her hands on a copy of *The Color Purple*. Turns out that her aunt had taken her to see the play, but she didn't realize that it was based on a book."

"That's great." I resume eating, relieved that we've switched to a neutral topic.

"You'll make readers of them all." He unscrews the top of his bottle of ginger beer. "Good job, honey."

"Thanks, Dad." Morgan smiles, obviously feeling pleased about her book give-away. She may not want children, but she obviously cares about them.

"Anything new happening on the homestead?"

"Jared came by to see your uncle," Dad says. He looks at me as if I might have something to add, but I keep sipping my tea.

"Elaine, have you changed your mind yet? Because if *you* don't want that man, I'll happily take him off your hands." She waves her chopsticks in my direction. "It's not every day that you come across a fine-looking working man who happens to be a lawyer who is crazy about you."

"Really, Morgan." I bite into my eggroll. "I already told you that we aren't compatible." Little does she know that beneath Jared's conservative appearance is an angry man who can't accept rejection.

"You okay, Elaine?" My father takes a swig of his beer.

"He's *not* the right man for me," I say emphatically and concentrate on my pork fried rice as I recall Jared's sudden mood shifts.

"Then who is?" Morgan replies. "That's what I want to know." She tilts her head. "I think you're married to this place."

When we hear a crow squawking outside, Morgan and I turn our heads and stare out the large rectangular window. We may both be looking through the same glass, but what she sees is different from what I do. I see the lushness of the magenta bougainvillea trees; its delicate flower petals twirling like *papier mache* in the breeze. The distinctive aroma of the thirty-year-old eucalyptus tree that supported our first tree house provides a warm, familiar scent. I imagine three generations of elders that lived, loved, and invested their dreams and hopes into this land. For her, it's where she lives, nothing more and nothing less.

"Dad, everything will be fine," I say.

"I'm not worried." He pats my hand.

"Sometimes I wish I could be more like you two," Morgan adds. "I want more." With a wistful expression on her pretty face, she pushes her food away. "I chose a teaching career partly because I want the freedom to work anywhere, not to feel like I'm tethered to Santa Lorena. There are other places I want to live."

"Which is fine. Everyone doesn't have to see things the same way." Dad's tone is that of a wise man who understands his daughters so well, including my need for the continuation of the legacy my ancestors began and Morgan's for adventure and new experiences. "This land, this lifestyle, isn't for everyone."

"Well, I love it and never want to leave." I fold my paper napkin. "This is our home. I'll do whatever it takes to make certain that Hartland is around for many years."

"In that case, you better make it right with David Cole." My father turns toward me.

"I know." I look down, embarrassed that I lost my temper earlier. "He was so impatient. I couldn't finish my presentation without him looking at his cell phone every few minutes." I set down my chopsticks. "And then, he had an attitude about Betsy."

"Who's David Cole?" Morgan asks.

"Your car was loud." Dad sets down his fork. "I've been telling you that you need to get a tune up."

"Anyone I know?" Morgan's eyes dart from our father to me. Exasperated, she throws her hands in the air. "Anyone care to fill me in on the mystery man?"

"David Cole is a banker," I say flatly. I can still see his face—nice one minute, then looking like a piece of solid stone when it came to business.

"*You* got to meet a banker?" Morgan abruptly stands, hands on hips. "You get all the luck. It's not fair." She pouts. "I only meet teachers and most of them are women." She plops back down in her seat and rolls her eyes. "You've been holding out on me. I've been home for more than an hour and I'm *just* hearing about this now." She points a finger in my direction. "Give me all the details. At least I can live vicariously through you."

"I've heard this story." Dad gets up and heads toward the glass patio doors. "I'm going to have a cigar while your sister fills you in." The one thing I haven't been able to get my father to do is quit smoking, but since he doesn't have any other vices, I can't complain too much.

"Okay, Dad." I face Morgan. "I blew it." I fold my hands in my lap.

"No surprise there, really. First, you toss out a perfectly good-looking lawyer and now it sounds like you blew it with a banker. Way to go, Sis." She pats me on the back.

"The banker was not a dating prospect." If only we could switch banks. But it's too late for that now and we're in too deep. Even though we'd still be financially behind, at least I wouldn't have to interact with David.

"That's too bad." Morgan looks confused. "Was he too old or what?" She stares at a fortune cookie before biting into it. "These are strangely addictive."

"You *know* you have a weakness for any type of cookie."

"You're right…" She pauses, eyes open wide, before she grimaces and holds out her hands. "Stop!" She practically yells the word. "Before you go on any further, you have *got* to tell me why you are still wearing that necklace. I thought we both agreed that it's meaningless."

In the craziness of the day, I had forgotten to tuck the locket that was a good-bye gift from our mother inside my bra. Usually, you can't see it inside my shirts. I gently touch the etched gold heart shape that holds a picture of our mother. "It's the one thing that she left for us. Is it too much to do what she asked and wear it close to our hearts so that we know we are always in her thoughts?"

"Um, let me think. The answer to that question would be a resounding and unequivocal *yes*. It *is* too much to ask. She was not there for us when we got our periods, had our first dates or went to the prom, so, therefore, she did not have the right to ask anything of us."

Morgan had been only one when our mother left and has no memory of the woman who gave us birth. If only I had been a better daughter my mother would have stayed to raise us and love my father. But one horrible mistake caused her to walk out on her daughters and her husband.

"Well, *I* think it was a nice gesture." I sip my green tea. "I'm not ashamed to admit that I still wear it sometimes."

"Suit yourself. Mine got lost." She shrugs and runs both hands through her thick, curly hair. "Let's get back to something more pleasant, like your banker. What was wrong with him and exactly how did you blow it this time?"

"He isn't my banker; he's *our* banker." I smooth down my bangs. "I tried to share my business plan, but he didn't have time for it. So, I decided to show him the orchards and he was unimpressed."

"I get that." Morgan pops another cookie in her mouth. "Don't look at me like that. Not everyone is turned on by trees."

I glare at my sister. "You two would make a perfect pair."

"Really?" She sits up straighter, looking alert. And from the look in her eyes, her mind has already taken off, imagining the possibilities of a love match. "Describe him for me. Maybe I'll go to your next meeting—oh… if only I didn't have to show up to my darn job. Children can be so demanding." Morgan insists that just because she's a schoolteacher, it doesn't mean that she's particularly fond of children, even though she's always buying books for her students or taking them on field trips. She finishes unwrapping another fortune cookie. "Seriously though, do you think he's my type?"

"Morgan, honestly, I don't think you have a type, do you?" I think of the different men she's dated over the last year. "There was a technician at the computer repair shop, the new school psychologist, the strange guy you met on the dating app who always came up with some lame last-minute excuse why he couldn't make it—"

"Okay, you've made your point." She holds her hands out. "My dating life proves that I'm open to different possibilities." Leaning back in her chair, she glares at me indignantly. "However, I don't like just *anybody*. He has to at least have a job. We were talking about *you* and the mysterious banker."

"He's tall, with dark brown skin and broad shoulders." I pause, remembering those eyes. "He's not the friendliest person." Except that he was just what I needed to get Jared to back off, but I'll stick to his business persona. After all, it's the business side that matters to our future. "I'm not sure if he's anyone's type. I… well, I didn't exactly lose my temper, but I know I didn't make the best impression either."

"Don't look so worried, Elaine." She grabs another cookie and offers it to me. "I see you *are* really stressed. Try one of these; they always make me feel better."

"If only it were that easy." I shake my head, take the cookie, and crack open the crispy confection. Unfolding the narrow strip of paper, I read the words out loud. "Let's see what my fortune says. 'Those who are humble in spirit lead a fulfilled life.'" My shoulders slump as an uncomfortable knot twists in my belly. "Even this fortune cookie is telling me something."

Morgan begins clearing the table of the scattered empty cartons. "What do you think it means?"

"Isn't it obvious?" My shoulders tense as I silently reread my fortune. Clearly, I need to practice being more humble and giving our banker ultimatums isn't going to lead me to having a fulfilled life. I meet Morgan's inquisitive glance. "It means that I'm going to have to swallow my pride and make it right with David Cole."

Chapter 3
The Family

This is not how I would have preferred to begin the next day, but it doesn't really matter because standing stiffly in the kitchen, his back turned away from the window, a disgruntled expression on his surly face, is my cantankerous uncle. No two brothers could be more alike physically, both are average height with the same once-black-now-mostly-gray hair and skin that gets more reddish brown with each passing year, especially my father's from spending so much time outside in the unyielding sun. However, their dispositions could not be more different. My father is as mellow as his older sibling is cantankerous. Uncle Robert's pessimistic view of my plan to increase our profits didn't help the meeting with David. If there is anything he can complain about, he will. Maybe if he had settled down and gotten married, he'd be a happier man. However, since he's now sixty-seven, I've given up any remnants of hope that there is a super-patient, wonder woman somewhere out there who can fulfill his expectations. But it's really my father's divorced status that weighs heavily on my mind. If it weren't for me, my mother wouldn't have abandoned us twenty years ago and we would still be an intact family—which is why I have to figure out a way to remedy the current crisis.

"Thought I'd find you here." He looks at me

sheepishly.

"Yep. Just fixing myself some coffee." I measure out the coffee before casting a quick look in his direction. "I know you usually have your coffee before you get here so I won't ask if I should make enough for you." Even though Uncle Robert's house is on the opposite end of the large corner lot the family owns, he arrives at our house at exactly six thirty most mornings.

"Well, there you're wrong." He takes a seat at the island counter. "I haven't had anything to drink yet. So, sure, make enough for me."

Something is off here. For one, he avoids eating and drinking anything I prepare, making it clear that he doesn't think highly of my cooking.

"You sure?" I ask, eyeing him suspiciously.

"Yes. I said I'd like a cup." The sudden twist of his lips and flare of his nostrils shows that he's getting impatient with the conversation.

"Okay." I shrug, having abandoned any attempts to understand my uncle's mercurial moods years ago.

A few minutes later, I pour myself a cup while Uncle Robert removes a mug from the cupboard, inspects it and, determining that it is not clean enough for him to drink out of, he grabs a sponge and liquid soap and proceeds to scrub the cup and rinse it with hot water. Only then does he pick up the coffee pot and pour himself something to drink. He takes one quick sip, looks around frantically, then rushes over to the sink where he leans over and loudly spits out the coffee.

His hand clutches his throat before he chokes out the words, "Girl, that's *too* damn strong. Can't you do *anything* right?" He scowls and shakes his head in disgust. "Guess not. You mother—*that's* another story.

She could make a *great* cup of coffee. When she was around, I'd have two cups, maybe three." As he reminisces, his lips curl into what I believe is a rare replica of a smile.

"She didn't teach me her coffee making tips before she left." I'm tempted to add that I was only five at the time, but he *is* my father's older brother and I have been raised to respect my elders or else, "I'd give you a good piece of my mind."

Oops, now that I've accidentally spoken the words out loud, I put my hand over my mouth—hoping that the bad taste in *his* mouth has clouded his hearing. Between the mounting concerns about the orange groves, it's getting increasingly difficult to stay pleasant all the time. I mean, really, did he *need* to spit the coffee in the sink? I don't know, it seemed over the top to me. A simple, "It's too strong" would have sufficed.

"What did you say?" Uncle Robert's eyes pop open as he cocks his head to the side. "I must not have heard you correctly—"

"Could be." I smile innocently, hoping he'll buy the act. "I just said that I wouldn't *mind* if she had taught me how to make coffee."

"I just bet you wouldn't." He swipes his mouth with the back of his hand.

I try not to chuckle as I notice coffee dribble on his chin.

He pulls his trusty, antique pocket watch out of his pants as he struts into the living room and does the same thing he does every morning.

From the kitchen I clearly see him standing in front of the large brick fireplace, closely scrutinizing the smattering of old photos that my father insists on displaying on the mantel. Pulling a cigar from his shirt pocket, he places it between his lips. He doesn't light it though; that will come later after dinner when he'll join my father on the patio for a cigar.

Next to Morgan's and my grade school pictures is our only family photograph. That day, we'd been dressed alike in our fancy pink, knee-length church dresses with matching barrettes and wide, silly grins plastered on our faces. Dad, wearing a dark suit, looked handsome as usual, his hair already beginning to gray at the temples. Perhaps he already knew that my mother was busy plotting her escape. In the photograph, she looks off to the side, away from the camera, as if to say, *I don't belong here. I'm not with them*—and then… she really wasn't. *Poof.* Like a magic disappearing act, she was gone.

"I'll check on Dad," I call out, eager to block out my mother's distant look captured for all eternity in this one picture.

"Before you get your father," he turns away from the picture and comes back into the kitchen, "I want to mention something to you."

"About what?" I raise my eyebrows. We never meet separately; my father is always here, being the mediator as needed. "A new complaint?"

"No, of course not." He chuckles and puts his hands in the air, as if in surrender.

Now I *know* that something is very off. He's not even acting like his regular self. I didn't know he possessed a sense of humor, and now he's chuckling. Something is definitely wrong with this picture. "What is it then?"

"I met with Jared." His eyes grow dark with

irritation; all attempts at good-natured joking are gone.

"Okay." At least my personal relationship with that man is in the past.

"He told me that you broke it off with him." His hands grip the edge of the table as if he needs to grasp it for support.

"That's right." What business is it of his if I'm dating someone?

"I'm curious as to why I would be the last to know." Nostrils flaring, he glares at me.

"I didn't make a general announcement, if that's what you mean." This conversation is becoming more peculiar by the minute. I stand up, signaling that I am done talking.

"I don't see why you kept it a secret." An unmistakable tone of irritation underlines his words. I know that he's fond of Jared, but that doesn't mean that he has a right to give me feedback on my relationship with him.

"Uncle Robert, I'm twenty-six years old. My personal life is just that—*personal*. Why would I discuss that with you?"

"Sit back down." He points at my now vacated chair. "Don't get offended. I'm not in your business, but Jared is a damn fine attorney and an outstanding young man. You could do worse."

I don't comment, even when he looks at me as if I'm expected to say, *Oh, you're so right, Uncle. What was I thinking*?

"I've got a pile of work to do…"

"All I'm saying is that you owe it to yourself to give him a second chance, that's all." Uncle Robert practically growls out the words.

"Okay, so now I know *your* opinion," I say tersely. "*I* knew what I was doing when I ended it with Jared." Pacing the floor, I glance down and see the red welt that circles my wrist.

"I strongly disagree with you and, because of that, I made Jared a promise." He looks defiant, almost proud.

I stop in my steps, fold my arms across my waist, and look at him suspiciously. "*What* are you talking about? Any promise you made to Jared has nothing to do with *me*. That's between you and Jared."

"I promised Jared that you would go on one more date with him." This time he laughs as if we just shared a joke.

"What?" Has he lost his mind? He promised Jared *what*? And *why*? "Well, I'm not doing that. You'll have to break your promise to him. This has nothing to do with *me*." Heat infuses my face and I take a deep breath to keep myself from yelling.

"Elaine, you are making too big a deal of this." He spreads his arms out. "You dated the man for how long?" He pauses, looking sheepishly at me before continuing, "Well, it must have been at least a year. It couldn't have been that bad." He points a finger in my direction. "One more date won't hurt you."

"You tell him no since you're the one who told him yes." Each word comes out stilted as if the sentence has been broken into fragments. "I'm not seeing him anymore, except in a business setting." I wrap my arms tighter around my body.

"Okay, okay." He softens his voice. "I get it. You can tell him that tonight because he's coming by to pick you up for a late dinner. He's in a meeting with the other partners at his law firm and can't be contacted during the day." He walks to the door, tossing those last words over his shoulder like some kind of random afterthought. "Look, little girl, tell my brother I couldn't wait anymore. I have to get going. I'll talk to you later."

Even taking a deep breath and silently counting won't still the emotions frantically coursing through my veins, sending a surge of anxiety and anger that has me trembling from my legs to my arms. I shudder, recalling the threatening words hurled in my direction when I'd told Jared that we were better off being friends. I honestly don't know if I will be able to survive one more evening in his company.

****

The term *unmitigated gall* comes to mind. Does my uncle think he can manipulate me to his will? Luckily, there's a Parent/Teacher Association meeting this afternoon at Morgan's school, so she doesn't have to report to class until later this morning, which is a good thing because I really need to talk to her. Wait until she hears what our uncle has done now. Noticing that her door is open, I peek into the room. Seeing her sitting lotus-style in a sea of neatly stacked books immediately calms me. There are more important things in life, like students and learning, than my uncle's odd actions.

"Hey, Sis, do you think you have enough books?" I walk in and take a seat on the floor directly across from her.

She tilts her head to the side as if contemplating my question. "If not, I can always get more." Her serious tone reflects how committed Morgan is when it comes to being there for her students.

Maybe it's because Dad was usually too busy

working to help us with our homework, so we had to fend for ourselves.

"I got up early this morning so I could sort through the books I want to distribute to the students later today."

"You are such a good teacher, buying all of these with your own money." Picking up a copy of *Siddhartha*, I absently leaf through the pages.

"It doesn't take any effort to order a few extra books for the students." She looks up and tucks a stray curl behind her ear.

"Uh huh." I decide to not mention that this is significantly more than a *few* extra books.

"Do you know that some of these kids wear athletic shoes that cost over a hundred dollars but have never owned a book? It drives me nuts."

"You have a point; that really doesn't make any kind of sense." I think of public libraries where they can check out books for free. "Well, it's still generous of you."

"How did you sleep last night, or should I say, *did* you manage to get any sleep?" Folding her hands in her lap, she stops sorting and fixes me with a penetrating stare.

I shake my head dismissively. "Not really." I decide to tell the truth *this* time.

What's the use in pretending? The shadows under my eyes are worse than hers. Unfortunately, unlike our father, she's a light sleeper and sometimes the dreams—no, I should say the *memories*—that haunt my sleep have me crying out and waking both of us even though her room is down the hall from mine.

"Elaine, you can't continue like this forever. You

should consider talking to someone." She holds her hands out. "Don't go getting all defensive. Just consider it. It can't do any harm."

"That's not going to happen."

Contrary to reality television shows and social media rants about everyday occurrences, I don't find it necessary to share my personal business with anyone. What would be the point? Plus, Santa Lorena is a small community where many of the people have resided for most of their lives. Except for the seasonal tourists, everyone knows each other. The last thing I want is our family's secrets to be the subject of small-town gossip.

"I worry about you." She shakes her head. "This has been going on for years."

"Well, stop worrying." I know she means well. But Morgan has no idea how lucky she is to be in the dark about certain events. "You have enough on your mind with your students. Besides, we have more important things to consider. Did I tell you that I've figured out how to increase our profits?"

"Don't even try it." She frowns and transfers two books from one stack to another. "You know that talking about Daddy's farm is my *least* favorite subject."

"Again, it's not a farm and it's our legacy, and *if* either of us decides to have children, it will be passed on to them. I know that we aren't even *beginning* to think about that now, but we still have to consider the future."

"Look, I can enjoy men without having to bear their children. You seem to be forgetting that I only like *other* people's children. I don't feel any compulsion to procreate. Most of the kids in my classroom seldom, if ever, see their fathers." She pauses before nodding. "Kind of like our missing-in-action mother. Not that she bothered spending time with us. She barely waited until I was out of diapers before deciding she'd had enough of the motherhood role and left." She looks at me defiantly, daring me to deny the truth of her sobering words. "I'm not big on the whole family legacy thing."

"Even though Mom left, we're still here. I'm doing everything I can to make sure that we don't lose what we have." I'll never understand how Morgan continues to be flippant about the possibility of losing our home. "Banks aren't real big on businesses lagging behind on their loan payments."

"I know, you're all about saving the farm— oops, I mean ranch." Morgan's eyes glaze over. It's clear she's not interested in talking about anything to do with Hartland. "I'm not invested in this place the way you are. If Hartland *wasn't* here, I'd be fine. More than fine, as a matter of fact. I can always live somewhere else. As long as it's sunny, I won't have any problems packing my bags and hitting the road." She smiles mischievously. "I like the thought of that—meeting men, enjoying wild, wonderful sex, preferably outdoors."

"Really Morgan?" My frustration surfaces as I listen to Morgan's dismissal of the seriousness of our problems. I don't know why I keep trying to get through to her to force her to understand when her mind is clearly on other, more frivolous matters. "That's your response to our situation—sex on the beach?" My voice involuntarily rises. "This is no joke. This has been our home our entire lives."

"Exactly my point. I don't plan to be stuck here forever. There are too many other places to explore beyond the boundaries of Santa Lorena. Hawaii, Spain, Rio de Janeiro, to name a few. I hear that Cape Town is incredible." Her hazel eyes change colors when she's excited. Right now, they're sparkling like brand new Christmas tree ornaments. "I'll leave the worrying about Hartland to you, Dad, and Uncle Robert. Truth is, I'm more concerned about you, *not* the land." She reaches up and gives me a quick hug. "I've said this before, and I'll say it again. You should talk to someone about whatever the hell it is that keeps you up at night."

"No way, but I love you, too." I return her hug. "I appreciate your concerns, honestly, I do, but there's a lot more at stake here than my lack of sleep."

Morgan nonchalantly shrugs. "You'll *never* catch me complaining about the sun. I can't get enough of it. It's one of the reasons I became a teacher—to enjoy long summer vacations, with as much nude sunbathing as possible."

"Never mind." I halfway turn away, more than ready to change the subject before I wake my father. "Uncle Robert is in rare form this morning. I can't believe he's trying to interfere in my love life—as if he has a say in who I choose to date."

"Hey, only I'm allowed to do that." She smiles and playfully shakes her head.

"We both know you're joking. He's serious. On top of that, he actually spit out the coffee I made, as if it was toxic waste."

"Never mind him. I am grateful that you love to cook." Morgan glances down at her hips. "You can tell that I'm not complaining. As far as Uncle Robert is concerned, we'd go into shock if he let a day go by without finding something to bitch about."

"Never at you though." I think back, trying to recall a time when Uncle Robert raised his voice at Morgan or even expressed displeasure with anything she had done. How is it that she has managed to escape his wrath all these years? How could I not have noticed before now? "What's your secret?"

"It's no secret. He knows better than to mess with me. You are a whole lot nicer than I am so he feels he can get away with saying anything to you."

She grabs her red cardigan from the closet and tosses it into the box.

****

Box in hand, she heads downstairs while I head to our father's bedroom and knock on the door. As usual, I don't suppress the inevitable chuckle that bubbles up whenever I view the ragged remnants of Morgan's and my school days taped on the outside of his door: report cards, pictures from parties, and art projects.

The room he shared with our mother is at the opposite end of the hall. I don't know how long Dad waited before locking their bedroom door and that part of his past away—the part where he fell in love, asked a girl to marry him and they started a family together. Still, he seems happy enough with his books and the orange groves. I take my lead from his silence about the woman he loved and how she abandoned not only their two daughters but him, too. He's never spoken a word about the past and, so, neither do I. I remember him walking, head slightly bowed from one room to the other, transferring items as he quietly moved into one of the spare rooms on the second floor, setting up his collection of cowboy hats across the dresser and a stack of books, mostly westerns and espionage stories, near the lamp on his nightstand. I don't know where or when he got that lamp, with a bent over cowboy on horseback for the base.

"Dad, are you awake yet?" My knuckles tap a steady rhythm against the door.

"Come in."

Seeing my father never fails to make me smile.

Sitting up, he leans back against the headboard, a paperback in his hand. "How's my girl doing this morning?"

"Great." I kiss him lightly on his weathered cheek. "What're you reading? Anything I might find interesting?"

"I don't know." He places a hand over the cover of the book. "It's about a cowboy."

"Really, Dad?" I look at him skeptically, knowing how much he loves to tease me. He'll do anything to make me smile. "Speaking of cowboys, I've been meaning to ask you about this lamp you brought home last week." I touch the bronze base, noting the clear delineation of the horse's legs and the defined flare of the nostrils. "Where'd this come from?" He loves all that stuff—cowboys, rodeos, or any books that portray the Wild West.

"Joe Ramirez's son had a garage sale last weekend. I got to help out a kid who's trying to raise money for college." He swings his pajama-clad legs over the side of the bed.

"I can see that."

He smiles and caresses my cheek. "If you want to know more about this book," he holds up the book, his hand moving aside so I can read the title, "you'll have to read it yourself."

As he slowly rises from the bed, he lets out a raspy chuckle as if some of the smoke from his cigars have permanently curled around his vocal cords and altered the timbre of his voice.

"I can hardly wait. I have a book for you, too. I'm going to fix us some breakfast while you're getting dressed."

"Sounds good. I called the man about the water irrigation system for the trees not working properly. He'll be here in about thirty minutes."

"It really doesn't make sense." I frown, puzzled by challenges we've had in addition to the drought. "I'd like to be in that meeting."

As my hand reaches for the doorknob, he calls my name. "Elaine—"

"Yes, Dad?" I pause and scan his face, noticing how tired he looks. Is the farm getting to be too much for him?

"I don't say this often enough, but I sure appreciate your cooking and everything else you do around here. I don't know how we'd survive without you taking such good care of us."

"Thanks, Dad." I softly close the door behind me. Pausing for a few minutes, I close my eyes, sigh, and allow a feeling of gratitude to wash over me. If one parent had to leave, I'm grateful that it was my mother and not my father.

****

There's a light tap on the office door. Great. Didn't my new secretary read the Do Not Disturb sign on the door? I need to get these ledgers balanced. Dropping my pen, I force my attention away from my work as my twin Amanda, looking as if she stepped off a Paris runway, cautiously peeks her head inside.

"Busy?" she asks, not bothering to wait for an answer before she struts into my office and plops onto one of the two black leather chairs facing my desk.

"Would it matter if I said I was?" I ask as she stretches out her long legs.

"Not at all," she responds before leaning forward and whispering conspiratorially, "Look, I did you a big favor and stopped at the coffee shop in the lobby. I gave your secretary-of-the-day, a macchiato coffee, or some such fancy drink, *and* a blueberry scone. Maybe if you were kinder, they would stick around for more than a few days." She runs her fingers through her short, spiky hair. Oddly enough, the bold style, complete with dashes of neon blue streaks on both sides, accentuates Mandy's striking beauty. "What's this one's name anyway?"

"Damn, if I know," I say, bothered by the interruption and the interrogation.

"Just as I suspected. You don't even know the young woman's name and she's been working for you for almost two weeks." She makes a disapproving utterance under her breath.

"What's your point? I'm busy." I pick up a pen and start making notes. If I ignore her long enough, maybe she'll get the message and go back to her own office. It worked when we were kids and I wanted her to leave my room.

Mandy reaches across the desk and takes the pen from my hand. "Oh no you don't, David Allen Cole. During the last few months, your secretaries have fallen into one of two categories. Don't give me that innocent look. You know full well what I'm talking about."

"I don't believe in coddling employees." I pick up another pen and highlight four of the stock options I'm considering investing in.

"That's an understatement." She holds up two of her long purple-tipped fingernails. "There are the ones you fire and the ones who up and quit without so much as a goodbye." She points one of those talons in my direction. "*Now* we've got a situation. The employment agency is threatening to stop supplying us with a steady stream of secretaries if you don't treat them better." She digs into her gargantuan purse that's the same size as a piece of carry-on luggage and pulls out a nail file which she points in my direction before she begins filing her nails. "*I* know that your bark is worse than your bite, however you're single-handedly giving our company a bad name. Pretty soon, no one will want to work for us and then what will we do?"

"Are you finished with the lecture? Because I don't know what you're talking about." I look defiantly at Mandy, who is older than me by a whopping three minutes, a fact she never lets me forget. Of course, I *know* what she's talking about, but I'm not going to give her the satisfaction of admitting it.

"By the way, I told your secretary, who at this time will remain unnamed, that the coffee and scone were from you," she says with a slight British accent, which undoubtedly and strangely has everything to do with our parents' high school graduation gift of a trip to London and Paris. London changed the way she spoke, and Paris altered the way she dressed.

"I didn't ask you to do that." Sometimes, Mandy

goes too far. "This one is working out fine."

"Sure, that's why you don't know her name. She couldn't believe you bought the coffee and scone for her because she said you were quite angry about her not being able to locate the Hartland file." Amanda kicks off her four-inch stilettos. "Ah, that's better." She wiggles her toes. I'll be damned if I can understand why she wears those sky-high shoes when she's already six feet tall.

"Don't go getting comfortable. I've got deadlines to meet."

I stand and look out at the view of downtown Santa Lorena. Currently a cross section of storefronts, including wine and specialty foods, clothing boutiques, and yoga and exercise studios occupy the palm tree-lined streets. But an influx of new businesses are expected to break ground as the exorbitant cost of more urban areas is hitting the roof and pushing people outward toward more affordable suburban and even semi-rural areas. More new businesses mean more loans and that's good for us.

Mandy walks over and drapes an arm across my shoulders. "I know you do. That's why we set up an office here because this area is rapidly growing and there are opportunities for development. But you haven't been the easiest person to deal with since Courtney left."

I give her my most menacing glare and intimidating growl, hoping she'll leave my office. "Don't go there." At an early age, I had to figure out a way to get my twin to go bother someone else. The ploy didn't work then and doesn't seem like it's working now. Just hearing my ex's name makes my chest tighten and my throat constrict. I loosen my tie.

"Oops," she says, obviously not remotely intimidated. "I already did."

"I am *not* going to talk about my soon-to-be ex-wife with you," I say firmly. "Is there something related to work that you came to discuss? If not, I've got a packed day."

What Courtney did was inexcusable, and I won't have Mandy dissecting the myriad ways that my ex betrayed me. Hell, I still can't wrap *my* mind around how or even when things began to unravel. But unravel they did.

"Okay, fine. I can take a hint." Mandy shrugs while squinting at my desk. "You know I want to help. If we *have* to stick to work subjects, tell me how the meeting at Hartland went last week. Speaking of Hartland," she pulls a folder out from under a stack of papers on the corner of my desk, "was *this* the folder you were yelling at your secretary about?"

"Yes, it is," I reply sheepishly as I take the folder and open it. "I met with Mr. Hart last week about the loan being delinquent. We've already granted him more than ample time to bring the account current."

"What did he say?" Mandy raises her eyebrows and looks at me inquisitively.

"He assured me that they should be able to bring their accounts current within the next ninety days."

"That's good," she says. She rustles in her jumbo purse and manages to find a tube of lipstick and a mirror. "So why don't you look convinced?"

"I don't know if he can recoup his losses at this time. I believe he means well, but *I'm* not convinced."

"So will the property go into foreclosure if they

can't make their payments or are you considering giving them another extension?"

"I don't know if there's any point in doing that. I didn't see any evidence that they would be able to catch up."

As I reflect back on my time at the ranch, I get a flash of Mr. Hart's daughter, Elaine, being manhandled by some jackass. With her fringe of smooth bangs and that mass of curly, auburn hair and big brown eyes, I could see why the guy would want to get up close and personal. But he was clearly not respecting her wishes. What kind of moron doesn't get that *no* means *no*? It's guys like that who give men a bad name.

"That's too bad. If I recall correctly, that ranch has been in their family for a long time."

Mandy pauses in putting on several coats of lipstick, no doubt recalling the details discussed at our last shareholders meeting. "Wasn't it passed down from the father to the oldest son?"

"You're partially correct." As my stomach growls, I glance at the clock on the wall behind Mandy, noting that it's almost lunchtime. Too bad she didn't think to bring her brother something to eat. "Twenty-five years ago, the land was passed down from father to the youngest son."

"Hmmm." She tilts her head to the side. "That's kind of unusual, isn't it?"

"Yes, it is." I pause, perusing the contents of the folder. "From what I learned from Thomas Hart, his older brother Robert lives on the estate and assists in the running of the day-to-day operations. Thomas Hart has two daughters. Morgan is a schoolteacher and Elaine works closely with him in every aspect of the business."

"I suppose you spoke to her, too, then." Mandy folds her hands together and leans toward me, thoroughly interested.

"I did. In the middle of her report, she abruptly decides that we need to see the orchards. That wasn't a surprise since that was Mr. Hart's initial plan when he asked me to meet him at Hartland." I shake my head, remembering how she rushed out the door and expected me to get into her dilapidated car. "I reluctantly got into her car and the next thing I know, we're headed back to the house and her car is threatening to explode."

Elaine Cole is the most unpredictable woman I have ever met. One minute she's looking vulnerable, like she needs rescuing and the next she's irritated that I'm not impressed with oranges that even she admits are small.

"Explode?" Mandy scoots to the end of her chair and tugs on my arm. "So, what happened next? Did you have to call a tow truck or what?"

"We made it back, but just barely. I couldn't wait to get out of that jalopy."

Amanda clasps her hands together and lets out a loud laugh. "I wish I could have seen that. Especially knowing how much you like to keep your car so pristine, as if you just drove it off the lot."

"It was not funny." I stand in front of the window, but I'm no longer looking at the view. Instead, I'm remembering how perturbed Elaine was about me checking my cell. At first, I was looking for a text I was expecting and then I kept doing it because it was kind of fun to watch her get increasingly upset.

I come back to the present, store the image away,

and see Mandy smiling from ear to ear. "You can wipe that silly grin off your face."

"Okay, but only because you're insisting. So how did it end?"

"It was left up in the air. I wasn't sure the direction she was headed in before the car fiasco." I pause, thinking how one minute she'd been talking about oranges and the next, she'd switched subjects. "She said something about avocados." I rub the back of my head.

"What? I'm sure the crop was oranges. She doesn't sound like she was very clear about resolving their deficit."

"Exactly my thoughts. It was odd, since her father couldn't sing her praises enough. He was quite confident that his daughter would be able to sort things out."

"Think about our parents and how much they trust us. Parents have been known to put more faith in their children than they sometimes deserve." Mandy stuffs her belongings back into her suitcase/purse.

"Wait a minute."

I turn from the view outside and my gut twists as I stare at my own sibling. What is she implying? After all, our parents had been slowly giving us more responsibility for their business during the last two years. Was she questioning the wisdom of their decision? Or was it just *my* ability that she wasn't sure about? After all, my initial business investments were poorly thought out and had cost the company a lot of money. That's why so much was depending on me making the right choices now.

"You don't think Mom and Dad should have handed so much of the business over to us?" My jaw tightens and I'm not sure I want to know the answer, but I've got to ask the question. "Or do you think they are placing too much trust in *me* specifically?"

"No, I'm not saying *that* at all. How could you even think that? We're both committed to keeping the company solvent. More than solvent, we want to see it *grow*. But not every child wants to follow in their parents' footsteps. Maybe this... Elaine would really rather be doing something else like her sister. Maybe she feels obligated, but her heart isn't really in it."

"Hmm." I rub my jaw, relieved to know that my sister wasn't alluding to my past mistakes. "I hadn't thought of that. You could be right. She's not the easiest person to talk to. She was all over the place. I'm thinking thirty days should be enough time for Hartland to produce. That's it—"

Before I can finish my sentence, my office door is shoved opened, and standing in the doorway, is none other than the lovely Elaine Hart. The rise and fall of her breasts is apparent as she breathes heavily and puts her hands on her slender hips.

"Sorry to interrupt, but I didn't see anyone at the desk outside," she says.

"Really?" I raise my eyebrows because, somehow, I don't believe she's sorry at all. If I had to describe how she looks at this very moment, I'd say she was proud and possibly defiant as if she's just found the last missing piece to a puzzle.

I lean against my desk, arms crossed, waiting to see what she'll do next.

"I need to speak to you right away." She approaches my desk.

"The secretary must have gone to lunch," Mandy

suggests, smiling and curiously eyeing the unannounced visitor. "You're here to see Mr. Cole."

What the heck is she doing here without an appointment? As soon as the secretary returns, I'm firing her for incompetence. The least she should have done was buzz me on the intercom to inform me that she was taking her lunch break.

"I would ask you to come in and have a seat, but you've already taken that liberty," I say dryly, as she walks over and sits on the chair vacated by Amanda.

I have to admit, Elaine looks incredible in a blue and white wrap dress that clings to her slender curves, and I can't help noticing her shapely legs as she crosses her ankles.

Mandy extends her hand. "I'm Amanda Cole, and you are?"

"Elaine Hart," she says. "I didn't mean to interrupt you and your husband."

Before Mandy or I can correct her, she abruptly stands, almost knocking over a sculpture on my desk. I barely catch it before it falls to the floor. She looks back, points to the door.

"I *accidently* heard you as I opened the door. I don't make it a habit to eavesdrop, but if you think you can waltz into town and take over our ranch, you're in for a surprise." She pierces me with a scathing glare, while her voice rises with each word. "We need *more* time, not less."

Does she even know what she's talking about? Her family is already months behind on their loan payments. "I'd say we've been more than patient."

"You would, wouldn't you?" She rolls her eyes and shakes her head. "Well, I disagree with you. You can't come into town and take over people's homes and dreams." She spins around, heads back toward the door, then abruptly stops, turns around, and marches up so close to me that I smell a light fragrance on her skin. She jabs a finger in my chest. "You are hereby warned that I won't let you take Hartland away from my family. It's *not* about to happen." She smooths down her dress and looks at Amanda's shocked expression. "It was nice to meet you, Mrs. Cole." And with those parting words, she again stomps toward the door, pauses as if remembering one more last thing, then, facing me, she adds, "I'll see you in court, Mr. Cole."

Chapter 4
Le Petit Bistro

"Elaine, please tell me you're joking." He runs a hand across his brow. He's wearing one of his blue-and-red-checkered shirts and brown trousers. His usual western-style hat casts a slight shadow across his eyes. "I know you didn't go to Mr. Cole's office without an appointment."

I inhale deeply as we stroll through the groves, examining the fruit which is almost at peak ripeness. It will be picked, packaged, and delivered to the market within the next few days. I sigh and inhale two of my favorite fragrances: orange blossoms and my father's cigars.

I link my arm through his. "Yes, I'm afraid I did. Honestly, I went there with the best of intentions. I had even rehearsed the words I would use to apologize, but when I got near his office, I overheard him talking to a woman who I later found out was his wife."

They looked like a perfect match. Both of them were tall, slender, and stunningly attractive. I don't know why I'd felt a pang of disappointment when I saw her. I suppose I had assumed he wasn't married because he hadn't had a wedding ring on the other day. I shouldn't have been surprised, since not everyone advertises his or her marital status. The truth is, I'm not looking for a new romantic entanglement, especially not with anyone connected to our business. I'm enjoying being on my own again.

Picking up one of the fallen oranges, my father purses his lips and tilts his hat back so I can better see his eyes. "I hope I don't regret asking you this, but what did you hear?" He peels the orange and offers me half.

"Well." I peer up at the cloudless blue sky as if the words are etched above. "I didn't hear everything he said, but it was something about taking over our ranch in thirty days."

"That doesn't sound right." A look of confusion passes over my father's face. "Maybe you heard wrong. He was reasonable when I spoke to him."

"No. He sounded firm and that's why, the more I thought about it, the more upset I became. The next thing I knew, I found myself in his office, letting him know exactly what I thought of his deadline."

"You have *got* to learn to control your temper." He gently taps the side of my head. "Think first, act later. It's important that you take all options into consideration before reacting."

"You're right," I reluctantly agree. "But *thirty* days? Really, Dad, that's not enough time. I know we'll be fine in sixty days, but thirty is impossible. I've calculated that next month we'll be in the black after our first avocado harvest."

"Did you share our strategy with David, or did you just complain about the deadline?"

When my father looks at me with those probing eyes, I know that I can't even fudge the answer.

"Okay, so you know me too well." Inwardly cringing, I reflect on how I stormed into David's office while he was meeting with his wife. Really, his marital status should not be my focus. The man was beyond handsome and sitting behind his mahogany desk and in that large leather chair, he emitted some kind of strong animal magnetism that had me feeling flushed. From all appearances, I'd guess he probably worked out at the gym *when* he wasn't crushing family-owned businesses.

"I didn't actually get to the avocado part." I squeeze my father's hand. "As a matter of fact, I'll apologize to him right away. I'll even go so far as to call and make an appointment first. Does that sound better?"

"It sounds excellent." Taking off his hat, he pauses and wipes his brow with the back of his hand. "Getting old. I won't be taking these long walks with you much longer."

"You're not that old so don't try to rush things." His skin looks somewhat ashen. "I'm a little tired, too. Let's take the shortcut back."

"Good idea." After several minutes of silence, he asks, "So what's this I hear about you getting back together with Jared?" He holds his hands up. "Hey, you *know* how I feel about him. There's something about that man that rubs me the wrong way. But if *you* like him—and are back together—that's your decision. There's no denying he's a good lawyer. Robert did a good job of bringing him on to handle our legal documents."

"Dad, you don't have to worry about me going down that road again. I've got this under control."

****

Later that evening, I take a shower, select one of my favorite dresses, and prepare to see Jared, but *not* for the reason that Uncle Robert has in mind. When Jared suggested we meet at the new French restaurant, I hadn't thought about the fact that it was across the street from David's office. The last thing I need is another run-in with David and Jared. I can only handle one irritating man at a time. Come to think of it, I also don't feel like running into David and his wife, the dynamic duo who look like they could win a contest for the world's most stunning couple. I do my best with what I have, but there's no competing with *that* type of beauty. The two of them are in another league of their own.

After parking my car in the lot, I take my time, slowly making my way across the street, in no rush to see Jared. I'm not completely confident that meeting him is a good idea, but I have my own reasons for giving it a try.

The restaurant's dimly lit windows are adorned with hanging baskets of cascading purple, blue, and yellow Southern California wildflowers. A wrought iron *fleur de lis* symbol is displayed on a rustic door and French music can be heard from inside. Jared, dressed impeccably in a navy-blue suit, white shirt and narrow red tie, greets me with open arms— which immediately irritates me.

"You look beautiful," he says. Before I can protest, he grasps my hands, pulling me toward him and presses his lips first to one of my cheeks and then the other. "Since we are going to be eating French food, we might as well practice their customary greeting. *Oui*?"

I roll my eyes upward. "No, this is strictly business." I snatch my hand away and step out of his reach. I didn't want him to try anything, which is why we are meeting in a public place. "I thought my text was clear."

"It was," he says, shrugging and looking mischievous. "I got carried away. You look good enough to eat." He smiles sheepishly, looking like a schoolboy who just got caught stealing candy from the corner store. "As a matter of fact, I remember exactly what you taste like. No doubt it's part of the reason I fell so hard for you." He licks his lips. "A man could get hooked on your nectar."

"Really, Jared, do you have to be so crude? Let's go inside," I say tersely. I'm not about to stand outside and explain to him why he needs to keep his lips and his memories to himself. Why did he have to start the evening off as if this was some kind of a date? Hopefully, I won't have to remind him again that I see beneath his boyish charm and deceptively preppy appearance.

"The name is Jared Chandler. We have reservations," he tells the waiter, who promptly leads us to a private table behind a large fern. "Robert told me that you wanted to see me. I have to admit I was surprised."

"He told you *what*?" I can't believe my uncle would go so far as to lie to get me to see Jared. I shake my head. "Look, I can't imagine why he would tell you that. Nothing could be further from the truth."

"He obviously can see what I already know. We make a great team." He pulls out the chair for me before taking his own seat.

"Everyone has a right to their own opinion," I mumble before turning my attention to the menu. Glancing at the price list, I conclude that this is not a restaurant for those on a budget. "I'll have the chicken Caesar salad."

"Money is no object, you know that. Order whatever you like." He signals to the waiter to return to the table and prepares to give him our order. "I'm having the steak and lobster. Are you sure you don't want more than a salad?"

"The salad will be fine. I *am* ordering what I want."

Once the waiter leaves, Jared's expression changes, becoming almost vulnerable. "So, what is it you wanted to see me about?"

Is he expecting me to have changed my mind? "I told you, this wasn't my idea. My uncle told me that you wanted to see me." I can't imagine what the man was thinking. I don't meddle in his social life, so he has no business meddling in mine. "However, since we are here, there's something I wanted to run by you."

"I'd like to go first. There are a couple of things that I need to share with you." He sits up straighter in his chair and adjusts his tie. "Do you mind?"

"Be my guest." What is this about? I never know what to expect from Jared and tonight is no exception. He almost looks uncomfortable. He never fidgets and that's what he's doing now. "What is it?"

"I've had some time to think about how I reacted to you breaking up with me." He clears his throat, looks down, and shakes his head. "I went about it all wrong. I shouldn't have gotten... you know, physical about it." He tugs his tie. "I sincerely apologize. Can you forgive me?"

My mind goes blank. I'm stunned. I can't believe he is actually apologizing and looks contrite. But I can't forget what he did, even if he's truly sorry now. Too much has happened, and my wrist has the welts to show for it. "Yes, of course."

"You don't know how relieved I am to hear you say that. I wasn't sure I'd be able to stand it if you didn't forgive me."

The waiter brings our food and neither of us says anything as we eat.

"I probably shouldn't push my luck, but there's more. My behavior was unconscionable. I *was* being an ass." He runs a hand through his hair and offers me a sheepish grin. "But the truth is, I'm miserable without you. We are perfect together, both college graduates who deeply care about Santa Lorena. You'd do anything for the town and so would I." He holds up his hands before I can respond. "Don't say anything; I know you do. This is our home. Look at us. I know we can make this work. We were good together and some part of you knows that, too." He pauses and cocks his head to the side. "I'm not sure why we're not still together."

"Because I don't agree with you." Here we go again.

"Ouch," he says, wincing. "You're really giving it to me straight."

"Right, because apparently I have to. We already went over all of this. You are a great guy—for some other woman, but not me."

Okay this is not a true statement, but it just popped out of my mouth and, besides, it will probably keep him from going ballistic. He says he's a changed man, but is he really? I don't plan on being around him long enough to find out.

"There is no other woman for me. I handled it clumsily. I should have given you more time before bringing up marriage. I obviously scared you off."

"Not really. You just confirmed that we are on two different pages and we needed to cut our losses."

He pushes his chair back from the table. "You almost have me convinced, but not quite." Smiling, he takes a sip of his red wine.

"I almost have you convinced of what?" I'm confused now. Jared is talking in riddles.

"That you don't still care for me. If you don't want me, you wouldn't have dressed up for our date. That red dress is pretty damn sexy, as I'm sure *you* know. And do you really expect me to believe that it was your uncle's idea and not yours that we meet tonight? I can tell you still want a piece of me and all that I can offer you."

I blink back the shock as I inwardly acknowledge his complete arrogance. "Wow, you are really full of yourself, aren't you?" This egotistical side of him is exactly what turned me off even before he got violent.

"And you know full well how I love the perfume you're wearing. It drives me wild. Don't tell me you didn't put that on just for my benefit." He licks his lips suggestively. "Because I *know* you put it on for me."

"You really think you have everything figured out, don't you? For your information, I did not set up this meeting, or whatever you want to call it. I always dress for myself and I chose to wear my favorite fragrance because *I* like it. News alert: everything is not about you."

"You expect me to believe that?" He laughs. "You just happened to forget how much it turns me on." He shakes his head. "Girl, you do not need to play hard to get. It's a little late for that."

"Jared, listen to me. I only came because I wanted to give you a heads up."

I'm so ready to go back home, slip on some warm pajamas, and curl up in bed with a good book. But I came here for one reason only and I'm not leaving until I've given him an update on his status as our lawyer.

"A heads up about what, my love?" he asks innocently.

"About how I'm going to have you removed as our attorney," I say triumphantly. "Tonight is a perfect example of how you don't listen to what I'm saying. This," I point a finger at him and then me, "is clearly not working and I think it's best if we terminate your services as our attorney."

"What?" His loud laughter causes several patrons to turn in the direction of our table. "Believe me, your uncle will never allow *that* to happen. You can't get rid of me that easily, even if you wanted to."

"What are you talking about?"

"Let's just say that, unlike *you*, your uncle is very fond of me. It's about more than my work ethic. It's about something you could never understand since you always knew who your parents were. Even with your mother out of the picture, you were raised in a home with your sister and father. One day, I told Robert about the foster homes and—well, he sees me like *his* family." He sips his wine. "So, it's deeper than you think. He's never had a son and I've never had a father, so I don't plan on going anywhere any time soon."

"Oh." I fold my arms and sit back in my chair at a momentary loss for words. I'm not sure what to make of this new revelation. When we were dating, Jared had confided in me that he never knew his biological parents. When he was nine months old, his mother had left him at a neighbor's house while she went to buy some drugs. When she hadn't returned two days later, the neighbor contacted the Department of Children and Family Services. His father's name was unknown and since no one ever came looking for him, he ended up a ward of the court and spent his youth in a succession of foster and group homes. Now that I think about it, his past probably explains why he has so much difficulty with rejection and feeling unloved, but it doesn't alter my decision to move on. "I never knew my uncle felt that way about you."

"Now you do and should understand that it will take more than your wishing I'll disappear for me to go away." He raises his glass. "I'd say that calls for a toast, wouldn't you?"

"I'm not sure what we would be toasting. Your relationship with my uncle?" I don't pick up my glass.

"No." His eyes glow with victory. "To our future."

****

I had no intention of working until seven, but sometimes that's what it takes to get the job done. I pick up my burger and fries from the coffee shop and have just stepped out the door when I stop and do a double-take. Damn and double damn. Directly across the street, standing in front of the new French restaurant is none other than Elaine Hart. She looked good before, but now, she looks... hot. She's wearing a bright red dress, high heels, and all that curly hair falling around her shoulders. There's no mistaking those curves. She must be waiting to have dinner with her family. Man, she cleans up nicely. I might as well say hello to her. I press the signal and wait for the light to change so I can cross the street.

Sure, she has a habit of losing her temper when she talks with me. Oddly enough, her temper is part of her appeal. All that passion for her family business that she just can't keep bottled up. Makes a man wonder if some of that passion spills over into other areas of her life. It's got to, right? But this isn't about business, so she should be able to calmly respond to a simple *Hello*. Just as I'm about to cross the street, take-out bag in hand, the jerk who was at her house pops up from out of nowhere, wraps his arms around her, then commences to slobber all over her face. *What the hell?* I can't believe it. Not after the way he was talking to her and grabbing her wrist, and now she's going out on a date with him as if nothing happened. Hey, if that's what she likes, then I wouldn't be the man for her anyway. Beats me why I'm thinking of her in *that* way in the first place. It's a crazy random thought that materialized out of nowhere. Probably because she's so unpredictable that I can't help but being confused.

Damn if I understand women. I quickly turn away, hoping she didn't see me, and head straight to the parking garage. She can suit herself. She comes storming into my office all angry and ready to sue me, which is ridiculous, but she's ready to go out on the town looking all sexy as can be with some Neanderthal. I'm done trying to figure out how to please a woman. I'm good on my own and don't need the additional grief, especially not now when I'm on the verge of taking the business to a new level.

Problem is, my mind won't shut down even after

I've showered and gotten into bed. I keep seeing Elaine standing there, looking so good that I was willing to go over there and make a fool of myself. I don't know what I was going to say, but with the way she looked, I probably would have asked her out. Obviously, that would have been a huge mistake. I didn't expect her to put up with abuse from any guy. Clearly, that guy didn't know the first thing about how to treat a lady. Just goes to show that I don't have a clue about women. Didn't with Courtney and don't with beautiful Elaine.

****

The next morning, I nick my face while shaving which doesn't do anything for the crummy way I'm feeling. Before heading to work, I walk a man's *true* best friend which, in my case, is my two-year-old Terrier Mix, Roscoe. Dogs are a totally different story.

"Right Roscoe?" He's always happy to see me. No funny moods, unpredictable behavior or mixed messages.

Before I am all the way in the office, my secretary Linda frantically approaches me in obvious panic mode.

"Mr. Cole, I tried to have her take a seat in the waiting area, but she wouldn't listen to me," she says anxiously as she frantically waves her hands in the air.

"Who are you talking about?" I peruse the large, beige-and-tan reception area. "I don't see anyone." Based on Amanda's comments that I'm impossible to work with, I intentionally speak as calmly as I can, considering that Linda is obviously worked up.

"Exactly." She flaps her hands some more. "She wouldn't wait out here." She folds her arms decisively across her waist. "That woman would not take *no* for an answer." She squints her eyes toward my office.

Growing impatient, I say, "Look, I don't know what you're talking about. There's no woman here."

"Of course not. That's what I'm saying." She looks apologetically in my direction. "She insisted on letting herself into your office."

Now I'm getting angry. Linda did everything she could to prevent the intruder from barging into my office. What could be so urgent that this person couldn't sit in the waiting area? Amanda decorated the reception area so people would be comfortable while they wait; tall ficus and ferns are on the end tables and stacks of the most recent magazines are on the coffee table.

"I'll take care of this."

"Should I call Security?" She looks at me nervously as she reaches for the phone on her desk.

I shake my head since I can't imagine a need for security. Suddenly, I feel a surge of anticipation. Why didn't I think of it sooner? It's probably Elaine. It would be just like her to make another grand entrance. She's probably sitting in there fuming while anxiously waiting to see me. I suppress a big grin. "Did she give you her name?"

The young secretary flushes bright red. "Why, yes. That's the other odd thing I was going to tell you. She said she was your wife, but I didn't believe her. If you were married, I figured you would have a wedding ring on and would have probably mentioned it, you know?"

Suddenly deflated, excitement and anticipation are replaced with a flash of disappointment and irritation. "Thank you, Linda."

What did Courtney want now? I moved out of the mansion and into a two-bedroom condominium several months ago. She got to keep the new Rolls Royce and the Audi. I even gave her the yacht. I want the marriage in my past. The only thing I kept was the dog. Roscoe was more loyal to me than she had ever been. What was there left to want? She had everything—including her lover.

"She's my soon-to-be *ex*-wife."

"Oh." Linda gasps, clearly surprised. She stumbles back into her chair. "I am so sorry. I had no idea, sir." She looks mortified.

"Of course, you didn't. You did the right thing." I pat her on the shoulder. "I'll handle this."

Courtney is peering out the window. She's wearing what appears to be custom-made jeans, the kind that cost thousands of dollars, complete with strategically placed holes revealing bits of her golden-brown skin on her thighs and calves. The matching denim jacket is tailored to accentuate her petite curves.

Finally, she turns and, noticing me, teeters across the room to throw herself into my arms. "Oh, my love, you don't know how much I've missed you."

The heavy scent of her perfume envelops me as her slender arms wrap around my neck. Did I ever really like that heavy fragrance? I can't help comparing it to Elaine's clean fresh scent.

"What are you doing here?" I free myself from her embrace. "I can't imagine how you've missed me at all. I'd think that James would keep you pretty busy."

What kind of woman decides to have an affair with her husband's best friend? Apparently, my ex-wife. While I was busy securing our financial success, she was sleeping with my best friend.

Sitting at my desk, I lean back and shake my head,

remembering the sweet young woman I'd met in my psychology class when I was a sophomore at San Francisco State University. She was a shy freshman with a cap of very short, ebony curls that perfectly accentuated her heart-shaped face. She'd made it clear that she preferred to keep things simple, refusing to bother with fancy hairstyles or layers of make-up. Courtney had grown up in a ten-story Oakland housing project. That was back before gentrification totally changed the landscape and rents soared sky-high in that historic, beautiful city across the bay. At that time, she'd been at her home with her mother and five brothers and had been working her way through college. She'd been a sociology major with a goal of becoming a community organizer who would help impoverished youth achieve their dreams. What I can't figure out is when she changed from being that sweet, innocent woman to the materialistic and dishonest person standing before me?

"Please don't be that way, David." She coyly looks down and places her hands over her heart. "I have never stopped loving you. You've got to believe me." Her voice is as sweet as honey.

"Yes, but apparently you couldn't love *only* me." I had let her break my heart once, but never again.

How can I ever trust another woman after all the crap that Courtney put me through?

"You don't understand how it was," she pleads. "I had never been with anyone before you. You know that I was a virgin when we met. And you were gone away so much I'd get—"

"Stop right there." I abruptly hold up my hand. "I don't need to hear your excuses. What do you want?"

Courtney is still attractive, but not in the way she was when we'd first met. Now, she wears false eyelashes, long acrylic nails and even her face looks different, as if she's had work done on her cheeks and her lips. Of course, she has the right to do whatever she wants with her appearance. Call me old-fashioned but I had admired her natural beauty. The cosmetic changes are one thing, but the infidelity wasn't something I was able to tolerate or brush aside.

She twists her hands together nervously. "I *know* I made a huge mistake." Coming to my side of the desk, she touches my hair. "Remember how I use to shampoo your hair and massage your scalp? You used to *love* that."

"*Used to* is the operative term." I move my head out of her reach. "Now, if there's nothing more to discuss, I have work that needs my attention."

At least we never had children to drag into the mess that was our marriage. I had wanted some, maybe two or three, but Courtney never felt the time was right. She was always too busy with her social life and maintaining her perfect size-six figure.

"Don't the years we spent together mean anything to you?" She pouts, looking at me innocently. "You're willing to throw it all away?"

"I can't believe those words came out of *your* mouth." I look at her incredulously. "Remember, *I* was never unfaithful to you. Not once. My lawyer says I'm the injured party, Courtney, not you."

When had she become so self-absorbed? Perhaps, it's my fault. I had indulged her every desire. But I'd loved her and wanted to treat her like a queen. Because that's what she was, my queen. She'd never had any desire to work outside of the home. No problem. She'd had weekly massages and manicures at the most exclusive private spa in Northern California. She'd attended monthly book club meetings that were held at one-hundred-dollar *high teas* in San Francisco's swankiest hotel and played tennis at the most prestigious country club on the West Coast. We had a housekeeper and a personal chef who prepared our meals four nights a week and usually the other three nights we either ate out or ordered in. I take a deep breath, before breaking the pencil I'm holding in two.

"That's true," she admits hesitantly and at least has the decency to look embarrassed. "But I didn't think you were the type of man to hold a grudge."

"Well, now you know." I look into her hazel eyes, those eyes that I use to think were so pretty, but now I see a shadow of the young woman who captured my heart when I was twenty years old. I turn on my computer and begin to review some files.

"So, it's like that?" She stomps her foot. "You are really going to ignore me? Act like I'm *not* in the room?"

"I only have one thing to say and that's sign the divorce papers. You should have them by tomorrow." I push the intercom on my desk. "Linda, please bring me the Hartland file."

"Fine, if you want to be that way." Courtney pushes out her chest while tossing back her hair. "I still love you, David. I know that you still love me, too, even if you're unwilling to admit it. I'm not giving up on our marriage without a fight."

Chapter 5
Moses & the Revelation

Sorting through my closet, I finally decide on my one business suit for today's *properly* scheduled meeting with David: the beige print blouse, tailored dark brown slacks, and tapered jacket. As I slip on my brown heels, my mind keeps returning to my dinner with Jared. The minute he'd kissed me outside the restaurant I should have known that he hadn't heard me when I said our relationship was over. It's as if he has it all figured out in his head and can't absorb anything else. I'm *not* one of his court cases where he can just keep talking and win the verdict he's hoping for. He obviously didn't take me seriously when I told him that I felt it would be better if he weren't our attorney. Finally, something from the past I *can* undo. The one thing I hadn't expected to hear was how close he was to Uncle Robert. The way Jared explained the whole family thing kind of made sense, but they can keep their father-son relationship, as long as Jared understands that I'm not part of some family "bundle".

Today is the day that I rise up to *my* father's expectations about how I conduct business. I'm not normally this easily riled, but it's the possibility of losing the family legacy—the legacy of love—that has me going to extremes. Did I *really* say, "I'll see you in court," to David? What was I thinking? Probably wasn't. The embarrassing—but honest—truth is that it's difficult for me to think clearly when I'm in his presence and that fact alone is irritating. I have no idea what goes on behind those mysterious eyes, but I know that he exudes some kind of masculine energy that could easily reel me in *if* I let my guard down. Now that I've admitted the ugly truth to myself, I'm ready to look beyond his distractingly good looks and finally explain my plan. Of course, my father is proud that I called David's secretary and scheduled this 10:00 a.m. appointment.

In the kitchen, I scrounge around for something that won't require more than a few minutes to prepare. Opening the refrigerator, I reach in, take out the cream cheese, and spread it on a sesame seed bagel. As I'm biting into the bread, Morgan takes a stilted step into the room. I can immediately see that something is wrong. Her breathing is heavy, and it ends with a small whimpering sound.

"You okay, sis?" As I sip my green tea, I recall that it's Back-to-School-Night, so the school day starts later which explains why she's still home. "Everything ready for tonight?" I flash her a thumbs-up sign.

"We have a situation…" Her eyes scan the room as if looking for something she's lost. "Oh my God, my God."

"What is it?" Frowning, I rush to her side and place my arm around her tense shoulders. "Did something happen to one of your students?"

Morgan shakes her head.

I'm getting worried. It's unlike her to not have something to say.

"Is it you? Are you all right?" Something is clearly

wrong, and she is afraid to say it. Could she be pregnant? Of course, she *could* be, but *is* she?

"No, it's not me." Her voice is low, making it hard to make out the words.

"Great," I say, relieved. "So why do you look like you lost your best friend?"

"It's not me or one of the students... It's Dad."

Before she can finish her sentence, I swiftly brush past her and run out of the kitchen into the hall and up the stairs. Panting, I'm finally standing in my father's bedroom doorway, taking in the familiar objects—the books on the shelves, the hats on the dresser, the brown bedspread, and my father sitting up in bed. I clutch my side and steady my breathing. Nothing has changed. What was I thinking? Morgan didn't actually say something was wrong with our father. My imagination just took off and went in all kinds of crazy directions. Morgan probably got freaked out because he's still in bed which isn't normal for him. I thought he was already outside checking the orange groves, but, obviously, he needed more rest. So, why then, am I trembling, afraid to actually step *in* the room? I force myself to approach the bed, but I can already see that he looks the same yet startlingly different at the same time. He's not moving, just sitting up, looking at something I can't see.

A bright image explodes in my mind, a three-dimensional vision so real and horrible that it's as if I'm once again two years old and my mother is hitting me until my father rescues me from her enraged blows. That awful night, she blamed me for my baby brother, Julian's, asthma attack and death, adamant that it was my responsibility to watch him and keep him breathing.

But something had gone very wrong that night and something was wrong now.

"Good morning, Dad." I force myself to step into the room, ignoring the trembling that's moved up from my legs to my arms. I reach out to hug him but hesitate and, instead, lightly touch his shoulder. "How are you feeling?"

He doesn't say anything, just looks out at nothing in particular. I can see his mind is somewhere else and I swallow the panic that has me curling my fingers into fists, my nails digging into the palms of my hands. I pull my cell phone out of my jacket pocket, begin to dial 911, knowing now without a doubt, that my father needs urgent medical care.

"I dialed the emergency number before I came to get you." Morgan comes in and stands beside me, her shoulder leaning into mine, reminding me of when she was little and would want comforting because she had skinned her knee or fallen off her bicycle. "I came into the kitchen to tell you... and then, for a moment, I couldn't talk." She smooths down her curls. "I just couldn't say it, Eli, but the ambulance should be here any minute."

It's been a long while since I heard my childhood nickname. Looking at her, I see the tears in her eyes that she blinks back before they can fall. I remember what it feels like to be responsible for doing the right thing when there's a crisis. I recall begging my mother to not hit me anymore, tearfully telling her how sorry I was for what I had done. I force myself to return to the present, not wanting Morgan to feel responsible. No one should ever have to carry that burden.

"You did a good job." I wrap her in my arms and

feel her breath catch as the tears flow. Hearing the quiver in my voice, I'm not sure who I'm comforting— her or me. "He'll be okay, won't you, Dad?" I turn, take a step back, and peer at my father's familiar face.

His eyes frantically seek out mine for a brief moment before he reaches up, frantically clutching his heaving chest, while heavily breathing and swaying slightly as if he's overcome with vertigo. His slow and steady moan echoes in the room as beads of glistening sweat form on his forehead.

"He's going to be fine." Actually, I'm not sure of anything, but it's what I hope—for all of our sakes. Had I missed the signs? He had seemed more tired than usual lately, but I didn't think that was a big deal. Doesn't everyone's energy fluctuate daily?

"Do you think so?" Morgan looks skeptical.

"Yes," I say, wanting to believe it's true. Riding that same wave of optimism, I cautiously sit by the side of his bed.

"Can you speak?" I ask, searching for some sign that he recognizes my voice, but with the exception of his deep groan, he doesn't utter a word. "I know you're in pain. Medical help is on the way and will be here very soon."

Morgan and I sit as if we're bookends, one of us on each side of our father, ready to prop him up if the need should arise. I'm afraid to move him or to look away, as if he'll disappear or crumble to the floor if I don't stay vigilant. I don't realize that I've been holding my breath until I hear the high, shrill pitch of the siren, and let out a long exhalation. Morgan bolts up, and, together, we speed down the stairs before the doorbell has rung. We fling open the door, signal the two paramedics to follow us up the stairs. I have to believe they are as efficient as they appear in their dark navy uniforms, carrying large square boxes of what has to be life-saving equipment. Once they are in the room, they quickly introduce themselves, while going directly to my father.

"Good morning. I'm Moses Perez and this is Tran Nguyen. What happened here?" the older of the two men asks as the one with the crew cut—Tran— begins to check my father's vitals.

"I came into my father's room to say good morning and…." Morgan pauses, folds her arms tightly around her waist, as if holding herself together. "He was not moving at all."

Morgan somehow manages to look smaller, her large personality seeming to have shrunk under the pressures of the morning.

"I asked him if he could speak, but nothing." I shrug helplessly.

"You both did a good job." Moses's eyes briefly make contact with mine before he continues administering to my father. "Tran and I have this now. You did the right thing by calling us." With their backs to my sister and me, they spend several more minutes working on my father before they load him onto a gurney. Securing him with thick straps, they carry him down the steps and out to their waiting emergency vehicle.

"Only one person can ride in the ambulance," Moses says as the back door to the vehicle swings open and Dad is hoisted in.

"I'll ride with him." I look at Morgan as I step inside. "We'll meet you at the hospital."

"Okay." Morgan nods her head.

Before I can caution her to drive safely, Moses and Tran are in the ambulance and the doors are closing. The wail of the siren blocks any thoughts of me bombarding them with questions. I reach out and grasp my father's hand, giving it a gentle squeeze.

"It's okay, Dad." I keep repeating the same sentence as if it's my new magic mantra.

****

I have no idea how long Morgan and I have been waiting in the sterile, crowded waiting room at Mercy General Hospital. The fluorescent light washes over us, casting us all in a yellowish hue. At some point, we agree to offer our seats to an elderly couple who would otherwise have to stand, since all of the other chairs are occupied. This is where the buck stops. It doesn't matter how much or how little money you have; this is the place when we realize that we all walk the line between being sick or healthy, regardless of income.

We edge past a dark-haired little girl rocking her stuffed doll while two people who appear to be her parents sit huddled together, whispering frantically in a language I don't recognize. Finally, we make our way to the window, which looks down on the hospital parking lot. Everyone pauses and anxiously looks up when a doctor walks through the door, eager for news on the status of their loved ones. I know we've only been here for hours, but it feels like days. A vending machine and a water fountain are directly across from the reception area.

"Are you hungry?" I open my purse. "I can get you something from the vending machine."

Morgan shakes her head. "I can't eat anything now." She chuckles and smiles weakly. "That's a first for me."

"I'm not hungry either." I link my arm through hers as we stand silently looking at the cars.

Out of the corner of my eye, I see Uncle Robert enter the room. "Darn. I didn't think of calling him. My focus was on Dad."

"I called him before I left the house." She raises her hand, signaling for him to join us.

"Thank God you did. He needs to be here." I brace myself, knowing that he must be worried sick about his only brother.

The scowl on his forehead appears deeper than before as he strides into the room, and, catching my eye, he walks over to us. It's not concern that emanates from him as much as it is anger. Anger that I now see is directed at me.

"What did you do *now*?" Disgust underlies his every word. His face is flushed, and his breathing is labored. He pants out each word as if he had to run a marathon to get to the hospital.

I turn away from the hatred I see in his eyes. Was it always there and I hadn't recognized it for what it was until now? I guess it took a real crisis for him to reveal his genuine feelings.

"Nothing," I utter. My father is laying in a hospital bed somewhere and I have no strength left to fight his brother's hostility.

"Pitiful," he mumbles loud enough for several people to turn and look our way. He turns to Morgan. "What happened?" Less agitated he addresses Morgan. "I can't get a thing out of that one. Maybe you can shed some light on why my baby brother is in this place."

"It's exactly what Elaine said." She glances at me.

Her voice is stern. "We're waiting to find out more." She crosses her arms and turns away from him. Morgan has never been able to tolerate the way Uncle Robert speaks to me.

Finally, a middle-aged woman with gray hair neatly pulled back in a bun walks in and scans the waiting area. "I'm looking for the family of Thomas Hart."

"That's us." My hand shoots into the air as if I'm a student eager to let the teacher know I have an answer, but, really, some illogical fear has me thinking that if I don't quickly speak up, she'll turn around and leave without telling me what's happening to my father.

She indicates that we should follow her out to the hall where there are no pictures on the wall or hushed words of anxious families attempting to stay calm while waiting to know the status of their loved one. A slight hint of antiseptic lingers in the air. She makes an effort to smile reassuringly, but it doesn't work. The fear that's lodged in the middle of my chest grows larger. Uncle Robert steps forward and brushes against my shoulder, almost knocking me over in the process.

"I'd like to speak to a doctor." He bellows, his voice echoing off the walls as if he's speaking to a person who's hard of hearing.

"I'm Dr. Patel." She pulls out a pair of red-framed eyeglasses and reviews the folder in her hand. "I have met the daughters and you are…?"

"The older brother, Robert Hart."

"I see," she says, while focusing her attention back on the green folder. "Mr. Hart's condition is in the process of being evaluated at this time. However, it appears that there may have been an area of blockage in one of the arteries leading to a myocardial infarction."

"Do you mind speaking in *plain* English?" Uncle Robert says. "I don't know *what* you're talking about."

"In other words, it appears that Mr. Hart has experienced a heart attack." She takes off her glasses, folds them before placing them back into her pocket. "I'm sorry I can't provide you with any more details at this time. When he's out of surgery, we'll know more."

"Surgery?" I repeat the words as if I must have heard her incorrectly.

"Yes. We need to go inside to be able to determine exactly what's happening with your father's heart."

"When can we see him?" Morgan asks while wringing her hands.

"It will be some time before the anesthesia wears off. He won't be awake for several hours." She looks at her watch. "You have time to get something to eat. By the time you come back, I'll have more information for you."

As Dr. Patel turns away, my legs wobble and the walls start to close in on me. "I need some air."

Everything is happening so quickly and in slow motion at the same time. How could my father be well one minute and having surgery the next? I look to Morgan and see that she's in shock as much as I am about the sudden downward turn of events.

"Dad is strong. He'll get through this." I'm saying this for myself as much as for Morgan. "And Mercy General has an excellent reputation."

Uncle Robert makes a clucking noise and shakes his head. "Is it too much to ask to see a *real* doctor?" He paces the floor. "That's one of the reasons I hate hospitals, all of the incompetence."

Ignoring his sexist comment, I nudge Morgan along toward the neon exit sign at the end of a long hallway that leads to the elevators.

"We both could use some air," I say.

The sun is starting to set, casting a gray shadow over the sky. It sounds like an ordinary day; a car horn slices through the air, a cheerful voice yells out a greeting, and the firm thud of shoes hits the pavement. Yet my legs feel heavy and weighed down as if I'm moving in quicksand. All I can think about is my father lying under the bright lights of a surgical table and having his chest cut open before they operate on his heart.

Morgan briefly closes her eyes while her hand goes to her stomach.

"You don't look so great." I peer at her more closely.

"I feel queasy, like I could throw-up." Her face drains of its usual color.

"Of course, because we haven't eaten all day." I squeeze her arm. "Most people's stomach growls when they're hungry, but you feel like throwing up. We've been in the hospital for hours. Let's get you some food."

Morgan shrugs. "You're right. I could use something in my stomach."

****

Not wanting to be far from the hospital, I glance around and see the closest place to get a bite to eat is the coffee shop in David's office building. That's right, it slowly comes rushing back to me, all the things I had planned to accomplish today, like meet with David to finally set the record straight—make good on my promise to my father so that the bank could give us more time to show a profit.

Walking toward the small café, I can understand it if he thinks that I'm completely unreliable for not showing up or bothering to call to cancel the meeting. I need to talk to him and explain why I didn't show up. All I can do is hope that he'll understand that emergencies happen, and events don't always go as planned.

Coleman Bank is spelled out in silver chrome lettering on the top of the skyrise building that dominates the block. David's office is on the twenty-fifth floor. But that will have to wait for now. The automatic glass doors open and we immediately see a sign with the words, One Stop Café written in purple, cursive letters. An arrow indicates that we should proceed straight down the hall and then turn right.

Inside the cozy diner is a long line of customers at the counter who are getting their coffee and pastries to go.

"Don't be put off by the line." The hostess, a small woman with big, blonde hair and a southern drawl, reassures us. "I got a seat for y'all. Just follow me." She leads us to a vacant booth toward the back of the bustling café.

"You all can take a seat right here. I'll get you some water." She hands us the menus and disappears.

Morgan and I sit there silently for a few minutes, both of us lost in our own thoughts, worried about our father. How could everything change so quickly? He was fine yesterday when we drove from the first rows of trees to the last. At least, he'd appeared fine. When was the last time he had a physical? I'd always assumed he was on top of his health and took good care of himself, but I know that's no guarantee that something like this can't happen.

"Toast and chamomile tea is all I need." I peruse the menu.

"I don't know what I want yet," she says, her head buried in the menu.

"We've got some time. The doctor said the surgery would take awhile."

Sitting across from us is a familiar profile that has to be David. His stunning wife with the cobalt blue streaks of hair listens intently as he speaks. When he looks up, our eyes connect. He squints slightly as if trying to see me better. I flush and take a quick sip of water.

"I need to do something," I say to Morgan. David needs to know I didn't intentionally miss our scheduled appointment. My father would want me to go over and apologize.

"Elaine, what are you talking about?" Morgan sets down the menu. "What do you mean there's something you have to do?"

"Never mind. They're coming here."

Here they come, all long strides and oblivious to the curious stares that people cast in their direction. They seem completely unaware of their striking good looks.

"How nice to see you again, Ms. Hart." David's wife smiles at me before casting an inquisitive look at Morgan. "You two look so much alike, you must be sisters."

"Yes, I'm Morgan, Elaine's younger sister."

"These are the Coles. David represents our bank." I

force myself to stop staring at David. He looks regal and sophisticated in his black-and-white striped shirt and black slacks. Suddenly, I'm aware of how disheveled I must appear. I've been so preoccupied with my father's health that what I look like is not a priority. Staying by my father's side has been the only thing on my mind. "David, you may have been wondering about me not showing up for the appointment. We've had a family emergency."

The café seems suddenly silent as if everyone is now listening to our conversation, but I know that can't be true.

"I'm sorry to hear that," Ms. Cole says. She sounds so sincere. For a reason that I haven't had time to think about, I *want* to not like her, but it's impossible. "I hope everything's okay."

"Not really," Morgan says before I have a chance to respond. "Our father had a heart attack early this morning and we've been at Mercy General for the last twelve hours."

"Goodness," David's wife says. "I hope that he'll be okay." She nudges David's arm, as if encouraging him to say or do something. "If there's anything my brother and I can do, please let us know."

"Your brother?" I ask, liking her even more now that I've learned that she's his sister and not his wife.

"Yes. Who did you think I was?" She chuckles knowingly. "You thought I was his wife. I use my maiden name for business. David is my baby brother."

David, who has been staring silently at me, loudly clears his throat. "I am not your baby brother."

"Yes, you are." She folds her hands across her middle. "Technically, we're twins, but I was born three minutes before him so that would make me his older sister."

I like her more by the minute. They're not married? They're twins? And all this time I was under the mistaken assumption that he was taken, but now... now what? I need to remember that he's still the enemy, threatening to take our property.

"They don't want to hear about that." He glares at Amanda. "I'm sorry to hear about your father." He looks at me and when he speaks, his voice is surprisingly filled with genuine concern. "Don't worry about the meeting. We can reschedule at your convenience."

"Really?" Relief washes over me. I know the thirty days are practically up, but there's more I have to say. I look into those dark eyes, surprised to see that they're filled with compassion I wouldn't have expected. So now I feel crummier. This is the second time I have misjudged David. "I'm sorry for the way I came barging into your office the other day." There, I said it. My father would be proud that I've finally apologized. There's no excuse for how I interrupted their meeting and said whatever thought happened to pop into my head. In the future—no, right now—I'll do better. It's as if a weight has been lifted off of my shoulders.

"Don't worry about it." She laughs while patting David on the back. "It was my absolute pleasure to watch someone put my brother in his place. It made my day."

Morgan squints at David and Amanda. "I wouldn't have guessed that you two are twins." I can see that she's soaking it all in. They don't really look alike.

"Mandy never misses an opportunity to share her

three-minute lead with the world," he adds dryly. "Elaine, there's no rush with the meeting."

Even with my thoughts clouded with worry, I feel something stir inside when he says my name.

"You understandably have more important things on your mind. Let's revisit the topic when your father is released from the hospital."

Chapter 6
Man's Best Friend

"I'm sorry to hear about their father's heart attack." Mandy looks solemn as I pay our bill and head out of the restaurant and into the brightly lit lobby. I glance up and see that the elevator has stopped on the nineteenth floor, so we'll be waiting for a while.

"I agree. I thought I saw her when she walked in the restaurant with her sister. But I wasn't sure. They were understandably distraught."

When she'd first entered the restaurant, I could tell that Elaine wasn't her usual self. Something about the way her shoulders were slumped, and her face looked drawn as if she hadn't slept in hours told me that something serious had happened. The few times I've seen her were like she'd been fueled with boundless energy, but not today. A part of me wanted to go over and wrap her in my arms, but, of course, I don't know her like that. It was this irrational impulse, though. Heck if I know where that thought came from. She's so confusing, all fired up and angry one minute and then the next contrite and apologetic. Is it a wonder that I don't understand how I feel about her?

"Just thinking about how things can change so quickly is scary, especially when it comes to someone's parent suddenly becoming ill." Amanda tosses her handbag over her shoulder and looks at me curiously. "I must say, I was proud of you. You were very understanding."

"Why wouldn't I be?" I frown at Amanda, wondering why she's looking at me suspiciously. "I'm a considerate guy."

"Well, you certainly can be, as we just saw. But let's face it. You are the man who recently fired several secretaries."

"That's because they were incompetent." I move aside to let Amanda get on the elevator before I step in, glad that no one else has gotten on. I press the button for the twenty-fifth floor.

"So you say." She shrugs. "When you spoke to Elaine, I sensed a different vibe, that's all."

"What are you talking about?" I ask.

We discontinue the conversation when the elevator stops on the sixth floor and a group of noisy people gets on and begin chattering away about some happy hour they'll be going to after work today. Finally, after three more stops, we get off on our floor.

"Like I was saying, I was giving both of them a little extra time."

We stand outside Amanda's spacious office. Despite all of the mauve and lavender furniture, the space looks professional and inviting. Initially, I teased her that it looked more like a therapy room than a business office, but it suits her personality. No secretaries here. She prefers an open-door policy and handles all of her clerical tasks herself.

"No big deal," I continue. Leave it to my sister to complicate matters.

"You totally ignored Morgan. I don't recall you saying one word to her. It was obvious you only had eyes for Elaine."

"That's because she's the one I'm working with, not her sister." Sometimes Amanda's assumptions are too much. She has a vivid imagination. Always has. But, damn, I didn't think she could see through me that easily. I'm not admitting anything to her.

"Wow, so that's the way it is?" Amanda asks, looking at me quizzically. "What's with you and Elaine? And don't you dare try to pretend that you don't know what I'm talking about. There was something happening between the two of you."

I follow her into her office. "Are you saying you think she has a thing for me?" She did say she sensed something happening between the two of us, so it wasn't just my feelings that she was picking up on. Interesting.

"I'm saying that something was obviously going on between the two of you." Sitting down at her desk, she pulls the phone in front of her, looking up at me while beginning to dial a number. "I've got some calls to make and you…" she points a finger in my direction, "have to decide what, if anything, you are going to do about what's happening between the two of you."

"I don't need your advice," I say, even though I know she's right.

"Oh, I know that. It's just that, as your big sister, I feel obligated to help you out with friendly suggestions whenever I can." She smiles innocently.

"At this point in my life, I don't need any suggestions, thank you very much."

"I agree. However, I do have one last piece of advice—don't forget that we have the Strawberry Festival in two weeks."

How can I forget about the Strawberry Festival? Our mother has talked of nothing else for the last two months. She read about the annual event in the local paper and is looking forward to being able to eat her favorite fruit in a variety of recipes, including pies, smoothies, ice cream sundaes, and who knows what else.

It was her and my father's idea to leave the hustle and bustle of San Francisco behind and live in a smaller community as they prepare for their departure from the company. Those two continued to be as romantic and in love as ever, barely able to keep their hands off of each other, which was a bit embarrassing for Amanda and me growing up. Not all of us were so lucky when it came to love and marriage, as witnessed by the fiasco that my marriage turned out to be. I've learned my lesson. I *like* living alone. It's peaceful.

***

By the time eight o'clock comes around, I'm ready to head home, but, first, I'm going to head over to the hospital. Earlier, I'd ordered a plant to be delivered to Mr. Hart's room, but I want to see how he's doing for myself. He's a good man who spoke highly of both his daughters, but had made it clear that much of the success of the ranch was due to Elaine's efforts.

I couldn't stop thinking about her all day. Her concern for her father was visibly taking a toll on her. Could I be missing her erratic behavior? Nah, that wasn't it. I just feel bad for her.

****

Something about hospitals makes me uncomfortable. Probably because it reminds me of when I was ten years old and had visited my grandmother in one. It was the last time I saw her alive and, in my young mind, it wasn't the ovarian cancer that had killed her, it was the hospital. Of course, as I matured, I knew better, but a lingering discomfort surfaces as I make my way to room three-eleven.

A small lamp on the nightstand dimly lights the room. Something stirs in me when I see Elaine and observe the worry etched on her lovely face as she sits by the side of her father's bed. At the sound of the door opening, she looks up, startled, and, for the briefest of seconds, our eyes lock before she smiles and signals for me to come into the room. Grabbing an extra chair that's by the unused hospital bed on the other side of the room, I bring it over to sit next to her.

Looking at her father, I wonder how it's possible that he's changed so much in a short amount of time. He's a shadow of the man I'd visited a few days ago. Lying in the hospital bed, his skin ashen and devoid of its previous rich hue, he appears frail, his chest and arms connected by multi-colored, intravenous tubes to a large, steadily beeping monitor. Elaine slowly stands, arches her back and motions for me to follow her outside to the hall.

"Hi." She smiles as she stifles a yawn. "I feel like I've been sitting there forever."

"If you've been here since this morning, it *has* been hours."

"It's like a Las Vegas casino here; you lose all track of time." Faint shadows form dark crescents under her eyes.

I bring my hand up and then down as I suppress the desire to pull her into my arms, offer her some comfort. She looks like she could use a shoulder to lean on. I'm glad that she no longer sees me as the enemy. Where is her uncle or even her sister? Maybe they've already come and gone home. It *is* late.

She looks away before letting out a deep breath. "There's nowhere else I could be right now, except by my father's side." She raises an eyebrow. "You didn't have to come."

"I know, but I wanted to. I enjoyed talking to your father." While this was true, I'd also needed to see her. "I wanted to see how he was doing."

She glances down the hallway at the long row of open doors. "I don't want to disturb anyone. Let's sit over there." We make our way to a row of blue seats not far from the nurses' station. "Thank you for the plant. That was thoughtful."

"How's he doing?"

She takes her time, as if she isn't sure of the answer. "He's slept most of the day... It's the anesthesia."

She absently brushes her hair off her forehead and then, as if realizing that she's exposed a small, z-shaped scar, she bites her bottom lip and quickly smooths her bangs back into place.

I'm curious. Wonder if it's from a childhood injury, such as a bicycle fall, but since she obviously likes to keep it covered, I decide not to comment.

"Has he been awake at all?" How in God's name had I not noticed that her skin was such a beautiful rich shade of brown? *Focus, man, and not on the fullness of her lips*. I clear my throat. "I mean since you came back from the coffee shop?"

She shakes her head and her eyes sparkle with joy. "He woke up about two hours ago and squeezed my hand. I called for the doctor to come in, but he was already out again by the time she came to the room."

"Where's Morgan?" I've got to ask, knowing that it isn't any of my business.

"She's at the school where she teaches." She takes her cell phone out of her purse and frowns. "Oh no. My battery is dead. I've been keeping Morgan and my uncle updated on my father's status. Morgan came back to the hospital after class, but I encouraged her to return to school for Back-to-School-Night." She bleakly re-examines her phone before shaking it.

"I don't think shaking it will charge the battery."

She laughs and nods her head. "You're right. I'm so tired that I can't think straight. I need to be able to communicate with Morgan and Uncle Robert."

"You can use my phone to call her." I pull it out of my pocket.

"Thank you, but Morgan won't answer if she doesn't recognize the number. She's had problems with crank callers in the past."

"What kind of phone do you have?" I ask, thinking that she can use my car charger.

"An Android." She eagerly raises her eyebrows. "By any chance, do you have a charger I could use?"

"I wish I did, but my phone isn't an Android." A couple of thoughts take shape, and, before I can think it through or dismiss it as a crazy idea, I speak up. "Look, we need to get your phone charged so you can communicate with your family."

"True." She distractedly runs a hand through her hair. "I told Morgan I'd give her a call later."

"I don't know about you, but I'm hungry. Have you eaten since this morning?"

She looks thoughtful as if she's trying to recall the last time she ate. "Now that you mention it, I only had tea and toast this morning." She sighs heavily. "It seems like it was days ago instead of earlier today. What time is it anyway?"

"It's past eight." I'm concerned that she hasn't eaten all day. She won't last long or be there to help her father with his recovery if she doesn't take care of herself.

"Really?" She twists her hands together. "I didn't realize it was so late."

"Elaine, I've got an idea. It sounds like you're running on empty. You need to put some food in your stomach and get your phone charged."

"You're right." She places her hands on her stomach. "Now that we are talking about food, I feel ravenous. I don't know if the hospital cafeteria is still open."

"I doubt it, but I was talking about a real meal. How did you get to the hospital?"

"I rode in the ambulance with my father. Morgan is going to pick me up after Back-to-School-Night ends sometime after nine."

"She's got to be exhausted, too." I glance at my watch. "Since your father is still sleeping, why don't we get a charger for your phone and some food for your belly?"

"I wouldn't want to be any bother." She gives me a sober look. "You must have other plans."

"I don't." I shrug. "I'm hungry, too. We can pick up a charger on the way to eat." I smile, eager for her to say yes so I can be with her longer. "And maybe you can sleep on the way."

"Dr. Patel did say that he's on heavy medication and she expects him to sleep through the night." There's a note of uncertainty in her voice as she looks down at her rumpled clothes. She swipes under her eyes. "I can't go to any restaurant looking like *this*." She makes a face while shaking her head. "But thanks for the offer."

"You look fine, but you need to feel comfortable. I live close by. We can stop and pick up a charger on the way to my apartment. And I'll prepare us something to eat. You will be back in your father's room in no time."

"I *am* exhausted." She yawns before abruptly rising to her feet. "Okay, let's do it."

She smiles brightly, and I feel as if I made a winning touchdown during the last ten seconds of the homecoming football game.

"Your offer is too tempting to turn down."

****

While we sat talking in the hospital, a cool breeze had replaced the warmth from earlier in the day. It was taking me a while to adjust to Southern California's temperature variations. Hot, balmy days are frequently followed by chilly, windy evenings. Large dark clouds speckle the sky as we make our way to my car which is parked in the lot across the street. Noticing that Elaine is shivering, I remove my suit jacket and place it around her shoulders.

"Thank you."

Our hands briefly touch as she accepts my jacket, and I'm caught off-guard at the unexpected spark of heat the contact ignites. After I open her door and get in the car, she faces me, her lips tilting up in a smile.

"This *is* nice." She scrutinizes the car's interior.

"I bought it before moving down here." Pulling out of the parking lot, I'm thinking of which store we'll need to stop at to get her a charger.

"I don't know much—really *anything*—about cars." She absently runs her fingers across the dashboard. "You already know that, though."

I glance in her direction. "I remember something about riding in I think her name was Betsy."

I grimace remembering the rumbling engine. Even though the car obviously was on its last leg, at least it showed that Elaine wasn't status conscious which is a plus in my book. I always leased Courtney's automobiles because she never wanted to be seen driving a vehicle that was more than two years old.

"Well, that's the thing. I would keep it forever, but the last time I had to renew my registration, it barely passed the mandatory smog test." She stretches out her shapely legs. "I like my car even if it doesn't run as well as it once did."

I pull into a twenty-four-hour drug store. "Do you want to wait here while I get the charger? You look pretty cozy over there."

She nods and I go inside the store where I head straight to the electronics section and select two chargers for her phone. One is portable and can be carried in her purse and the other is for emergency back-ups. When I return to the car, she's half asleep.

"That was quick." Looking slightly embarrassed, she sits up straighter. "I didn't realize how exhausted I was." She rubs her hand across the back of her neck.

"It's been a stressful day." I plug in the new charger. "Let's start charging your phone now so you can let Morgan know what's happening."

"Right. I don't want her to worry." She connects her phone to the charger. "Thank you. You're a lifesaver."

We drive the rest of the way in silence. I smile when I look over and see her nodding off again. "Hey, sleepy head, we're here."

I pull into the garage and we make our way to the underground elevator. As we enter the townhouse, I hope that I didn't leave the place in too much of a shamble since I wasn't expecting company. Roscoe rushes out to greet me, but, first, he sniffs around Elaine's ankles.

Elaine reaches down and strokes him between his ears. "Hey, who's this fella?"

"That's Roscoe, my dog." I grimace, realizing that I should have asked if she was okay with dogs before inviting her over. From the looks of it, Roscoe has found a new best friend. He never liked Courtney, but his tail rapidly wags as he licks Elaine's hand. "Seems he approves of you."

"He's adorable. What kind of dog is he?" She continues to stroke his back.

"A terrier mix." I think back to the mangled, infested fur ball he'd been when I'd first laid eyes on him as he'd followed me home from my jog. I couldn't get him to go away. "He followed me home one day. He was in pretty sorry shape and the rest is history."

"He's adorable and so friendly, too." She scratches behind his ears. "Aren't you boy?"

"The thing is," I rub my chin, "he's not that way with everyone."

Roscoe trots behind Elaine as she makes her way across the living room before she stops to peruse the books in the built-in bookshelves. She doesn't comment but picks up a few nonfiction ones covering history and politics. After leafing through several pages of Barack Obama's autobiography, she sets it back on the shelf. Taking her time, she makes her way over to my music collection that's neatly stacked against the living room wall right beside my large screen television.

"You have eclectic taste. Looks like you've got a little bit of everything." Kneeling down, she sorts through the pile of old albums and CDs. Picking up an Erykah Badu album, she glances at me. "I love her music. If you listen closely, you get that she is very deep."

"She's great." I walk over to stand by her side, pleased that she can appreciate my taste in music. "How about this?" I pull out a Blake Shelton album. "Bet you weren't expecting this?"

"Hmmm." She takes the vinyl from my hand. As our fingers briefly touch, I know she has to feel the undeniable spark as strongly as I do. "I can't say that I was *expecting* it, but I like country, too. My father's people were originally from Texas. He likes country music—and we would listen to it as children. Some would say that it undoubtedly originated from the blues. You know, singing about your heartache is definitely part of the African-American tradition."

"I didn't know you were into music like that." I take a step closer, smelling the freshness of whatever perfume she's wearing.

"It's not like you really *know* me." She yawns and steps away.

Of course, she's right, except it feels as if I've known her for a long time. It's as if she belongs right here in my home.

"I like these." Her eyes roam over the brown suede sofa and matching chairs, the wet bar, the black-and-silver chrome appliances and granite counter tops. Her eyes are half-closed, and she appears ready to collapse.

"Make yourself at home." Removing the jacket from around her shoulders, I point to the wet bar. "What can I get you to drink? Would you like a glass of wine?"

Looking sheepish, she smiles. "That sounds great."

I go to the refrigerator and remove a bottle of Sauvignon Blanc that I opened last night. I hand her a glass. "I'm going to start dinner. Are you a meat eater?"

She nods. "I eat a little of everything."

"Okay. That makes this easier." I remove two steaks from the refrigerator. "I have never met so many vegetarians since I moved to this part of the state."

"Well then, it won't surprise you that I use to be a vegetarian myself," she confesses.

I join her as she throws back her head and unselfconsciously laughs.

"But occasionally, I needed to have some chicken or even a hamburger." She holds her hands up. "I know Southern California is made up of a lot of health-conscious people." She chuckles.

"You can say that again." I put the steaks in the microwave to defrost. "Steak, baked potato, and a green salad. Sound okay?"

She walks over to where I'm standing in the kitchen, an intent expression on her face. "Do you have sour cream, chives, and bacon bits?"

"Let me check on the sour cream." I head to the refrigerator and scan its contents. "I'll have to make the bacon bits."

"Wow! That would be great." She rubs her hands together. "I can hardly wait. I think my stomach just growled again."

She peers over my shoulder as I stand at the sink and rinse two large Idaho potatoes.

"Can I help?" she asks eagerly. "I love cooking."

Her nearness distracts me and I'm glad I don't have a knife in my hand as I drop one of the potatoes.

"That one's yours." She looks down at the potato rolling across the floor.

I chuckle, turn, and see that she's standing so close that I could bend down and press my lips against hers, but I won't. Her father is in the hospital and she's exhausted. Right now, I'm being a friend. I may have to keep reminding myself of that fact.

"I don't need any help. Relax." I get another potato, before removing the lettuce, tomatoes, and bacon from the refrigerator. "This is your chance to nap."

"Okay. I'll text Morgan first, and then I'll get out of your way." When she's done texting, she makes her way to the balcony and looks out the sliding glass doors. "What a view of the town. Did you know that it's raining?"

"A few drops came down when I walked into the store. I love this view. It's the main reason I bought this townhouse." After setting the sour cream down, I turn around to find that she's left the kitchen.

Twenty minutes later, I see that she's sprawled on top of my king-size bed, fast asleep. Roscoe lies across the foot of the bed, his paws covering Elaine's feet.

"So, it's like that, huh, Roscoe? Dump me for a

pretty face." He looks at me and whimpers. "I can't say I blame you."

Dinner can wait; she obviously needs sleep more than she needs to eat. As I turn off the light switch, I hear her voice, soft as a whisper. She's still asleep, though. Wonder if she's dreaming about the jerk at the French restaurant. How do I know if he's really an ex, especially if she dreams of him at night? It only takes a minute to decide that I'm not going to leave the room—yet. Besides, as I walk closer, I see that what I thought was a dream, may be more of a nightmare.

She frantically shakes her head back and forth. "I'm sorry. Please don't hurt me anymore," she begs as she raises her arms protectively over her head.

I've heard enough to see that she's pleading to not be hurt. What kind of man would so terrorize a woman that even when she's trying to rest, she's haunted by his violence?

I sit down on the edge of the bed and gently touch her arm. "Elaine."

She doesn't wake up at the sound of her name, so I caress her shoulder. She frowns before slowly opening her eyes and, blinking rapidly, looks around the room, clearly disoriented.

"You were having a bad dream." I rub her arm, trying to soothe the frightening images of whatever had her cowering in obvious fear. "You okay?" God, her skin is so soft.

She sits up, breathes deeply, and averts her eyes. "I'm fine. Thank you for waking me." She swipes a tear from the corner of her eye. "I didn't plan to fall asleep." She sheepishly shrugs and runs her hand across the black velvet comforter. "It looked so comfortable." She holds a thumb up. "It passed my test."

"Good to know. Anytime you need a bed, you know where to find me." That didn't sound right, especially since I'm trying to stop myself from wrapping her in my arms right now.

"Are the steaks ready?" She looks up, composed, having brushed off the images that were haunting her only moments ago.

"Yes." I nod my head. "Waiting for you."

We walk into the kitchen. "Silverware is in this drawer and plates are in this cabinet." I'm glad to be back in the kitchen. I was starting to imagine her *in* my bed, not *on* it.

While eating in silence until our plates are almost empty, I decide to avoid discussing anything intense. It's good to see her relaxed, especially after witnessing her in the middle of a bad dream.

"What got you interested in agriculture?" I eat my last piece of steak.

"It's hard not to be when you grow up on a ranch. It's really all I know and all I ever wanted to do." She finishes her food, and, when she looks at me, she's beaming. "Even as a little girl, I felt there was something innately magical about planting a seed in the ground and watching a little branch break through the soil." She laughs, pure joy in her voice. She clasps her hands together. "Do you know what I love the most?"

I roll my eyes. "Is this a trick question?"

"No." She laughs at her own game. "I don't know why I even asked you that. How could you know?"

At this moment, I want to know everything there is to know about her: what was she dreaming about, how did she get that scar on her forehead, how her lips taste, what her skin feels like on the inside of her arm and the back of her thigh.

"Do you want to guess?"

"Not really." Although, I would if it kept her eyes sparkling and her being relaxed and happy. "Do you love playing in the dirt?"

"No, silly." She laughs again while playfully nudging my arm. "I love watching the trees break through the ground, the leaves starting to form, and the blossoms emerging before the fruit does." She makes it sound like some kind of magic.

We both hear the sound of the phone going off at the same time. She jumps up, Roscoe on her heels. She unplugs the phone from the charger and glances at me. "It's fully charged now. Morgan sent me a text. She'll be picking me up in about fifteen minutes."

"It's raining hard out there right now. Not a good night to drive." I don't want her to leave. "I have a guest room you can use." I want to be clear that I'm not suggesting anything more than a good night's sleep before she returns to the hospital. I start removing our plates from the table.

She shakes her head. "I've already put you through enough, stopping at the store to buy the charger, cooking dinner, sharing your dog and your bed..." She frowns realizing how that sounds. "I mean... you let me *use* your bed."

"I know what you mean." I rinse the plates before placing them in the dishwasher. I like the sound of the first statement better. *If only she* was *sharing my bed— with me in it.* "I was going to eat anyway, and I didn't go out of my way. I enjoyed your company." I take her hands in mine.

111

"Good company doesn't fall asleep." She gently pulls her hands away.

I feel angry as I think of her nightmare and fear. "You needed the sleep. Glad I could help."

She smiles. "You're nicer than I originally gave you credit for." She glances down at her phone as it beeps again.

"I could say the same about you. You were pretty intense when you came storming into my office."

She rolls her eyes and places a hand to her forehead. "Please don't remind me. I *did* apologize. Sometimes I get carried away and need to take a minute before I react." She smooths her bangs. "Morgan is downstairs, waiting for me." She holds up the phone, as if I need evidence that she has to leave.

"Take my jacket at least." I remove it from the hall closet, wrap it around her securely, buttoning it and pulling up the collar. "It's a little big on you, but it will keep you warm."

"Thank you." She rolls up the sleeves. "I'll return it."

"Promise?" I smile and pull her close, finally pressing my lips against hers and wrapping my arms around her, feeling the warmth of her body as I hold her. When she responds with a soft moan and wraps her arms around my neck, I know my willpower is gone. The longing I feel is reflected back to me when I gaze into her eyes. I place small kisses on her mouth, until it opens, and my tongue meets hers, touching and exploring.

"David." She places her hands on my chest. "I have to leave." Taking a step backward, she creates distance between us.

"I know." Placing a finger under her chin, I lift her head, so that she has to look at me. Right now, this feels good... right, even. No troubling thoughts of business, illness or anything else, just her in my arms.

"Thank you. This reprieve—time away from the hospital—it was just what I needed." She shakes her head when her cell phone beeps and looks down while reading the screen. Tilting her head to the side and looking at me with her big brown eyes, she says, "Morgan is threatening to come get me if I don't hurry up."

"I'll check on you and your father tomorrow." I give in to the impulse to run my fingers through the reddish-brown curls cascading down her back before I slowly trace the outline of those tender, full lips with my fingertip, their softness as intoxicating as any aphrodisiac. Every part of me aches for her with an urgency I've never experienced before.

The minute she's gone, the condo feels different— too large and too empty which doesn't make sense since I love this place and everything in it. After all, this is my first home on my own since the divorce. Elaine's fresh scent lingers. I turn off the kitchen lights and head to my bedroom, where I note that her luscious body has left an imprint on my bed. Damn. How did this woman make her way into my thoughts?

Roscoe makes his way over to me and nudges my thigh. "I know. It seems empty around here, doesn't it?" Roscoe answers with a yelp. "No offense meant." I pat his head. "You're still my best friend."

I kick a shoe that I've left on the bedroom floor. I don't need these complications. My divorce isn't even final.

One kiss. Okay, the fact that it was the one kiss that happened to be the best kiss I've ever had does not change the fact that her family is delinquent on their loan. *But what kind of jerk would I be if I kept them to their thirty-day obligation while the father is in the hospital recovering from surgery?*

I kick the other shoe, tossing it all the way across the room. My first obligation has to be to the business not to the most interesting woman I've ever met. Damn, damn, damn. I've messed up in the past. Caused the family to lose, hell, I don't know how much money. I was young, just starting out after business school and my father had allowed me to make some investment decisions that failed miserably. I had made the mistake of going by decisions that felt right as opposed to using statistics and quantifiable facts. Feelings got me in trouble in my marriage and in business. There isn't room for feelings in my life now. I've learned my lessons the hard way. Tonight, I slipped. Gave in to my desires. Wrapped her in my arms and held her, so close I could feel her heart beating against mine. I can't put myself in that situation again. From now on, I'm keeping my distance. No matter how enticing she is, *and, man, is she enticing*, the business must always come first. What happened tonight with Elaine will never happen again.

Chapter 7
Dr. Patel's Call

"Before you tell me how you happen to be at David's house, I want to know how Dad was when you left the hospital." She looks in my direction before changing lanes. "Nice jacket, by the way. A tad too big for you, but it has that boyfriend-girlfriend vibe about it. It's only missing a letter. Remember those letter jackets? Did your new boyfriend give it to you?"

"Very funny, Morgan. To answer your first question, Dad was sound asleep. Dr. Patel said the anesthesia would have him out for hours, so there was no need for me to hang out. She told me it was too early to have any results from the surgery."

"That sounds good." She nods. "I'm thinking he should have a smooth recovery. It's not like he was sick or anything. Now, if he had been ill, that would be different, but he wasn't."

"That's what I think, too," I say to reassure both of us. "Mercy General has a really good reputation, so that helps." I don't add that I wouldn't have been surprised if Uncle Robert had ended up in the hospital. He was older and led a much more sedentary life than our dad. Of all people, I should know that life can be unpredictable and, sometimes, bad things happen not just to older people, but also to those who are younger, too—like my baby brother.

"What happened back there?" Morgan gives me the side-eye as she steers her car onto the on-ramp leading back to the house.

"How was Back-to-School-Night?" I avoid answering her even though I know what she's talking about. I'm not sure how I ended up kissing David, but one thing's for certain: I thoroughly enjoyed it. That man can kiss—which has me wondering what else he does well.

I don't know if I'm ready to say what happened at David's place. I'm not sure how I ended up in his arms and his bed. Sure, he wasn't in the bed with me, but if I had stayed there any longer, anything could have happened. When I woke up and saw him standing over me, I was tempted to ask him to join me under the covers. What I don't understand is how I felt so comfortable with the man I originally saw as my enemy.

"Back-to-School-Night was exactly the same as every other Back-to-School-Night. Some parents were angry that their child isn't doing better in school and they didn't know it before tonight. Other parents brought me a special treat and appreciated how well their children were performing. There are some brownies in the backseat." She removes one hand from the steering wheel and points a finger toward the back. "Help yourself and then stop stalling and tell me how you end up at the super hunky banker's house, 'cause if I'm not mistaken, you gave me the distinct impression that you hated the guy."

I reach over and bring the box of brownies to the front seat. "These are delicious. I love walnuts." Stalling, I chew slowly. "You should give more students high marks so we can get more treats."

"Very funny. Don't pretend you can't talk with your mouth full." She pauses at a red light and gives me a hard look. "Just tell me how you ended up at that beautiful man's place before we get back to the ranch."

"Honestly, I'm not exactly sure." I brush the crumbs off David's jacket, wrapping it more tightly around my shoulders.

"You are going to have to do a lot better than that." This is Morgan's *I am the teacher-master of the universe, don't mess with me* voice. I'm sure it works wonders with the students, but with me, not so much. She pulls into our driveway. "Spill it."

"It's too late to go into all the details, but the bottom line is, he came to check on Dad. When he saw me at the hospital and learned that my cell phone was dead, he offered to get me a charger and feed me." I loudly yawn, hoping that she'll stop asking questions. "That's it. Nothing more." I shrug, not willing to say anything else. I need time to sort out what happened first before I can even *begin* to explain anything to Morgan or anyone else. I'm not about to add that being in his arms felt like a little bit of heaven, that his kiss sent electrical currents soaring through my body, sparking a desire that I had never experienced. "I'm going to get some rest before I check in at the hospital tomorrow."

"Okay, *for now*. At least school will be dismissed at the usual time and I can get to the hospital earlier."

****

After managing to sleep for a few hours, I arrive at Mercy General and see Dr. Patel in the room by my father's bed. Any anxiety I was feeling about his

117

condition disappears as I walk into the room and see that he's sitting up and looking more like himself. His face and body look a little thinner and his complexion is sallow but, other than that, he looks good.

"Elaine. Good morning, Daughter." His voice is more raspy than usual, probably from the tube they'd inserted in his throat when he first got to the hospital. "Come and give your father a hug." He holds out his arms. "Don't worry, I won't break."

He feels smaller, as if a couple days in the hospital has already shrunk him, but I can always plump him up with his favorite meals when he returns home.

"Dad, I'm so glad to see you awake." A wave of relief washes over me as I drink in the sound of his voice.

"Me, too." He takes my hand in his and squeezes my fingers. "We need to talk."

"I'm going to leave you two alone," Dr. Patel says.

"How is he?" I look from my father to his physician. "If he's fully recovered, does that mean he can come home?"

I press my palms together in a prayer gesture. With him out of the house, I recognize how much my father is the center of our lives. Everything revolves around him, not just the running of the business, but the connections between each of us. Without his younger brother to keep him calm, Uncle Robert's barely controlled anger grows larger each day. Morgan and I look to our father as the one solid source of love and support we've had our entire lives.

"Well…" She draws out the word, so that it sounds like it's two syllables, then tucks the tablet she was looking at under her arm. "Your father is much better than he was when he came in here. As you know, he suffered a major heart attack. I have already shared that with your family."

"I thank God that I lived to see another day." He holds out his hands and smiles.

This had to be frightening for him and, here, I've just been thinking how his health has affected everyone else, not what it must be like for him after being cut open and operated on by a team of surgeons.

"The operation was successful, but that doesn't mean he is free to go home today. We have to keep him here for a couple more days for observation. We put in a pacemaker and we need to see how his body accepts it."

"Oh." I feel as if the wind has been knocked out of me. What was I thinking? It makes sense that he needs more time to recuperate before returning to the ranch. I shake my head. "I don't know what I was thinking." I take a seat near the bed. "It's just that I miss you so much, but, of course, Dr. Patel is right. You need time to recuperate from everything your body has experienced."

I squeeze his hand. It makes sense for him to stay in the hospital, at least for a few more days. I shudder, thinking about what he went through on that operating table. I'm grateful for modern medicine and can already see how much better he looks than he did twenty-four hours ago.

No sooner has Dr. Patel left the room than Uncle Robert storms in. Without acknowledging my presence with so much as a nod or a greeting, he swiftly brushes past me and rushes over to the bed. As usual, he's wearing a long-sleeved dress shirt that is stretched across his middle, making me wonder why he doesn't purchase a larger size.

With a loud sigh, he takes the other chair up to my father's bed. I have to prevent myself from coughing when I get a whiff of the heavy aroma of cigar smoke that clings to his clothes.

"How're you feeling? You had me worried for a minute, but you look good as new." He loudly clears his throat before squeezing my dad's shoulder.

My father's eyes are filled with love as he gazes at me before taking my hand in his. "Your niece has been taking excellent care of me."

Uncle Robert casts a cursory glance in my direction while managing to avoid direct eye contact. He shrugs dismissively, clearly not in agreement with my father's statement. That's fine with me; I'd be a complete wreck if I sat around waiting for my uncle's approval.

"So, what did that woman doctor have to say anyway?" He chuckles under his breath while leaning back in his chair, hands folded across his protruding stomach. "Are you going to live?"

"Uncle Robert, my father's health is no laughing matter." Inhaling deeply, I force myself not to get into an argument with my uncle about his inappropriate comment. "He's recovering from open heart surgery so watch what you say."

"Don't go getting all defensive." He smirks while turning his attention to my father. "He's my brother and I know how to talk to him. You may think you know how to run a farm, but you don't know how I need to talk to my brother. We understand each other, don't we, Thomas?"

Dad smiles, his eyes crinkling at the corner. He appears completely unperturbed by his older brother's callousness.

"Yes, we do. Elaine, it's okay. I know your uncle is only kidding. That's just his way. Always has been. But I love you and appreciate you for always having my back. Now, why don't you go and get yourself a bite to eat while I talk to your uncle for a few minutes." He points a finger in my direction. "You and I will talk later after Robert and I have visited."

I find a vacant seat in the lobby area and pick up a magazine, but I can't concentrate on the words. Now that I know my father is going to recover, my mind wanders back to how comfortable I was in David's bed. It felt right. Not uncomfortable like I would have expected, so right that I fell asleep which is strange considering I frequently don't sleep soundly in my own bed. Even his sheets smelled good, a mixture of woodsy and musk scents that smelled as good as he did.

It's not like me to trust a man I barely know and feel comfortable going to his home. That isn't my style, but I did it and felt safe. Protected, even. Is he thinking about me half as much as I'm thinking about him? Something stirs deep in me, reflecting on how aroused I was from the five—no, ten—star embrace and kiss. This is a complication that I can gladly do without.

Speaking of what I *don't* need... Uncle Robert, a scowl on his face, hands balled into knotted fists, steps out of my father's room. He mumbles under his breath as he strides past me, his steps firm and decisive. What happened in there?

I rush back to the room. Thank God, my father looks relaxed.

"Everything okay?" I touch his hands cautiously, careful not to disturb the intravenous tubes taped to his skin.

"Great." He briefly closes his eyes.

"I saw Uncle Robert out in the lobby, and he looked…" I struggle to find the right words, "…a little upset." I smooth the light blanket across his chest. "I could be wrong."

This is true, I could be reading more into it than there is. After all, slightly irritated is the norm for Uncle Robert, particularly when it comes to me. But he was with his brother who just survived a life-threatening heart condition, so why would he be angry with him? We should all be grateful that everything turned out so well.

He shakes his head and sighs. "I doubt you're wrong, but how he reacts to *anything* is not your concern, you understand?" His expression is somber as he looks at me.

"Yes," I say, but I don't know if I do. I had to learn early on not to take Uncle Robert's barbs personally. After all, what had I ever done to offend him?

"There's so much I need to tell you." He squeezes my hands in his. "I'm not sure where to begin." His eyes almost close again. "However, I'm tired now and can barely stay awake."

"Dad, I'm sorry. Of course, you need your rest. Morgan and I will be back this afternoon when she gets off work." I kiss his cheek. "I love you and am so glad you're better."

"I love you, too. You and your sister are the best daughters in the world. Tomorrow, you can update me on the loan." He looks at me eagerly. "Oh, before you skedaddle, did you make it right with David?"

I pause, wondering if I did, or was falling into his bed and arms too much? "Yes, I believe I did."

I haven't heard from him today and hope he doesn't think I crossed a line. All I need is for him to think that I storm in and out of men's beds. Hopefully, that's not what he thinks. That would make matters worse.

"Good." He clasps his hands as much as possible with the tubes running along his arm. "I'm glad to hear that. That's my girl. I think he's a good man. Sensible. You just have to explain that you know what you're doing."

If only I had as much confidence in myself as my father does.

****

After I get home, I check the orange and avocado groves. Everything looks good. Not great, but, with an additional sixty days, I'm still positive that we'll be able to sell enough fruit to get out of the hole we're in. When I finally explain the entire strategy, not just fragments of the plan, David will see it's darn near foolproof. Last night wasn't the right time to explain anything, but soon.

Morgan and I celebrate our father's recovery with a glass of merlot with our linguini dinner. It sounds like he'll be back home by the end of the week. Just as I'm about to crawl into bed, my cell phone rings, and I immediately think of David.

"I wondered if you were going to call," I say.

"Pardon?" a familiar voice replies. "Is this the Hart residence?"

It's Dr. Patel. What is she doing calling at this time

of night? Apprehension settles in my chest.

"Dr. Patel?"

I fight the urge to disconnect the call, turn the phone on mute, and put off whatever she has to say until tomorrow. Could she still be at the hospital? How many hours a day does the woman work?

"Yes, this is Dr. Patel. I apologize for calling you at this late hour, but I wanted to give you an update. There's been a change in your father's status. He's had another heart attack."

"What?" I probably should have told her that he was a little tired today. Nothing more. "Are you sure?" My mind races with a trillion jumbled thoughts, most of them probably not making sense, but I'm desperate enough to want to explain away what she's saying. "He already had a heart attack, remember? This is probably heartburn. He has that sometimes. You probably didn't know that. I'm certain that's what it is. Do you know what he ate for dinner? I'm asking because spicy food really messes with him. It could mimic a heart attack, couldn't it?"

"No, I'm afraid not. Patients can experience multiple heart attacks in a relatively short period of time. We've moved him to the intensive care unit. The family can visit him early tomorrow."

There's no use trying to sleep now. As I make my way to the kitchen, I vacillate on whether I should wake Morgan or let her rest. I decide on the latter. Tomorrow will arrive soon enough and we'll both have to face Dad's second medical crisis in less than a week.

Opening the pantry, I take out the oatmeal, raisins, chocolate chips, baking powder, and other ingredients I'll need to bake my father his favorite cookies.

By the time the sun rises over the horizon, I'm sitting at the kitchen table, drinking my third cup of hot cocoa and nervously munching on my fifth cookie. I figure it has the same nutrition as a bowl of cereal, so it's kind of a healthy breakfast. I can't fool myself as easily when it comes to my father, but I honestly believe he'll be fine when he recovers from this challenge. After all, he takes good care of himself and has managed to survive one heart attack. I'm sure he can survive another one, especially since it happened while he's at one of the country's best cardiac hospitals.

When Morgan wakes up, she finds me in the kitchen, a container of cookies sitting on the counter.

She rubs her lower back. "I've been lifting too many boxes of books lately. My back is sore." When I don't say anything, she pauses and looks apprehensive. "I don't suppose it was one of your nightmares that had you up baking all night?" It's more of a question than a statement.

I shake my head, while nervously clasping my hands together. "Not a nightmare this time. Have a seat." I pat the chair next to me. "Dad had another heart attack last night. We need to head to the hospital."

Morgan looks crestfallen, her eyes drooping at the corners. "Okay, but I thought…" Her voice trails off. "It doesn't matter what I thought. You're already dressed; I'll throw on something and be ready in two minutes. I'll call for a substitute teacher when I'm in the car."

Less than five minutes later, she's back down the stairs, standing in front of me wearing crumpled gray sweatpants and a hoodie obscuring her cap of dark curls. Her eyes are rimmed with red and her nose has a rosy tint, an obvious give-away that she's been crying. I get it. It's been an emotional roller coaster the last few days, not knowing from one minute to the next how our father is faring. He looked so much better yesterday, causing me to let my guard down and my hopes to soar, but now, I don't know. Dr. Patel had been brief on the phone.

****

Not speaking at all on the drive to the hospital is a first for the two of us. Our usual carefree banter is absent, replaced by an unacknowledged and unspoken fear. Better to stay silent and hope for the best. The hospital parking lot is unusually crowded. Normally, there's plenty of parking on the first or second level, but not today. I swear under my breath as I drive around in circles, trying to locate a free space. Finally, I pull into a vacant spot on the fifth level. Morgan is halfway out of the car before I have a chance to turn off the engine. Grabbing my purse and pulling the strap over my shoulder, I rush to catch up with her. A sense of urgency propels us forward, through the wide double doors, past the visitor check-in desk and straight to the elevator doors. I'm anxious to see my father's face— eager to be reassured by the smile that's always dancing behind his eyes, as if he has his own private stash of joy that can't be concealed.

Dr. Patel meets us as soon as we step off the elevator and sighs as she looks at our faces. Stray wisps of black hair have escaped her usually impeccable bun which tells me that something is very wrong. "I'm so sorry. His body rejected the pacemaker. We tried everything." She looks genuinely sorry, as if losing a patient is difficult for her also.

"I'm sure you did." I try to swallow this big, painful lump that's lodged in my throat, making each word come out shaky and uneven, almost robotic. Instinctively, I grasp Morgan's hand.

Morgan shakes her head as her eyes cloud with uncertainty. She appears dazed and confused. She brings her hands to her face. "When did this happen? Maybe we should have gotten here sooner." The last words are followed by a loud sob, as if the timing of our arrival could have saved him. With a pang of guilt for the time I got to spend with him yesterday, it dawns on me that maybe she wished she could have seen him one last time.

"It happened a few moments ago." The doctor pauses and looks over my shoulder as Uncle Robert hurries into the hall. "I informed Elaine and Morgan that, despite trying everything we could, we were unable to revive Mr. Hart after he experienced another heart attack last night."

"I highly doubt you did *everything* possible or my brother would still be alive, wouldn't he?" Uncle Robert points a finger at the doctor. "I'm going to have my attorney look into malpractice. That was my baby brother and you all killed him."

Morgan and I gasp, appalled by his harsh words.

"That's enough, Uncle Robert," I manage to say. "Now is not the time for blame. We all need time to accept what's just happened." Even as I speak, I feel a numbness settling over me, giving everything a surreal quality.

"Humph. I've had enough. I'm sick of being surrounded by incompetent women and now my only brother is gone." He storms out of the hallway, his anger casting a dark shadow on an already sad day.

Even with the increasing sense of numbness that's clouding my thoughts, I know I have to apologize for Uncle Robert's harsh words. I'm used to him saying cruel things to me, but it's unacceptable for him to blame Dr. Patel for my father's second heart attack. "Please forgive our uncle. He didn't mean what he said."

Dr. Patel waves her hand. "Doctors understand that people have different ways of expressing grief."

"Like lashing out." Morgan sobs, reaches into her purse, then pulls out a tissue.

"I'm going to give you time alone." Dr. Patel folds her hands together and bows her head slightly. "I'm sorry for your loss and wish we could have done more."

Chapter 8
Uncle Robert's Speech

The next few days pass by in a blur of surreal activity, sadness, and tears. On some level, none of this seems real. Any minute now, I half expect my father to walk through the door, but, realistically, I know that's not about to happen. Instead, steady streams of people move in and out of the house. It's easier if we don't bother to lock the door. We've posted a small sign that says, *Please let yourself in—the door is open.* I guess that's part of small town life, trusting the overwhelming majority of people in the community to do you no harm, whereas, in the city, you trust almost no one, believing that the majority are capable of ill will. Still, most of the faces are familiar. A neighbor's daughter, home from college, drops off brownies. The butcher brings by a slab of beef ribs and one of the worker's teenage sons drops off a large pan of homemade enchiladas. The majority of people are from the church we attended for years and I feel a twinge of guilt for not having stepped inside a church since I turned eighteen, which was when my father let me decide if I wanted to continue to attend Santa Lorena All Denomination Community Church.

Cooking is at the bottom of our To-Do list, so the food offerings mean a lot. There is a long list of important tasks to be completed, such as notifying family and friends and selecting a burial site and casket. To say it's overwhelming is an understatement.

Morgan and I sit in the office, hunched over my computer. We've been staring at floral selections for more than thirty minutes and have been unable to decide what seems most suited for the occasion: chrysanthemums, roses, or a mix of peonies. I'm almost ready to close my eyes and pick out a random selection.

"We are probably making this too complicated." My eyes glaze over wearily. "I mean, it shouldn't take this long to make a decision."

"Yes, but don't forget, we've had so many things to do lately that we probably can't think straight." She frowns at the page. "However, I do know that I don't like any of those. They're all so over the top."

"Me neither." I scroll down to the page displaying the various floral arrangements for grief, loss or sympathy. Finally, there's one that catches my eye. "This is it—the one that would be perfect for Dad."

"That one?" Perplexed, she glances back down at the simple assortment of flowers that comprise the selection. "Are you sure this is the one you want? We could pick these from our own gardens."

"I know. That's what I like about it. These are natural flowers that are indigenous to Southern California in general and our ranch in particular. They remind me of Dad." I rub my temple, unsuccessfully attempting to massage away the headache that's just starting.

"I get it." She nods. "You're right; these are perfect for our father. Like you, he loved everything about this place, including the flowers that adorn the countryside and our property."

"Exactly. All of these other ornate arrangements are too much. They might be perfect for someone else, but not for the man who raised us."

"After I call in the order, we can work on the menu for the reception." She picks up her cell phone and prepares to dial.

"Sounds good, but, first, I'm going to take a break in my room for a few minutes. I haven't been sleeping that well and I feel a headache starting. We've gotten a lot done today."

"I know what you mean. I'm tired too, but this part will be over soon. You take a mini-nap while I make this call."

Once I'm in my room, I draw the blinds before kicking off my shoes and lying down face-up on my bed. In the past, my dreams were always about Julian, but now they include my father. I imagine that they are together, and that thought does bring me some comfort and even eases some of the guilt that lingers all these years after Julian's death. Just as I'm about to doze off, a light tap sounds on my door and I assume it's Morgan.

"Come on in," I mumble, my eyes still closed. "What is it?"

"Elaine, it's me." That distinguished deep voice has me bolting up in my bed, instantly alert.

I smell his warm scent and feel the pressure as he sits on the mattress, letting me know that I'm not dreaming.

"Morgan told me to knock on your door. She said you'd want to see me."

I self-consciously fiddle with my bangs, remembering that, this morning, I had decided to forgo putting on any make-up. Even knowing that I'm dressed in faded khakis and an old t-shirt, I am happy to see him. However, it would have been great if Morgan could have given me a heads-up so I could have at least prepared myself.

"She's right, I'm happy to see you." Since my father died, there's a wave of awkwardness that permeates conversations. It's as if people don't know what to say to me and I don't know what to say to them. My instinct is to put them at ease, even if I'm the one experiencing the loss.

"My secretary told me about your dad." He takes my hands in his. "I'm so sorry. I know this has got to be a difficult time for you and your family."

"It is." I hope he doesn't notice the messiness of my room. It's nothing like the orderliness of his condo. I haven't had the energy to hang up clothes or put them in drawers.

I take a deep breath, eager to explain some of what I'm feeling. "It was so out of the blue. My father always appeared healthy. I didn't know he had high blood pressure. Did you know that there aren't any symptoms?"

"No, I didn't." He rubs a callused finger across the palm of my hand.

"He had been more tired than usual lately." I swing my feet over the side of the bed and avoid looking at him while I stand up. "Maybe I should have made sure he'd gotten more sleep."

"I don't know that his daughter could tell him what to do." He stands behind me, gently massaging my shoulders. His strong hands smooth away knots I didn't know I had. I softly moan with pleasure as the tension slowly eases from my muscles. "I mean, it's a nice thought, but your dad was a grown man."

"At least I could have tried. I saw he was tired and didn't say anything." I turn to face him, eager for him to understand what I'm attempting to convey. "I should have insisted that he go to bed earlier or that he sleep later."

"Do you think you could?" He traces the outline of my jaw and stares at my lips for so long that I think he's going to kiss me, but then he steps back. "I'm just asking because my father gets absolutely no exercise— no golf, tennis or even walking in the park. I've been after him for years to do something physical. I've even offered to go golfing with him even though I hate it."

"Well, at least you tried." I shake my head. "I didn't try hard enough, obviously."

"Don't do that," he whispers before pulling me close to him.

"Do what?" It feels so good to be in his arms. I absorb the heat emanating from his touch and lose my train of thought. This man is like a drug that leaves me hungry for more.

"Don't blame yourself. Your father had a mind of his own. You couldn't control his sleep patterns any more than I can control my father's sedentary lifestyle." He brings me closer so that our lips are almost touching. Rubbing his nose gently against mine, he says, "Do you understand what I'm saying?"

"Yes, I do." But my mind is growing cloudier, thrown off kilter by his nearness—the inexplicable animal magnetism that draws me to him. Or maybe it's my own sleep deprivation that has me lifting my arms while my fingers seek out the soft hair at the nape of his neck to caress. I softly moan as our mouths come together and our tongues join. A longing sparks inside me, making me want more as my body presses against his, but he takes a deep breath and pulls away.

"I didn't come here to seduce you." His voice is firm as he creates distance between us.

"I didn't think you did." I shake my head. "I'm the one who kissed you. Sorry if that's not what you wanted." Now I feel embarrassed. No, that's too mild a term. Mortified is more like it.

"It *is* what I want… and even more," he says gruffly, passion glowing brightly in his eyes as he pulls me to him. "But this timing is all wrong—for a lot of reasons." He drops his hands. "I came to offer my condolences, not take advantage of your grief."

Before I can respond, he's out the door. I don't go after him. He was right, of course. I don't know what I was thinking. The house is packed with family and friends. I can't allow myself to forget that as soon as the funeral is over, he'll have every right to take over possession of Hartland. Can I really trust him? What do I really know about the man except that he's an excellent kisser and I get hot just being near him? Either of those reasons should be enough for me to know to keep my distance.

I probably need to sign up on a dating app or meet some new prospective dates. Now I know why therapists say don't make any major decisions when you're in the midst of a crisis. If he hadn't stopped me, I'd have probably seduced him right here in my junky bedroom—shoved him down on the bed and pulled those slacks right off of his muscular, beautiful body. Geez, what was I thinking? I practically threw myself at the man and he was just being polite, coming to pay his respects, yet I acted like an animal in heat.

Stripping off my own clothes, I step into a warm shower, giving myself ample time to cool off and clear my head. I shampoo my hair, allow the natural curls to do their thing, and while I blow dry and smooth my bangs, I reflect back on David's words—not the ones about our bad timing, but about how I've been unfairly blaming myself for my father's health, whether it was his lack of sleep or high blood pressure. I've been spending half of the last few nights ruminating about how if I had been a better daughter, my father might still be alive. But something about David's no-nonsense rejection of my logic got through to me and, for that, I'm grateful. Maybe it was my father's time to go and it's time for me to release the notion that I was responsible for his death.

***

"You're not mad at me for sending David up to your room, are you?" Morgan checks off another item on our To-Do list as we sit in the living room. It's past midnight and, now that everyone has left, the house is quiet, and we finally have a chance to check in with each other. "When he walked in, he asked to see you and, without giving it any thought, I told you were upstairs."

"No, I'm not mad at all." I say absently while reviewing the names of the people we've been able to reach. A part of me doesn't want to remember or talk about the disapproving look he gave me before he left. "It's fine. He just wanted to give his condolences."

"Nothing else?" She looks at me as if she knows that I'm withholding information. "I thought maybe…"

"Don't go making it more complicated." Folding my arms, I steer the conversation away from David's wants and needs. I'm more than a little confused about how he feels about me and, more importantly, how I feel about him. "Right now, I'm concentrating on getting past Dad's Going Home celebration."

"I don't know why we even call it a celebration." She takes a drink of coffee from her favorite mug that was a gift from one of her students. Bright red letters spell out No. 1 Teacher. We've set a tray of crackers, cheese, and grapes and, of course, her coffee and my tea on the coffee table. Stirring in her usual three teaspoons of sugar, she looks at me with sadness in her eyes.

"Dad had a good life." I don't know if I'll ever be able to adjust to thinking of him in the past tense. The house seems eerily hollow now and substantially larger. He wasn't a particularly large man, but his absence is enormous. "That's what we'll be celebrating tomorrow and the fact that he'll be in Heaven." I sip my mug of peppermint tea. "If anyone has a clear pass into Heaven, it's definitely our father. The man was as close to being a saint as anyone I have ever known."

"I know we're adults, but we are now orphans. It sounds crazy, but, in a way, it's true." Morgan looks down, frowning slightly. "I never imagined Dad dying. I know that sounds ridiculous, but it's true, even though we knew it would happen at some point. I thought it would be years from now."

"I know what you mean." How could I not? Our mother's absence never felt more present. My efforts to contact her through several of the women in town who, I was told, were once her friends haven't yielded any results. They haven't spoken to her in years and have no idea where she lives. So that was a complete dead-end. Short of hiring a detective, I don't know what else I can do to get in touch with her and fill her in on what's happened. "Dad has been our rock, more like a father and mother in every way. We were lucky to have him."

"Can you imagine what our childhoods would have been like without him?" Morgan shakes her head as she pauses and scans the room. She peers at the heavy beige drapes, the books haphazardly jammed into the built-in bookshelf and the rectangular, tan throw rug in front of the large reclining chair as if she's seeing everything for the first time. "His absence makes such a big difference. The house actually feels empty."

"I know." I study the photograph we've selected to be on the front cover of the funeral program. We selected a picture from when our father was in his thirties and didn't have any gray hair or laugh lines around his eyes. He had on a colorful pullover sweater and gray slacks. We also selected a favorite childhood picture to include. Morgan's picked a photograph of him pushing her on the makeshift swing he had hung on the eucalyptus tree in the backyard. I had spent over an hour sorting through faded and torn photographs until I found an almost forgotten department store picture of the two of us sitting on Santa's lap. I couldn't have been more than five years old. I shake my head, remembering that, throughout my childhood, I had only one wish and that was that my mother would come back home.

"It's odd. You'd think that someone would have kept in touch and been able to provide us with her address. I'm still not sure if we should have included a picture of her, but we only have that one and, frankly, she looks pretty miserable. She's not even looking at the camera."

"I wouldn't recognize the woman if I saw her walking down the street." Morgan stacks the programs in neat groups of twenty-five. "I don't even remember her living here. If it wasn't for the picture on the mantel, I'd wonder if I was adopted by our father."

"I remember her well, even when she was pregnant with you. I was young, but I do remember it so, no, you were not adopted." I laugh, recalling that every few years Morgan brings up this theory. "Our uncle has managed to be strangely absent at this time," I say, biting into a piece of sweet potato pie that a neighbor brought to the house. "I'm not sure how I feel about that. Part of me is relieved and the other part is… pissed off."

"I don't care if he *is* our uncle." Clearly exasperated, Morgan rolls her eyes. "It's his brother who has died. He should be here. You'd think the man would have the decency to at least show up to see how his nieces are doing."

"Although, it is easier without him and his snide comments." I hate to admit it, but Uncle Robert not being here has made things less stressful because, somehow, he always manages to complicate matters.

"Still, to just disappear without so much as a phone call or even dropping by the house." Standing, she walks over to look out of the front bay windows. "He left all the funeral arrangements and everything to us." She shakes her head. "I don't know how you can stay so calm about it."

"Is there really any choice? We have to get through the next couple of days. We've got the funeral, the reception and the reading of the will the following day." I rub the knots in my shoulders. "You'll be going back to work and then…"

"Right. And then what?" Morgan runs a hand through her hair.

"What do you mean?" The last few days have been draining and I long for sleep as a feeling of complete exhaustion washes over me. Maybe the memories of my past won't haunt me tonight. I just need to get through tomorrow.

"When Uncle Robert inherits the property, what then? We probably can't continue living here." She turns around and waves a hand through the air as if she's showcasing the house on a game show. "Uncle Robert will want to take over this house. It's much bigger than his."

I grasp her hands. "Our uncle won't kick us out." Even as I say the words, I know they lack conviction. Our uncle is a loose cannon and I can't honestly say what he's capable of. "He probably won't put you out, but me, well, that's another story." We both laugh, but Morgan doesn't know that I'm already preparing for that possibility. I've begun looking for apartments in the city and have started packing. I'm hoping that, at the very least, he'll allow me to continue my work on the orchards.

"Oh, he wouldn't dare put either of us out." Morgan wraps an arm around my shoulder. "I don't believe he'd do that. Our uncle knows how much you've contributed to keep this place running. We would have already lost the farm if it weren't for your efforts. And I couldn't live here without you. No, Uncle Robert is not that cruel."

"We'll know what Uncle Robert is up to whenever he decides to make an appearance." I reconsider his absence to come up with a plausible explanation. "Maybe Uncle Robert is wracked with grief and would prefer to mourn in private."

"I suppose that's possible. It's just that our uncle has never kept any feelings to himself in the past so why start now?" Morgan chuckles bitterly.

"Who knows?" I look at the dark circles under her eyes, thinking about how she needs to rest. By the time she returns to work, we'll be done with all these late-night debriefings. "We need to call it a day. Tomorrow is going to be very busy, with or without Uncle Robert."

By the time my head hits the pillow it's after one a.m. and, thankfully, I fall into a deep, exhausted sleep. No restless questions about where I'll live once I've moved out of the home I love because I know, without a doubt, that my uncle has never and will never approve of my plans for the orchards. As the new owner, he's free to do whatever he wants, and my avocados will undoubtedly be one of the first things he eliminates... and I will probably be the second.

****

Morgan and I have agreed to forego the traditional all-black funeral attire and, instead, have selected a navy blue color which was our father's favorite. As I'm walking down the stairs, I get a text saying that the limousine is on its way to pick us up to take us to the church. I open the door to check the weather and see an elaborate and stunningly beautiful and fragrant floral arrangement sitting on the porch. It's an exotic mixture of birds of paradise, hyacinth, freesia, and many more that are too numerous to name. Taking it into the house, I set it on the long glass table in the formal dining room.

"When did those arrive?" Morgan walks into the room wearing the conservative pantsuit she bought for the occasion. "I followed the scent here. They look as lovely as they smell." She opens the small envelope and reads it. "These are from David and Amanda."

"I have to agree with you; these are the most beautiful flowers I've ever seen." I can't say the man isn't thoughtful. Although my opinion may be changing in the near future, but, for now, I appreciate the gesture. "I'll have to be sure to thank him and Amanda the next time I see them."

"Do you think they'll be at the church today?" Morgan asks.

"Maybe." I shrug, ignoring the rumbling of my empty stomach. I haven't had much of an appetite the last few days. "I don't know who will be there."

"This is it then, isn't it?" Morgan's voice is unusually somber, as if the finality of the day has sunk in. She takes my hand and rests her head on my shoulder. "Maybe we shouldn't have had a funeral," she says wistfully.

"Maybe, but it's a little late for that now, isn't it?" I manage a weak smile, although I, too, wish this day could be avoided. As long as I'm wishing, I wish that my father were still alive, but that kind of thinking isn't going to get us anywhere.

My cell phone chimes, indicating that the driver who will take us to the church has arrived. "The limousine is out front. We'll get through this. You and me, just like we always do. You can lean on me and I can lean on you and we'll make it to the next day. I love you."

"I love you, too," she says as we walk out the door.

It doesn't take us more than twenty minutes to get to the church. Not many people are here yet and we head to a room that's been designated for family members. On a small table someone has thoughtfully set out water bottles and a large box of tissues. Just as I'm stuffing a handful into my pocket, I hear a loud commotion outside. Before I can open the door to see what's happening, Uncle Robert bursts into the room. Unlike Morgan and me, his eyes are bright, and he has a new, shorter haircut. He looks very well rested, as if he has just returned from vacation. Maybe he has. For all I know that's how he copes with grief, but it would have been nice if he had been around to assist with some of the funeral arrangements.

"How are you and Morgan holding up?" He asks this question as if he just saw us yesterday, not more than ten days ago.

I'm in shock. When has he ever asked how I'm doing? That would be never. Maybe it takes a crisis for him to be a kinder person. If that's the case, I'm relieved that I can finally stop having to deal with his caustic comments. Now that my dad is gone, I'd love to have a better, more positive relationship with his one brother. Nothing would please my father more.

"As good as can be expected." I try not to eye him suspiciously, instead, I hold onto the possibility that things will be different between us now. Maybe knowing that the property and everything on it belongs to him has made him a better person. Was that what all his past bitterness was about, him not inheriting the property from my grandfather? Whatever the case, he's now sounding like a decent human being.

"Long time no see." Morgan's eyes are furious as she saunters past him and heads toward the door. "Glad you could make it. We weren't sure we were going to see you today."

"That's nonsense." He fumbles with his tie. "I wouldn't miss my own brother's funeral. What kind of person do you think I am?"

"You don't really want me to answer that, do you?" Morgan turns and faces him directly. She couldn't believe that he hadn't bothered to call or send a text since that day in the hospital, and she'd started to worry that something had happened to him. Several times, she'd made the half-mile trek to his house, only to discover that there'd been no signs of him anywhere. His car had been gone and the lights were out. Newspapers had piled up on the porch and the mailbox was full. "Did it ever occur to you that maybe we were worried about you?"

"No one told you to worry about me." He runs a manicured hand down the front of his black tuxedo style suit. "I'm doing well, as you can see."

"It was a fine time for you to do a disappearing act." She shakes her head dismissively. "I don't know why I expected more of you."

Before he can respond, I step between the two of them, ready to dispel the escalating tension. "We need to head to the church now. We don't have time for any of this." I pierce them both with the sternest expression I can muster. "We need to get through the next couple of hours."

He picks up one of the programs and scowls. "I don't see my name as a speaker anywhere in here. I'd think I would have been included."

"Of course. I'm sorry I didn't add your name to the list because I didn't know... Well, I hadn't seen you since my father died." Those are the words that are still difficult to get out. My dad died. The permanence of death. No euphemisms, no fancy terms, just plain and simple. He died. He's not here anymore. I don't have a father. But that's not true; my father lives on in my heart forever. He'll always be with me. "When would you like to speak?"

"Last will work," he says smugly, smiling. "I've prepared a few words to share about my baby brother."

Morgan and I sit in the front row, avidly listening as people share their stories of what our father meant to them. Sometimes we laugh and other times we cry, but mostly, we feel pride, especially when we hear how he helped several workers by giving them grants to put down payments on new homes or cars. Everyone in Santa Lorena, knowing how our mother had deserted us, had great respect for the way our father raised us on his own.

Filled with a range of emotions, we slowly make our way to the podium. Morgan gives an emotional testimonial of our father's love and the special relationship she had with him. Wiping away the tears, I take a deep inhalation and, with a quivering voice, share what my father meant to me and how much I will always love and miss him, even knowing that he lives forever in my heart.

Finally, it is Uncle Robert's turn to take the

podium. Now that my anxiety has dissipated from having to stand in front of this packed church and talk about my dad, I've had time to recover from the shock of seeing him here. I take my time and get a good look at my uncle. Some changes have definitely been made that I hadn't noticed earlier. His black shoes are polished to a high sheen and his suit is obviously new and looks custom-made. It even appears that he may have lost a few pounds. Maybe that's what a new suit will do for you. I peer more closely at him and fight back the shock of the stark change of hair color. Both brothers had grayed prematurely and had sported more gray than black hair since I was in elementary school. But now, my uncle's wavy hair had been died as glossy black as a raven's feathers.

Taking a folded piece of paper out of his pocket, he smooths it out on the podium. All eyes are on him as he looks out at the attentive faces waiting to hear what sentiments he'll share today. The murmur of voices stills as he's given their full attention. He takes his time drinking from a glass of water that a church usher sets in front of him.

"I'm not going to take long, but I do want to share a few words about my younger brother. I always felt responsible for him, being the oldest and all. I guided him the best I could." He holds out his arms. "Judging from what I've heard today, he learned well. He followed the example that I set for him at an early age. Everyone needs someone to clear a path for them, to provide them with direction and support."

Morgan gives my hand a hard squeeze and I gasp as she leans over and whispers, "I don't believe this. I should walk over and snatch that microphone right out of his hands. He's got some nerve, trying to take the credit for our father's accomplishments."

"We both know that's a bunch of bull and so does everyone else." I notice a few people peering at us. Hmmm, they probably overheard our conversation. I press a finger to my lips, signaling that we shouldn't talk now. The room is once again as quiet as a library on a Sunday morning as everyone focuses on my uncle's words. Anyone who knew my dad knows that he was his own man, not some person that Uncle Robert molded to do his bidding. This man has no shame. "We'll talk later."

"Together, we raised Elaine and Morgan, which is undoubtedly why they turned out to be the fine young women they are today." He points in our direction.

Morgan clutches my fingers so hard I'm afraid they might break. "Liar," she hisses under her breath. "He did not raise us."

I carefully pull my fingers from her bone-shattering grip. "I know. I know."

Uncle Robert continues, "So, in closing, I'd like to assure you that although there will be necessary changes at the ranch, those of you who are employees have nothing to worry about. You still have your jobs at this time as we all adapt to the change in ownership. Nothing will happen that my dearly departed baby brother would not have approved of. We frequently spoke about our vision for the future of our family legacy. He would be touched to have you all here today, as am I. I look forward to making Hartland Ranch bigger and better. I know that's what Thomas would have wanted."

"What the hell was that about?" Morgan says as we

make our way downstairs to the Fellowship Hall where the food is being served.

"That's our uncle—always coming up with some twist on reality, making him the hero." I shrug. "No doubt he'll be giving us our marching papers soon enough when he's done pretending he's a benevolent caring relative."

Our conversation will have to continue at a later time because we have to acknowledge the hugs and condolences of friends and family as we make our way to the serving table. Concentrating on the food, I have the time to sort through the mixed emotions just below the surface. I'm upset at my uncle, sad about my father, and relieved that this day is almost over.

Morgan, standing in front of me, adds potato salad to her plate. "The potato salad looks good."

"Yes, he does," I say, spotting David talking to the owner of the local grocery store. With his height and build he stands out even in a crowded room. I force myself not to stare.

I hadn't noticed him when he entered the church, but I was in the front row and he could have been sitting in one of the back pews. Even after the awkwardness of what happened—or should I say *didn't* happen—in my bedroom yesterday, I appreciate him being here. In retrospect, I know the timing wasn't right. Maybe it never will be, considering the circumstances. But which David is here today— the cold, calculating business banker who accepts no excuses when it comes to customers repaying their debt or the thoughtful, kind man who insisted I get some rest and let me crash at his place without expecting anything in return?

"Girl, *what* are you talking about?" Morgan sets a piece of cornbread on her already full plate before we finally take a seat at the head table. "Okay, I'm talking about the food and obviously you aren't. What are you looking at?" She swivels her head around and spots David heading in our direction as he pauses to speak to a few people. Nodding, she says, "I see now what's got your attention. Can't say I blame you. Talk about a much-needed distraction."

"That was a very nice service." He takes the vacant seat near me. "I hope you got the floral arrangement."

Morgan nods. "Thank you," she says and turns back to her plate.

"It was lovely." Why does this man always have to smell so good? "We really appreciate it."

Is it possible that he is more handsome than I remembered, with his broad shoulders, firm jaw, and eyes so dark they look like black ice? What happened to my *no mixing work and pleasure* rule? When I think back on that time in his apartment, we only shared one kiss so, technically, the rule isn't really broken. *A kiss is just a kiss.* And whatever happened in my room really doesn't count because it wasn't anything at all.

I make the mistake of glancing at his perfectly shaped lips and know that kiss was more than just a kiss… it was so much more. At least to me—

"Elaine, I really admired your father and his passion for his land and commitment to his family."

"Thank you for coming." Does he feel as uncomfortable as I do? Do I need to speak to him about the loan at all or is it up to Uncle Robert?

"I'd like to speak to you for a minute." He stands and looks at the door leading outside.

My palms sweat as I notice the stern set of his jaw.

"Okay." As I rise from the table, he places the palm of his hand on my back and leads me toward the patio.

"Let's step out here."

I have no idea what he needs to say outside that he can't say right here. No one is paying any attention to us; they're busy enjoying their food and sharing how they knew my father. At least, that's what I think until I notice my uncle standing off to the side and eyeing us curiously.

If this is about the loan, I'd rather deal with it right away. "About the loan…" I can't finish the sentence, because, right now, my heart is filled to bursting with grief and, after listening to my uncle, I'm not certain of my own future with Hartland.

"It's not about the loan." He takes those strong arms and wraps them around me until I'm nestled against his chest and can hear the strong, even rhythm of his heartbeat. "It's about you."

We stand there like that, his arms around me and then my arms around him, too, until I feel a sense of peace. It may be momentary, but I'll take it for now. I close my eyes, relax, and burrow into the comfort of his embrace.

He runs his hands through my hair and caresses my back. "I can only imagine how tough this is for you. I haven't forgotten—"

"What?" My voice is muffled. The question is *what* hasn't he forgotten, the loan or me?

"This. I haven't forgotten this." He holds me closer and kisses the top of my head. "The feel of you in my arms, of your lips on mine."

His breath is hot against my skin as he peers in my eyes, and I long to believe whatever he says.

"I just wanted you to know that. You've got guests in there. Call me when you are available to talk."

As he leaves out of a side door, my body is infused with a burning hot desire and a longing that's all-consuming. He's ignited a fire that makes me available for a lot more than a talk. Darn him. His touch is so arousing. Now my body and mind are in turmoil. I want to loathe the man, but my body craves his touch and the feel of his lips. I can't imagine what it would be like if we actually did more.

I stand up straighter, try to pull myself together, and focus on the moment. Time to return to the room before my uncle comes out to the patio to see what's going on. I'd noticed the suspicious look on his face as he watched us walk out the door. I don't know what's going on in his head because, even if he is grieving over the loss of his brother, at least he'll be able to do whatever he wants with the orange groves—at last.

****

Uncle Robert, Morgan, and I sit in Jared's spacious downtown office. It's ultramodern with glass everywhere, including the double doors we had to walk through. We sit at a long, beveled glass table that faces several mirrors, one hanging on each wall. We're waiting to hear the reading of the will. I have to stop myself from tapping my foot. Hartland will always be my home—my favorite place in the world—but I can't imagine Uncle Robert not wanting to move in and set up everything to his liking—probably as soon as possible. I can't blame him for wanting to get his life settled now that he owns Hartland. He's made it abundantly clear that he didn't agree with my father's decision to allow me to use a portion of land to grow avocados. Morgan and I have faced the cold, hard truth that he can now call all the shots, which has to make him one happy man. There's no need to wait for him to kick us out. We've finally found an apartment in town that will be much closer to Morgan's school.

"Is there a reason we haven't started yet? We're all here *now*," Morgan cast a side-glance at Uncle Robert, who had arrived his customary thirty minutes late. She still hasn't forgiven him for what he'd said at the funeral, sounding like he had molded our father into the man we all knew when nothing could be further from the truth.

Jared, who's usually so calm and confident, fidgets nervously with a pen on his desk. Gone is the usual bravado and cockiness as he takes on an all-business-only demeanor. No sly looks cast in my direction. No wink of the eye. He's behaving very professionally which is a relief.

"Yes, of course." He sorts through a stack of papers on his desk. "By the way, the service was well done."

"What does the *will* say?" Uncle Robert crosses his legs. He looks like the most relaxed, well-rested person in the room. "I've got a meeting in an hour. There's going to be a lot of changes and I'm eager to get started." He flicks his wrist at Jared. "Go ahead."

"Right," Jared says. "So, there is some legal jargon here, but it basically says that 'I, Thomas Hart, being of sound mind and body, leave the entire property of Hartland Ranch, at 4300 Bristol Road, Santa Lorena, California—'"

"There's no reason for you to read every little bit of minutia. We know where the ranch is." Uncle Robert abruptly stands and hovers over Jared's desk. "Just get to the part where he leaves me the land." He smiles confidently before sitting back down.

"We shouldn't assume too much." Jared clears his throat and mumbles something indecipherable under his breath.

"I don't know what you just said but get on with it and speak up so I can hear you." Uncle Robert scowls at Jared, his limited patience obviously wearing thin.

"Right." Jared pauses, squares his shoulders, and purses his lips before, once again, refocusing his attention on the stack of documents he's holding. "'I leave my entire estate, which includes the land, the house, and all the property therein to my two daughters, Elaine and Morgan Hart.'"

"What the *hell*?" Uncle Robert yells so loudly that I'm sure Jared's secretary and the other attorneys on the floor can hear him. His face is dark with rage. He runs a shaky hand through his newly blackened hair. "I probably heard you wrong. What did you say about my inheritance?"

Morgan and I stare at each other. Both of us are in a state of shock. Did our father really leave *us* the ranch and not his brother? Come to think of it, I've always wondered why our grandfather didn't leave the house to his eldest son. He obviously knew how much my father truly loved the land and he apparently didn't have that kind of faith in Uncle Robert.

"Did we hear you right?" Morgan stands now. "Do you mind if I look at that?" She removes the top sheet of paper from his hand before he has a chance to respond. She reads silently to herself before glancing up and saying, "That's absolutely what it states. *Everything*—and I mean *everything*—is left to Elaine and me." She looks at our uncle and smiles defiantly. "You taught him everything he knew, huh? Then I guess we should thank *you* for helping him make the right decision as far as Hartland is concerned."

"This is all your fault." Uncle Robert points in my direction.

"What?" I say. "Don't try to make this about me. My father made the decision he felt was in the best interest of the family." I had no idea what my father had stipulated in his will.

"Don't try to tell me that you didn't manipulate your way into convincing him that you should get Hartland. Everyone knows that Morgan doesn't give a crap about the orchards." With one swift move, he swipes the papers off Jared's desk. "This is bull crap, and this will was probably written when he was under duress. When that *female* doctor was treating him. Humph." His arms are balled into fists as sweat drips down his forehead. "I'm sure he wasn't in his right mind. That's what it was. He had already been in that hospital and they had him so doped up that he didn't know what he was saying." He takes a deep breath and cracks his knuckles, obviously attempting to control his rage. "Sorry about the papers. I was just a little shocked, that's all." He picks up the scattered documents. "When was this written?"

Jared looks apologetically at the man who'd hired him and has been his champion. No matter how close he may be with Uncle Robert, it's clear that he kept his client-attorney relationship with my father confidential.

"This will was written and notarized over five years ago."

"That's it." Uncle Robert stalks to the door, flings it open, then pauses before turning to glare at Morgan and me. "I've had it with this family. You are a bunch of ungrateful thieves. This property should have been mine all along. I'm the oldest son." He thumps his chest. "Legally, that entire ranch and the land it's on should be mine." He turns to me and shakes his head. "You'll probably mismanage it as badly as your father did. Talk about being *stabbed* in the back. I'm not surprised. First, my old man screws me out of my inheritance and now my own brother does. To hell with you all." He slams the doors so hard the framed certificates on the wall rattle.

"Wow." Morgan slowly stands, a dazed look in her eyes as she peers at me. "Talk about being blindsided. That was intense. I didn't see it coming. Good for Dad and good for us."

I join her as we laugh for the first time since our father's death. When we are finally able to contain our joy at the good news, Jared clears his throat, reminding us that we are still in his office.

Brushing a stray strand of hair from my face, I say, "I didn't see it coming either." I hadn't realized how depressed I was about losing my father and my home. For the first time since he died, I feel optimistic about the future. He hadn't forgotten how much Hartland means to me. "I guess that's it then. That's everything, right?" I can't imagine there's anything else we need to know.

"No, it isn't." He continues sorting through the documents before extracting a single page from the stack. "Mr. Hart also stipulated that before the land becomes legally yours, that *you*," he shifts his gaze from the paper and peers in my direction, "must notify your mother, *in person*, that your father has died. He makes it very clear that he has assigned that task specifically to you." Setting the papers down, he rubs his hands together. "That's it."

"That can't be possible. He couldn't have expected me to contact her. Not after all this time." I'm stunned. My mind races in several different directions. I haven't had time to process that the ranch now belongs to Morgan and me. How will I find the woman who abandoned two small children and a husband? She's never written or bothered to call to see if we were well. I always thought I wanted to see her again, but now, I'm not so sure. "You're kidding me, right? I don't even know where she lives. I haven't seen her since I was a little girl." I draw my shoulders up. "I've already asked people in town if any of them know where she lives." I throw my hands in the air. "I came up with *nothing*. It's like she disappeared from the planet."

"Jared," Morgan asks, "how is she supposed to find her if no one else can?"

Jared holds up his hand. "The address is here." He flips the paper over so that it faces us. "Your mother's address is right here. She resides at 4326 Magnolia Street in the city of Littleton."

"How is it possible that he knew where she lived this entire time?" I close my eyes as my mind goes blank. I'm lost in a fog of confusion. "I don't understand. None of this makes any sense."

Chapter 9
The Road Trip

"I can't believe Dad knew where our mother lived this whole time and didn't tell us." It's the day after the reading of the will and Morgan and I are sitting outside on the patio. "Are you sure you don't want me to go with you?"

I shake my head. "No. You've made it clear you're not ready to see her yet."

"I've survived this long without her in my life. I'm still adjusting to Dad being gone." She looks at the stack of condolence cards we've been reading since we woke up. "None of this feels real. I can't believe Dad didn't leave any of the property to Uncle Robert."

"Honestly, neither can I. I wonder if, during his time in the hospital, he tried to tell Uncle Robert about his plans. The day before Dad had his second heart attack, Uncle Robert stormed out of the room in a rage, practically knocking me down on his way out the door." I think back on how he had silently glared at me as I had walked into the room.

"Could be." She signs her name on a Thank You card. She shrugs and brushes a curl off of her forehead. "Obviously, Uncle Robert *didn't* believe he wasn't going to inherit the house—not with that speech he gave at the church." Morgan sets down one of the many condolence cards that have been sent to the house. "We can do this later. The question is, are you okay with going to see our mother?"

"Do I have a choice?" I gently massage my temples. "For some reason our father knew where she was all along but didn't feel the need to share that information with us."

"But don't forget—the feeling must have been mutual because we've lived in this same house our entire lives and she could have visited us."

"And now it's all about to change. For some reason, he decided that before Hartland can legally be transferred to us, I have to meet with our mother." My stomach tenses as I imagine coming face-to-face with the woman from my nightmares.

"It's strange." Morgan's voice brightens as she continues. "Maybe he knew that you, not me, have always been the one who faithfully wore that damn locket and held onto the hope that one day we'd have some kind of magical family reunion."

"But you—"

"Let's not pretend," Morgan interrupts me and holds up a hand. "Dad knew that I couldn't care less one way or the other about the woman who gave us birth." She takes one of my hands in hers. "I don't think that makes me a cold-hearted bitch. I know that at some point after she closed the door on us, I closed the door on her. So, I see why he'd want you to go and not me."

"When you put it that way, it does make sense." Little does Morgan know that the thought of seeing our mother again does not fill me with joy. It was clear that she left the family to get away from me, not from Morgan or Dad.

"We need to get this over with so we can know

how to proceed. I wouldn't be surprised if our uncle isn't consulting a new attorney at this very moment to figure out a way to have Dad's will made null and void."

"What?" I open my mouth but am momentarily at a loss for words. "I never thought of that, but, yes, I wouldn't put it past him."

"Neither would I. That man harbors some deep-seated resentments." She stands up and pulls me from my chair. "So, stop putting it off. You need to get going. We've been sitting out here for over an hour and getting nowhere closer to figuring out why Dad wants you to go to Littleton." She hands me my sweater. "The quicker you get this over with, the sooner we can move on with our lives."

****

It's no use delaying the inevitable road trip any longer. The clock is ticking, and the land won't be transferred to our names until I get through this meeting. Two chilled water bottles are in the cup holders and I've got a full tank of gas. I've selected my favorite upbeat music to listen to on the drive in the hopes that the lyrics will help me block out the distress I feel about seeing my mother again. Having no idea what to expect, I concentrate on the road and enjoy the snacks I've prepared for the three-hour journey: rice crackers, sliced apples, and mozzarella slices. Between the music and my munching, I'm amazed I can hear troubling sounds coming from the engine. It was only two days ago that I took the car in to be serviced. The mechanic had checked the engine, water and oil. So why does the rumbling escalate to a jerking motion and a loud clanging sound, as if someone has dropped their keys under the hood?

I mumble a silent prayer that my car doesn't explode before I can cautiously make my way over to the side of the road on the two-lane highway out in the middle of nowhere, U.S.A. Dry shrubs and twisted trees dot the landscape. There's not a green leaf in site. The drought hasn't been kind to this stretch of land. Not even a sign identifying the city is in sight.

Turning off the engine, I swear under my breath. *Really Betsy? You can't do this for me? Maybe you are on my side and don't want me to have to face my fears.* But I have to remember that I'm no longer the cowering child who was once terrified of my mother's harsh words or even harder slaps.

There aren't many cars on this obscure stretch of road which is exactly the way I'd wanted it and why I'd left early on a Sunday morning. At six a.m., most folks are on their way to church or sleeping in. But, right now, I'd give anything to see a friendly face who could give me a lift to the next town or, even better, could look under the hood and fix my car. Finally, seeing a truck coming my way, I put on my caution lights so the driver will know I need help. Frantically waving, I watch as a truckload of farm workers whizzes by without even slowing down. On to Plan Two: I could call the automobile club for a tow truck, but it took me two hours to get this far.

I step out of Betsy, tempted to kick her tire, but decide against it. I get back in and pull the lever to open the hood, but when I step out, walk around to the hood, and try to lift it, nothing happens. Opening the hood has never been this difficult.

I hop back in the car and use more force to tug on

the lever. This time, it opens. I look at all the chrome parts and recognize the engine in the middle and the battery on the left side under some other doohickey.

I'm scowling at each unfamiliar part under the hood, mad that I don't know a darn thing about cars, when I hear heavy footsteps slowly coming closer. It's been at least thirty minutes since a vehicle has passed and I'm stuck out here just as the sun is getting hotter. Maybe if I don't look up, the person will just keep walking right past me. I know that doesn't make any kind of sense, but it's better than the alternative, which is that it could be a murderer or an escaped convict. *Aren't these remote locations off the beaten path where prisons are usually built? Yes, they most definitely are.* Sweat drips into my eyes and my heart pounds so rapidly that I think it's trying to get out of my chest. As the steps come closer, I frantically see if there's anything I can grab to protect myself. Everything looks pretty stuck under there, so I'll just have to use my hands and anything I can remember from my fifth-grade karate lessons.

Before I assume my karate chop stance, heavy hands clamp down hard on my shoulders. I open my mouth to scream, thinking how ironic, that I survived my mother's beatings only to die over twenty years later while on the way to her house that's out in some prison field.

"You don't need to scream." The voice is even, deep, and familiar. "No one will hear you out here."

I abruptly lift my head, hitting it hard on the hood as I turn and see David smiling over my shoulder.

"I've never been so happy to see anyone in my life." I can't stop grinning as I shake my head in disbelief. "How did you get here? I didn't hear your car."

"My car is right there." With a slant of his head he indicates his car, not far from Betsy. "That's the way new cars are—quiet." He smirks and looks smug. "But you wouldn't know anything about that, not with good ole—what did you call her, Bitsy?"

"It's Betsy." I force myself to step back from him, knowing that I look like a sweaty mess. "What are you doing out here?"

"I could ask you the same question, especially since *Betsy* doesn't appear to be up for long *or* short distances for that matter.*"* He strolls around my car, inspecting her for any obvious defects. "You *know* you need a new car, right?"

I decide to ignore the reference to the past orchard tour fiasco. "Okay, you're right about Betsy." I shrug, way past the point of pretending that she's in good condition. After all, the truth is evident. Being sentimental about a car and giving it a name makes it harder to give her up. My next vehicle will be nameless. "I just need to get her to a service station so they can see what's wrong." I wipe the sweat off my brow, not caring that my bangs are probably sticking out every which way. "I just had her checked the other day."

"The mechanic who serviced your car owes you a refund." He takes my arm and steers me toward his Mercedes. "We need to get out of this sun."

When we're seated inside, he turns on the air conditioner and I lean back in the soft leather seat. Turning to face me, he says, "Elaine, why are you on the road to Littleton? Are you on your way to the Strawberry Festival?"

"I don't know anything about a Strawberry Festival." It's easier to answer that question so I tackle it first. This is the first time I've seen David in casual clothes, jeans, and a button-down, light blue cotton shirt. He manages to look spectacular in anything, whether it's a dark suit or denim. Hmmm, he doesn't seem like a Strawberry Festival type, but what do I know about him beyond his role as a banker? Not much. "*You're* on your way to a Strawberry Festival?"

"Don't look so surprised." He laughs softly. "My parents wanted a slower pace when they relocated from the hustle and bustle of San Francisco, so they settled in Littleton."

He takes my hand and brushes his fingertips against my palm. Who knew the palm could be an erogenous zone?

"It's a small town with a lot of community events like the Strawberry Festival this week."

"Sounds nice." So, my mother's town was not as remote as I had initially thought. I try not to moan as he continues with my hand massage.

"My parents, *especially* my mother, love it. They like the whole family to get together and make a day of it. So now you know why I'm here. What about you? If it's not the Strawberry Festival, why come out here... unless there's someone you're meeting—?"

When I don't answer right away, he looks at me suspiciously and drops my hand.

"Is there a new boyfriend here or are you still with the attorney?" He clenches his jaw and frowns.

"No, it's nothing like what you're thinking." I pause, not knowing how to continue. "The lawyer has been an ex for a long time. It just took him a while to get the message, but you already know that."

"Good to know." He picks my hand back up and continues his gentle caress.

If I can feel this good from the touch of his fingers, I can only imagine what his hands will do to other parts of my body. It's been months since I broke up with Jared and I haven't had any energy left to even think about dating anyone else except the man sitting beside me.

"So, you aren't here for a meeting with a secret lover?" He looks at me questioningly.

"No. I'm here to see my mother." After not talking to anyone except Morgan about my mother for so many years, it feels strange to bring her up now. After she left, even my father never brought her up in any discussion. It was almost as if she didn't exist.

He raises his brows as his dark eyes probe mine. "I had the distinct impression that your mother wasn't around."

"She wasn't and she isn't." My hands automatically go to the locket that I've been wearing all these years. There's no way I'm going to tell David that my mother hates me for allowing my baby brother to die. "It's very complicated." I chew on my bottom lip, dreading the upcoming meeting. I'm torn between wanting to see the woman who gave me birth and wanting to turn around and go back home, but, of course, I would never go against my father's wishes. "My father wanted me to see her, so here I am."

"Yes, here you are—an unexpected surprise."

His smile instantly calms my shattered nerves.

"We need to get your car off the road. You're sure it won't start?"

"It makes that rumbling noise and it's shaking a lot. I don't think I should drive it. You were right about needing a new car. I could call the automobile club and get a tow." I'm relieved to have a simple task to complete that will take my mind off the difficult mother-daughter reunion ahead.

"I know the mechanic in Littleton. His name is Jim and I'll give him a call while you check on the tow." Cell phone in hand, he steps out of the car while I dial my emergency roadside service.

It's hard to read his face when he returns to the car. "I have good news and bad news. Which do you want first?"

"I'll take the bad news first." Maybe he was unable to reach his friend. "Were you able to get Jim on the phone?"

"Yes, but everything, including his car repair shop, is closed today on account of the Strawberry Festival. Pretty much the whole town is closed."

"Okay." I grimace, wondering what that means for my car. "That's the bad news; so what's the good news?"

"He's willing to come into the shop later this morning just long enough for your car to be towed there, but he won't be able to work on it. He's got to leave and get back to the Festival where he's participating in a classic car exhibit. He won't be able to start work on the car until Monday."

I groan. "That won't work." I shake my head, thinking of how I need to get this meeting with my mother over with. I've been away from work long enough and I need to check on the orchards myself. I've been talking with the foreman, but I need to assess the situation first-hand. Neither of us is mentioning it, but the deadline is in four days for the bank loan. "What am I supposed to do until then?"

"First this." He leans over, pulls me into his arms, and gives me a scorching hot kiss that sends an electric current through my body.

"I like that," I say when I finally come up for air. This man's kisses are even hotter than his massages, but I need to focus. "Seriously. I wanted to be headed back home tonight. That's why I left so early."

"Well, that's not going to happen." He smiles mischievously. "You'll have to spend the night."

"No, I can't possibly do that." I think of Morgan and all the tasks I need to complete at home, including the sorting out of my father's things which I haven't been able to force myself to do. I had planned on a quick turn-around trip. "Morgan will be worried."

"Morgan's a big girl. I'm sure she'll be fine without you for one night. Why don't you call her now?"

"I don't know." I'm not sure how Morgan will feel being alone in the house for the first time since our father's death.

I turn away from him, quickly dialing Morgan's number, while, in the distance, I see a tow truck heading in our direction. She picks up on the second ring. I quickly explain the situation and she assures me that she could use some time alone. "You're right. Morgan encouraged me to do whatever I have to do. She said she'll hold down the fort in my absence."

"Great." Smiling, he squeezes my hand. "That's taken care of then."

"If I have to wait until Monday for him to repair

the car, I'll need to find a hotel."

"There's one inn and one bed-and-breakfast in town and they're both completely booked months in advance." His eyes twinkle and he laughs the deep, echoing laugh that I'm starting to get use to. "I'm not making this up. You can call and check for yourself if you don't believe me. Strawberry Festival is a big deal and people travel from out of town to enjoy the festivities. You'll have to spend the night with me."

The last thing I need right now is to spend the night with David. With the undeniable attraction between the two of us, I know exactly what will happen. My vow to not mix work and my social life has already gone completely haywire because here I am, sitting in the cozy intimacy of his car, Betsy is on the way to the mechanic's garage, and I'm stuck in a remote little town that I never knew existed until a week ago. On top of that, I'm with the most magnetic man I've ever met who manages to make me feel emotions that are simultaneously new, exciting, and frightening.

"I'm okay with that." He's the kind of man I can trust. It's me I'm worried about. If we're going to be in close proximity, I'm not certain I can keep my hands to myself. "Do you have a two-bedroom apartment in Littleton?" I try to sound nonchalant.

"No, I don't." He has a twinkle in his eyes. "I have a one-bedroom."

"Oh," I sigh, resigned to the fact that this is going to be a super challenging weekend. "We'll have to make the best of it then, won't we?"

He throws his head back and lets out a deep, robust laugh.

"What's so funny?" Here I am getting all sweaty,

nervous, and yes, even a little aroused thinking about the possibility of sharing a bed with him and he's laughing like it's a joke.

"Okay." He gains control of himself—finally pausing long enough to meet my eyes. "You should have seen the look on your face. As if it would be torture to have to share a bed with me."

"*That's* what's so funny?" I glare at his remarkably even features. If only he knew that I was wondering what kind of underwear he wore, boxers, briefs or God forbid, the man sleeps in the nude. "Better that you don't try to read my mind. Although, I'm glad to see that you have a good sense of humor."

"Of course I do." He gives me an odd look and his words are slightly defensive. "Who *doesn't* have a sense of humor?"

"Can we stick to the subject?" I tap my leg and glance at him inquisitively. "So… we'll be sharing a room is basically what you're saying?"

"Not exactly. I do have only one room, but it's in my parents' house. But you don't need to worry, they have a guest room you can use." He rubs a finger across the palm of my hand. "Does that make you more comfortable?"

"Of course." So why am I disappointed that I'll have my own room? Better to change the subject away from sleeping arrangements. On top of meeting with my mother, I'll now have to meet David's parents. Can this day get much worse? There's got to be a safer topic. "Where's Roscoe?" My eyes linger over his distinctive profile as he starts the ignition and we begin the next half of the journey to Littleton.

How odd is it that my mother lives in the same

167

town as his parents? My mother could have resided in New York or China as far as I was concerned. These new feelings of anger toward her are more comfortable and easier to bear than the ever-present longing and guilt.

"He's with my neighbor, Jessica." His eyes dart in my direction. "He likes it over there. Jessica has a mutt Roscoe plays with. They have a great time."

"That's good so he won't be lonely." I remember the frisky dog following me around as I explored David's condominium. "He's so friendly."

"Not to everyone." He doesn't offer further details, so I decide to change the subject.

"It seems like you're always rescuing me—from the first time we met until now."

"Hmmm," he says. He adjusts his rear-view mirror, before giving me a sideways glance. "I hadn't thought about it like that, but, sometimes, there's only one right thing to do."

"Yes, but you didn't have to." So maybe he's not as cold as I initially thought. Now I know that there's warmth and heat, too, if I allow them to burn. Maybe the ice side is reserved for business—which is a frightening thought considering my predicament. I haven't told him that we won't be able to catch up on the loan by his deadline.

I shove that troubling thought to the back of my mind, shelving it for later. The deadline will be here soon enough. "On that first day I met you, you didn't hesitate to put Jared in his place." I chew my bottom lip, remembering how embarrassing that whole front door encounter had been. "When I was at the hospital and ready to collapse from exhaustion, you provided me with food and a place to rest, and now you've found a mechanic to get my car fixed."

"I was raised to help a woman in need. Anyone would have done the same thing." He moves his hand from the steering wheel to take mine in his.

"Would they?" I think of Jared and other men I've dated. Would they have allowed me to sleep in their bed with no expectations of anything in return? I doubt it. I hesitate, knowing that this is a big ask, but I have to get this visit—no that's completely the wrong word—this *encounter* with my mother over and done with.

I sigh loud enough that David hears and chuckles. I haven't been able to eat or sleep well since the reading of the will, when the possibility of seeing my mother had gone from some vague wish to an anxiety provoking reality. I always thought this day would bring me joy, but, instead, my palms are sweating and the only thing I feel is apprehension, even though I know that I need to get this *meeting* over with, so I can move forward with my life.

"I have one more favor to ask… and it's kind of a big one. I'd like to go by my mother's house first before I do anything else." I rummage in my purse and pull out the scrap of paper that has her address on it. "This is where she lives. I don't know why my father wanted me to see her after so many years of *her* choosing not to be a part of our lives, but it's what he wanted, so would you mind taking me to her house before we go to your place?" I smile and try not to look as desperate as I feel. "I won't be long." I hold up my crossed fingers. "Promise."

When he doesn't immediately respond, I review all the reasons why he's probably regretting his offer to help me. Right about now, he may be wishing he could just drop me off along the side of the road. But he's not that type of person. Maybe I've gone too far now and asked for too much.

"Not a problem," he says, and that's when I realize that I've been holding my breath and need to exhale.

****

We listen to a jazz radio station as we head to my mother's home. Now that I know she doesn't live halfway across the country or the world, I can't help but wonder how she could live so close to her two children and never feel any desire to see how we were progressing in school or getting along with our friends. What kind of person does that? I'll soon be finding out the answer to that question.

Once we've exited the highway, I'm surprised to see that Littleton isn't anything like what I was expecting. There's a certain charm to the palm-tree-lined streets and quaint cafés and storefronts.

"Magnolia Street is about three blocks away." He raises his eyebrows while peering intently at me. "You must have left early this morning. Did you want to get a bite to eat first?"

"No." I release a shaky breath. "I can't eat now. Thanks, but let's just go there. I've waited for this moment for so many years and now I just want to get it over with. Does that make sense?"

"It does. You don't know what to expect." He takes his eyes off the road to give me a quick, reassuring look.

"I don't know why my father wanted me to come here or even what to say to her." I nervously wring my hands together. "'Hi Mom, remember me?'" I pause, struck by a sudden thought and I cover my hand with my mouth. "Of course, she won't know that her ex-husband has died, so I'll have to tell her. What if she somehow blames me?" I don't add that it wouldn't be the first time she'll hold me responsible for a death in the family. "What if she won't see me? Obviously, that hasn't been a priority for her in the past," I add bitterly as a wave of nausea washes over me and I clutch my stomach. "What should I do then?"

He pulls over and turns the engine off in front of a tan, one-story stucco house that's the last home on a narrow dead-end street. "Elaine, you'll do fine." He gently runs a hand along my cheek. "I've seen you in action. You've got this."

"You think? I'm not so sure. This is different." I look out at the inconspicuous ranch-style house. A lone palm tree barely casts a shadow on the compact yard. Whatever flowers once bloomed here are gone—only the naked branches remain, surrounded by beds of scattered brown leaves. A large white cat, its blue eyes half closed, sits in a cluster of tall weeds on what was once possibly green grass, but is now a bed of dirt.

"Hmmm. It looks like an ordinary house." What was I expecting? The truth is, I didn't know what to expect. Did I think she'd live in some sort of gated community and I would have to go through a security guard to be granted access? To think that, all this time, Morgan and I could have driven to Littleton and visited our mother at any time. In that case, since my father knew her address, did he sometimes visit her? Maybe they were on friendly terms. Questions cloud my mind, filling me with sudden inertia.

"You going in?" He gives me a reassuring nod.

"Not yet." Rubbing my hands against my shirt, I say, "Maybe I should have called first. It's kind of rude to just show up at someone's house without an invitation or letting them know you're coming by." I know he's aware that I'm stalling, but it doesn't make me stop. "Come to think of it, I don't have her number, so that's out. It's not like I had an email address or any other means of communication."

"Elaine." He faces me, concern evident in the tenderness of his voice. "You don't have to do this alone."

I would love his support, but his presence is already helping me. "I'm tempted, but I need to do this myself." I take a deep breath and will the anxiety to go away. "My father had his reasons for wanting me to come to my mother's house."

"Don't forget, I'm right here, waiting for you." He smooths down my bangs, and then traces my bottom lip with his fingertip.

"Hey, don't do that or I won't be able to leave the car."

I make my way to the door on wobbly legs. I press a rusted circular doorbell, uncertain if I'm imagining the sound of footsteps approaching from inside or just wishing to. That's when I notice that there's a small piece of lined paper taped to the middle of the door. It says that the doorbell doesn't work. Even after I've knocked twice, no one answers. Maybe no one is home. To the left, is an open garage, with two cars parked inside a cluttered interior area. Does she own two cars? Maybe she has a roommate. I don't know anything about her. I've always blocked out my meager memories. When they have managed to resurface, it hasn't been good. Perhaps she's out for a walk. I wait two, three minutes—that seems like more than long enough. Would it count in my father's eyes if I didn't actually *see* her? No, it wouldn't. He specifically said that I must notify my mother, in person, that he has died. I can't turn around and run now.

As I open my purse and scrounge around inside for something to write on so I can leave a note, I hear movement behind the door, the sound of muffled voices—a man's and a woman's. Their words aren't clear, but it sounds like they could be arguing. This is obviously *not* a good time for a visit. I should turn and leave, but I don't want to have to come back.

Taking a deep breath, I ball my fist and knock more firmly. I need to get this over with and behind me. They obviously know someone is here.

When the door abruptly opens, I'm unprepared for the person standing there looking at me with anger and fury on his face. "What the *hell* are you doing here?"

"Uncle Robert?"

I'm stunned. Could my father have given me the wrong address? Was this another one of my uncle's homes, a place where he comes to unwind, that I don't know about? "Obviously… there's been a mix-up."

"Obviously." He sneers and grunts, looking like he's about to explode. This is the first time I've seen him dressed casually. His gray sweatpants, white t-shirt, and leather house slippers contrast sharply with the impeccable suits and shirts he's usually wearing.

I pull the address out of my pocket and read it out loud. "4326 Magnolia Street. This is it." I'm trying to put the pieces together. Why would my father give me this address if it wasn't where my mother lives?

"Let me see that." He snatches the paper from my hand, quickly scanning the address before glaring at me with unconcealed anger. "Just what the hell are you doing here?"

"I could ask you the same question. What *are* you doing here?" I'm done trying to figure out what's going on. I certainly didn't come all this way to have my uncle shout at me. "You left before Jared finished reading the will. My father wanted me to come see my mother, and this is the address I was given."

I hear a gasp in the background. I stand on my toes and try to look over his shoulders, curious now to see who's standing in the room behind him. "Is… is my mother here?"

"That's none of your damn business. You stole everything from me." He stomps his foot, looking like he's ready to kick someone. "Isn't it enough that you let my son die, but now you have to come here to stir up trouble? You got my inheritance, too. Now you come sashaying up to Littleton ready to take what little peace I have away from me."

Speechless, I don't move, unable to comprehend anything he's said after he said the words, *my son.*

"What did you say?" My voice is calm, steady, while, inside, a flood of emotions swirls over me like a tsunami.

"You heard me right, girl." He steps closer toward me so that I can see the veins on his face, the deep lines branching out like horizontal trees from the corners of his eyes. "My *son*. The baby you let die was not your father's. He was *my* only child." He looks sadly triumphant as he reaches into his pocket and pulls out his pocket watch. He thrusts it in front of my face, then turns it over to show me an engraving on the back: the day Julian was born and the day he died.

I shake my head, still confused. How could my uncle be the father of my brother? "But Julian was my baby *brother*."

"He was my son, so that also makes you his cousin." He snarls and shakes his head disgustedly, then points an accusatory finger inches from my nose. "Leave it to my brother to screw me over just like my father did." He laughs and the bitterness contorts his features. "But I had a back-up plan and it almost worked, too. I figured a college gal like you would fall for some hotshot attorney like Jared. If you got the money, I could control it through him, but… nope. You thought you were *too* good for him and my plans went up in smoke. Oh yes, *and* the water pipes." He smiles maliciously, clearly enjoying himself, proud even of his conniving. "Let me tell you about the other plan that didn't work. I had already jammed the water pipes months ago, knowing that the trees couldn't grow without sufficient water. I was hoping you and your dad would finally give up on the land, but no such luck. Your dad had to go and hire someone to fix that."

"What?" I'm barely able to mutter a word as the vileness of his words sinks in. "You can't be serious. You couldn't possibly hate your own brother that much. Or could you?"

My fists clench as I fight the rage soaring through me on behalf of my wonderful, sweet father. Did he know? God, I hope not. I suppose I'll never know. And what kind of woman was my mother that she'd betray the man she married to sleep with her brother-in-law and have a baby with him?

"You're worse than I thought. All of these years... betraying your only brother." Instead of screaming at how outraged and shocked I am by his betrayal of my father, I force myself not to give in to the urge to give him a good hard shove, hopefully knocking him onto his ass. As much as I want to walk away and never look back, my father wanted me to come here to talk to my mother so I can't leave yet. But I can't stop the quiver in my voice as I ask, "*You* are Julian's father?"

"You heard right, little gal. Your daddy didn't get to have all the fun. Hell, I deserved something, *someone,* of my own. You and your high-and-mighty self, with all your book learning, never figured it out. *I* wanted a family, too. What the hell did you think? That I would be content to live in my baby brother's damn shadow my whole life?" His malicious laugh makes me want to throw up.

I put my hands up, as if to block the onslaught of his built-up hatred. "So, you stole my mother and broke up my family before deciding to sabotage the orchards, knowing what it would do to our bottom line?" My heart pounds and, for a moment, I can't catch my breath.

"Get it straight, gal." He puts his hands on his waist, red-hot rage in his eyes. "I didn't have to *steal* your mom. Noreen came to me because she wanted *me,* not that wimp of my baby brother."

"How dare you speak about my father that way." For the first time I yell at my uncle, anger coursing through my blood. He's gone too far now. My father just died, and he hadn't deserved any of this.

"You don't tell me how to act in *my* house." He points to the gray sedan parked in the garage. The make and model of the cars had not been the focus of my attention, but now I recognize his license plates. Would it have made a difference if I had known he was here before knocking on the door? Not really because I've come too far to turn back.

"Now, get. Go back to where you came from. This is my place. Ain't your place enough for you?"

He's about to slam the door in my face when someone shoves him aside.

"Enough."

The voice is weary, but faintly familiar. I fight the flashback of her yelling at me and try to blink away the images and sounds of her rage as she punished me for anything and everything, including the worst sin of all—not preventing Julian's death.

"Mom?"

She looks older now, more tired than the image of the beautiful woman in the picture on the mantel. A frayed housecoat covers her small frame and deep lines bracket her mouth. The once luxurious, full black hair is mostly white now, thinner and pulled back in a tight bun at the base of her neck.

She brushes past Uncle Robert, indicating that I should come in the house. "You've said enough. Let the girl come in. She's come all this way. I might as well talk to her."

Uncle Robert mumbles under his breath but moves out of the doorway and disappears into another room.

My legs continue to shake as I follow her slightly bent figure to a dinette area adjacent to a cluttered kitchen. She motions for me to sit at a table that's littered with ashtrays filled to overflowing with discarded cigarette butts. Smudged red lipstick on the

tips show that the cigarettes are hers. Black rubber
house shoes make a flapping sound as she shuffles to a
counter by a sink that's filled with dirty dishes. Not
bothering to ask if I would like a cup of coffee, she
pours us each a cup before slowly making her way back
to the table. Only then does she look me in the eyes.

"Should have known you'd show up one day." She
nervously swings her crossed leg while tapping a finger
against the table. "You're all grown now—Morgan, too,
of course. I've missed so much... missed raising my
two daughters." She fumbles in her pocket and pulls out
a package of cigarettes. Her fingers tremble as she takes
her time removing one from the package. This haggard
older woman sitting across the table from me replaces
the violent, yelling monster in the nightmares that have
plagued me my entire life.

"What was Uncle Robert talking about?" Even as I
ask the question, the answer, as disturbing as it is,
forms clear and sharp in my mind of Uncle Robert,
standing in front of the fireplace mantel, staring
adoringly at the one picture of my mother we kept in
the house. He always arrived early enough so he could
have his private moment gazing lovingly at his
brother's wife before that brother descended the stairs.

With a flush of anger, I remember how he
compared everything I prepared to the way my mother
had cooked for us—and was probably still cooking for
him. I look at the coffee mug filled with the coffee my
mother brewed, the coffee that my uncle couldn't say
enough good things about. "You obviously know that
your husband is dead, but did you *ever* love him?"

Twisting her dry, cracked lips until they form a
thin straight line, she stiffens her back and shakes her

head, as if my question isn't worthy of an answer. She snorts before releasing a low, bitter cackle. Her body language and what she isn't saying tell me all I need to know. With startling clarity, I understand why my father wanted me to come here—to get answers once and for all. Now I know that the unraveling of my family wasn't because of me. There were things happening in my home that, as a child, I knew nothing about—adult things that are now emerging. My poor father—had he known that his wife was having an affair with his brother?

"Did you ever love my father?" I ask again, even though I'm not sure I want to hear the answer.

A chair scrapes against the floor in another room as the sound of my uncle's cursing echoes through the wall.

"I tried." She shrugs and looks at her hands, then picks at the chipped red polish, breaking off pieces as she reminisces. "Your father was very handsome and wealthy." A faint smile appears, not quite lighting up her face. "That made him attractive." She stands, makes her way slowly to the coffee pot and tops off her cup before sitting back down. "But did I love him? It's hard to say for sure…" A frown crinkles her sparse brows, before she purses her lips. "I got pregnant with you and, being the gentleman that he *was*, he proposed. He *adored* you. He barely thought of me after that. *I* was the one who gave birth to you, endured the pregnancy, the pain of labor, and he ignored me while always talking about how perfect you were. I think that's when my hatred of you began. What was so special about you? You were just a little crying baby who stole whatever love my husband had away from me."

I shudder as a pain creeps into my chest, as if she's stabbing a knife in whatever hopes I'd ever harbored for some perfect *all is forgiven* family reunion. How did my father *ever* love this woman? Or... did he? Maybe he'd just done what he'd considered the right thing to do at the time.

"Don't look at me that way. I'm no monster. You came here asking for the truth so I'm giving it to you." She folds her hands over her waist, reaches into her beige housecoat pocket and pulls out a box of matches. Taking her time, she lights a cigarette, inhaling deeply before exhaling a stream of curling smoke.

"I was an extremely beautiful young woman and men always wanted me. I liked men and thrived on their attention. It made me feel special." She takes another long, slow drag of her cigarette. The smoke curls in front of me, creating an opaque barrier between us. "I wasn't used to being ignored and that's what my husband was doing after he had his *precious* little Elaine." She sneers. "It disgusted me, to be honest with you." Her face is transformed as she recollects something that makes her eyes light up and brings a smile to her thin lips. "But Robert... he couldn't praise me enough. He saw how his brother was taking me for granted. He'd go on about how he loved my hair, my body, everything about me." She runs her hands across her chest. "I needed that... that validation. You know, to be appreciated. When I got pregnant the second time, it was completely different. Julian was so easy to love, especially after Robert took a paternity test and we discovered that he was the father."

I've heard enough. In my haste to escape this room and my mother, I bolt from the table, knocking over my chair and mug. The dark liquid spreads across the table, cascading like a black waterfall onto the faded yellow linoleum.

"What the hell?" She gasps, eyeing me suspiciously as if I'd intentionally spilled her cherished coffee.

She'll have to clean up the mess because I'm having difficulty breathing. I bring my hand to my throat and undo the top button of my blouse. This house is suffocating me, and I don't want to hear another word from this woman. I shake my head, struggling to comprehend the knowledge that my father had been married to someone who'd never truly loved him; the same woman who sits here and has the nerve to shamelessly proclaim an affair with her brother-in-law.

"Spare me anymore details." I barely recognize the harshness of my voice. "I get the picture."

She clutches my shoulder. "Everything was *your* fault. Your father stopped loving me the day you were born, and *you* killed Julian."

Pulling back, I block her raised hand before she can strike. Hatred contorts her features as she stumbles back, defeated, and all I feel for her is pity. "Don't *ever* raise your hand to me again." I reflect back on the years when Morgan and I craved our mother's love. This shallow woman is incapable of loving anyone but herself.

Hands clutched tightly at her side, she glares at me as if seeing me for the first time and recognizing that I'm no longer that helpless child she once pummeled as if I was her personal punching bag.

"I can't believe I blamed myself for Julian's death." The words are difficult to say, but there's no use avoiding the details of the devastating event that has marred my life. "You expected me to stay up all night so I could keep an eye on Julian to make sure that he was fine."

"Damn right, I did. He had asthma and you were his big sister." She shakes her head in anger, twists her lips, and yells, "You should have been able to manage that."

"I was *three* years old." I throw my hands up, understanding now, for the first time, that I wasn't to blame for Julian's death. "How was I expected to stay awake? Maybe he should have been in the room with his parents, not another child."

"Don't you say another word about my precious Julian. His death should be on *your* conscience."

"It was, but not anymore." I take a step back and stare at her until she has to look at me. "I was a child. It was *your* responsibility, not *mine,* to take care of Julian."

"I needed my sleep. My looks were all I had." Her face crumples in a frown, making her look much older than her fifty-nine years.

And to think, all the time I've wasted thinking that I could have saved my family when I had never been the one to destroy it in the first place. It had already been irreparably broken before Julian had even been born. But I don't want to think about Julian now or if Morgan is my father's or uncle's child. All that matters is that she's my sister. I only have one more question before I leave.

"And what about the necklaces you sent to Morgan and me?" I feel the weight of the locket heavy on my chest as I hold it out to her. It feels like it weighs ten pounds instead of an ounce. "Did you give this to our father to give to us?"

"I don't know what you're talking about." Scowling, she squints at the chain before shaking her head. "Get that tacky thing away from me."

"On the first Mother's Day after you left, Dad presented each of us with a locket. He said they were gifts from you... But that's not true either, is it?"

She laughs the deep raspy laugh of a woman who's been puffing tobacco for most of her life. "That is so like your father, making up some sappy story to make you all feel better. I never sent you two anything and certainly not that cheap piece of crap, got it?" She practically hisses the last two words.

I nod my head. I got it—more, than I could ever imagine. I can't wait to get out of this place, away from this woman. My uncle and my mother are the perfect pair. Dad deserved so much more. How did he survive being betrayed by his brother and his wife?

\

Chapter 10
Comfort and Joy

Shock and disgust leave a bitter taste in my mouth as I quickly make my way out of the house. I stumble down the walkway, ready to drive away and never look back.

David stands by the car, worry etched on his brow. "Everything okay?"

"Let's get out of here." My whole body trembles with outrage. What horrible people. My father was protecting Morgan and me all along from the knowledge of our mother's true moral character. But did he know Julian was Uncle Robert's son? I massage my temples and close my eyes, trying to erase the image of my mother attempting to slap me even as I stood before her as an adult.

We drive for an hour in complete silence. I lean my head back against the headrest, unable to speak. I concentrate on breathing evenly—stilling the trembling of my legs. Sometimes, we don't know what we're asking for when we say we want the truth.

"I'm stopping here before we get to my parents' home," David says.

I slowly open my eyes to find that he has parked in front of a long stretch of the Pacific Ocean. The water is a deep blue under a bright sunny sky. White waves crest against the shoreline. A man in a red baseball cap jogs by with a black Labrador retriever on his heels, loudly barking in delight. A bikini-clad woman stretches out on a multi-colored blanket on the sand, a large straw picnic basket by her side and a magazine open in her hands.

I look at David, noting the concern in his eyes.

"You okay?"

"Yes." I inhale deeply while stretching my arms toward the beach. "This helps. Thank you."

Just looking at the waves' steady rhythm of washing up onto the shoreline makes me feel better already. The shallow and vain woman I spoke to was not who I'd been expecting. I'd had no idea my mother was such a horrible person. My shoulders tense as I reflect on what life would have been like if she had stayed. What kind of woman is jealous of her husband's love for his daughter? But why leave Morgan behind? She was barely one year old when our mother left. Surely, she couldn't have found fault with her, too. I'll never know because I'm never returning to that place again. Since my mother and Uncle Robert live together, she has to know that my father is dead. Not that it probably matters to her one way or the other. At least, as painful as it was, I upheld my end of the bargain and followed through on my father's wishes.

"You look like you've seen a ghost."

"Well, it was…" I stop myself from saying she was more like a demon than a ghost. "It was no illusion. I finally saw the real person that is my mother and it wasn't pretty." I blink back a single tear, but it's not one of sadness; it's more from disappointment about what my father had to endure. "My uncle Robert was there, too."

"What? I don't understand." He raises his eyebrows. "I thought he lived next door to you."

"Apparently, he also lives here with my mother."

He frowns and runs his hands through his hair as he puts the pieces together. "That's—"

"All kinds of jacked up." I finish the sentence for him. "And there's more, but I don't want to talk about it right now. I need time to sort out everything I just learned."

"Understood. Let's take a walk."

He steps out of the car and makes his way to my side and opens my door. He takes my hand in his and we stroll silently down the beach, soaking in the serenity that only being in nature can provide.

Once we've past the sunbathers and random joggers, David stops walking and squeezes my hand. "Let's sit here."

"On the sand?" I love the feel of the sand between my toes and am glad I'd slipped off my shoes a couple of minutes ago, but I don't want the sand all over my clothes. Now, if I had a bathing suit, that'd be different. "Nice idea, but we don't have a blanket. Don't get me wrong, I love the beach, but the sand?"

"Do you want me to take off my shirt so you can sit on it instead of the sand?"

He begins unbuttoning his shirt and I'm mesmerized by how good his chest looks. Does the man workout or what?

He smooths the sand, then sets the shirt down. Opening his hand and bowing low, he says, "My lady, your throne has been prepared."

I laugh and settle down on the shirt. "Care to join me, kind knight?"

"Don't mind if I do." He sits down close enough that our shoulders touch. When he wraps his arm around me. I feel his warm, bare skin and I nestle in closer. He lifts my chin with his finger and presses his lips against mine. Our tongues mingle and I let myself relax into this. It's exactly what I need. I can't think of anything else but him right now. His fingers against my back arouse pleasure, especially when they move forward, lightly caressing my breast through my shirt. I begin to moan as sensations wash over me in a flood of desire, so powerful that I can hardly breathe.

"David," I whisper in his ear. "We are on a public beach."

"Yes, and your point is?"

He sucks on my earlobe and, for a minute, I can't recall if I had a point.

As I'm caressing his chest, something large bounces off my back. "Perhaps we should continue this some place more private."

The shrieks of children's voices heading in our direction have me pulling back and straightening my clothes.

"I'm not going to put this shirt back on," he says, defiantly, as if I would object.

"Good," I whisper. "I love the view."

"I have a jacket that I can put on once we get back to the car." He brushes some sand off of my hair and tantalizes my mouth with his tongue. I moan as our tongues touch.

"Hey mister, can you get our ball for us?" a squeaky voice says.

I open my eyes and see a little red-haired girl standing nearby.

"It's over there." She points toward the water. Apparently, she's afraid to go too close to the waves.

After David has given the girl her ball back, we stand up and he brushes the sand off my legs before we head back to his car. The feel of his hands against my skin is soothing and arousing at the same time.

"It's just as well we stopped." He interrupts my musings. "You've got a lot going on right now and I don't want to take advantage of the situation. When we make love, I want it to be in the right place and time."

I look at him incredulously, but he just keeps walking, not skipping a step. Did he just casually make reference to us making love? I know my brain may be cloudy with all of my family drama, but I *know* I heard that clearly. My vow to keep my work and personal life separate is becoming more blurred by the minute. More tangled thoughts for me to unravel later, but for now, David's affection is difficult to resist, and the truth is, I don't even want to try.

David pauses at the car. "I should probably warn you, the house will be full." He opens the door for me before walking over to his side and getting in.

"Oh." I don't know if I can manage small talk right now with a bunch of strangers, but I can't say no when he's been the one positive thing about this weekend.

"My mom makes it a family event." He gives my hand a squeeze.

"So, Amanda will be there too?" I can handle seeing Amanda. "It would be nice to see her again."

"She likes you, too, especially the way you told me off that day in the office."

I clear my throat, still embarrassed by my past bad behavior. "Don't remind me. I've apologized, remember?"

"Yes, I do." He leans over and brushes his smooth lips across mine, instantly relaxing me. "Amanda's husband and two kids will also be there."

My chest constricts, thinking about having to meet his whole clan. The tightness increases when I notice my wrinkled clothes and feel the sand between my toes. "I can't see anyone like this. Do you mind if we stop somewhere first and pick up a few things?"

"You look beautiful just as you are." His dark eyes gaze at me appreciatively.

"That's a nice thing to say, however, I still need to pick up a few things." I pull down the visor and look in the mirror—which confirms my need to wash up. "There's a mini-mall with a boutique and a drugstore right there." I point in the direction of the next block, which contains a set of modest stores that will hopefully have something I can purchase to help me look more together than I feel at the moment.

I'm happy to see that the boutique has both clothes and accessories. I select a sleeveless, orange-and-yellow, long sundress and a matching clutch bag. I hadn't planned to spend the night, so I get clothes for tonight and something to change into tomorrow. I also buy a couple of matching bra and panty sets, blue satin baby doll pajamas, a purple linen blouse, and assorted toiletries. After paying for my purchases, I head into the dressing room and change clothes. Returning to the car, I see David is fast asleep.

He wakes with a jolt as I toss my bags into the back seat then get into the car. "I'm sorry I took so long that you fell asleep."

"It was worth it—you look beautiful." He kisses

my cheek. "I've been working long days and that little snooze just helped."

"So, it was a power nap?" I laugh, knowing that most men don't want to admit that they've been *napping;* it reminds them of kindergarten.

"Exactly," he says while winking at me.

****

Fifteen minutes later, he pulls up and parks in front of a two-story, terra cotta, Spanish-style home that's surrounded by a sprawling green lawn and blooming jacaranda trees, their purple petals scattered across a circular front porch. Before he unlocks the large red double doors, it swings open.

"Hello, son. I'm so happy you're finally here. I can't wait for us to go to the Festival." A soft and welcoming voice greets us as an older woman peers around David's shoulder and flashes me a brilliant smile. "Who's your friend?

"Mom, this is Elaine Hart. She's never been to the Strawberry Festival, so I asked her to join us." He pulls me close to his side. "Elaine, this is my mother, Catherine."

"Splendid. It's lovely to meet you, Elaine." Noting her regal stature, shoulder-length auburn hair, and hazel eyes, I understand where Amanda and David got their stunning good looks. "Welcome to our home. Come on in, both of you." She ushers us into a cozy and elegant foyer lined with glass shelves containing African and Asian sculptures.

"Your home is lovely." The deep russet, bright yellow, and rich orange pillows and curtains create an eclectic and vibrant effect.

"Why, thank you. I love it, too. We haven't been

living here *that* long, but I instantly fell in love with this house the first time I saw it. I told my husband, Edgar, that this would be our new home."

"I can see why." I instantly connect with the warmth of the home and its gracious owner.

We step outside to a lovely, circular patio area where a cluster of adults are busy eating, reading newspapers, and engaging in a lively discussion. A small boy and girl, who are focused on what appears to be mud pies, are plopped down on a mound of dirt in the garden and chattering away with each other. No one seems to pay any attention to the fact that their clothes are dirty, and mud is smeared on their pudgy, little cheeks.

David's sister, Amanda, looks up and, upon seeing me, rushes over to give me a warm embrace. "Elaine, it's so good to see you again. David told me about your father. My condolences to you and your sister," she says softly so that the others can't hear.

"Thank you. Our father meant the world to us."

"Of course." She pats my hand. "I'm glad you can join us at the festival." She raises her perfectly arched eyebrows, "I hope you like strawberries."

"I do." I manage to smile. There's an air of relaxed chaos here that makes me wish I had grown up in a home like this.

"That's my father over there. Dad," she raises her voice, "can you stop looking at the paper long enough to meet David's friend, Elaine?"

Mr. Cole reluctantly puts the paper down on the table. Taking off a pair of glasses, he pauses long enough to squint at me. "Hello, David's friend. Nice to meet you." He tilts his head in my direction before resuming his reading of the newspaper.

"Those two dirty little munchkins, Madison and Dillon, are mine." She rolls her eyes. "Another set of unruly twins I'm afraid. Stanley," she shouts at a rather conservatively-dressed, bespectacled man who is walking in the opposite direction before Amanda summons him. She gestures wildly with her hands. "Come here and meet Elaine. She's joining us at the festival."

"Hello." He pauses and reaches out a hand as if to shake mine before abruptly changing his mind. "Better not shake your hands," he says, apologetically. "I'm likely to get mud on them." He reaches down and manages to pick up his two children at the same time. They both giggle and squirm in their father's arms. "Got to get these two clean. Wish me luck."

"Come sit down with us, Elaine. Orange or cranberry juice?" Amanda asks as she plops onto the floral sofa and pats the space beside her.

I point to the pitcher of cranberry juice. Amid the scattered newspapers and the muddy children, is a strong bond of love that permeates their home.

"Good choice. Stanley just loves being a fulltime father. Lucky for me. I couldn't stand the drudgery of it all." She shudders. "Really, who could stand cooking and cleaning all day?"

"Amanda, I'm going to show Elaine the guest room. You can bore her with the mundane details of your domestic life later," David says.

"I'm going to get you for that," Amanda yells at David's back as he guides me out of the sun porch.

"All of the bedrooms are upstairs. My room is right there." He opens a door and steps inside. "Do you like it?"

I take in the thick brown comforter on a double bed. A large recliner chair is in the corner. "It's nice." It's obvious that he doesn't live here because it has none of the personal, sophisticated touches of his condominium in the city.

"Good because I'm hoping you'll want to spend some time with me here as opposed to the guest room next door." He rubs his hands up and down my arms, causing me to practically purr with pleasure.

"Tempting offer." I kiss him on his cheek, wondering how I got myself into this predicament. Is it a good thing or something to be avoided? Hmmm, he would definitely provide a much-needed diversion from the recent troubling information I just learned about my mother and uncle—talk about disgusting human beings. I shake my head and focus on the handsome man standing before me. "Let's explore the possibilities later. You have a great family, David." He probably has no idea how fortunate he is to have *two* loving parents.

"They're okay," he says. "Mandy is a pain in the butt and Stanley is a saint for putting up with her."

"How old are the twins?" I ask. Dillon looks like Amanda, while Madison resembles her father.

"They turn four in July." He continues rubbing his fingers across my arm.

"Really? They're only three?" I shake my head. "Do you mind if I sit down for a moment?"

"Of course not. What's going on?" He rubs my back. "Kids remind you of someone?"

"You could say that."

They remind me of when I was three years old and given more responsibility than any child should have to bear. How could anyone have expected a toddler to care for a child who had a life-threatening illness? My brother did not die because I, at three years old, hadn't done my job. My mother didn't leave because of me. She left because she wanted to be with my uncle.

I take a deep cleansing breath and feel lighter than I have in years. I bring my hands up to my face, liberated, at last, of a lifetime of guilt, shame, and tortured dreams.

"Care to share your thoughts?" His face is etched with concern.

Regardless of what happens with the business, I appreciate being with him, this reprieve from my own troubled past. "Not now." I wouldn't know where to begin. "Thank you for bringing me here." I hug him and just hold on for a moment, not wanting to let him go— not ready to share information about my family, but still wanting, no *needing,* to be held. Because of this detour, I've been given a new lease on some significant aspects of my life.

His breath is hot as he nibbles on my neck. "We all go through some tough times. You're not alone. We can just stay here if you don't feel like being around my family or hanging out at the festival."

"Oh no, nothing can stop me from going. I happen to love strawberries and being here with your lovely family who have already made me feel welcomed. It's exactly what I needed." I brush my lips against his. "Seeing the twins has been the best gift that anyone could give me."

"I think I can top that," he says, smiling mischievously.

****

The festival is better than anything I could have expected. Amanda and Stanley take Madison and Dillon to have strawberry images painted on their faces by Bobbi the Clown. David's parents decide to participate in a pie-eating contest while David and I go to sample strawberry cotton candy, strawberry popcorn, and strawberry fried chicken. That's right, chicken dipped in some type of strawberry batter and fried to a crisp.

By the time the sun has set and we're back in David's parents' home, I vow to never eat another strawberry in my life. "Look," I hold up my hands, "even my fingertips have strawberry stains on them." I laugh. "I think the strawberry fried chicken was the last straw—no pun intended."

"Cute." He chuckles before his expression sobers. "Stay here in my room with me tonight?" Desire and need burn in his eyes.

"I'm not sure." I force myself to look away because it's hard to say no when a part of me wants to take what pleasure I can in his arms.

In three days, I'll have to tell him that neither the oranges nor the avocados are ready for the market, which means we'll still be unable to make a full loan payment. We need a good thirty days before we'll be able to come close to catching up, but debt is the last thing I want to think about when he's looking at me with a sexy, pleading grin on his handsome face.

Just because I'm falling hard for him doesn't mean he won't do his job. And if he does, then what? I run a hand through my hair and feel my body grow warm with desire. At least I'll have the memory of tonight and this wonderful day that has given me a guilt free future. That, alone, deserves a celebration.

"I respect that." He steps closer so that my breasts touch his chest. His scent is warm and sensual. "You have to want me as much as I want you or this won't work. I want to make love to you, but if you don't feel the same way—"

"Enough." With my finger, I outline the perfect shape of his firm lips. "I'm on birth control for occasional migraine headaches." I smile at his amazed expression. "I want you, too. Now what are you going to do about it?"

"I happen to have condoms, but they aren't for migraines." He grins and his voice is husky. "I'd be happy to show you exactly how I use them."

Shaking my head, I laugh. "You're incorrigible, but you've aroused… my curiosity. Show me what you can do." I move even closer, giving in to the urge to run my fingers along his shirt buttons, then slowly undoing each one. "Let me help you get more comfortable." I begin to unbuckle his belt before carefully unzipping his pants. Smiling, I force my eyes to look up into his smoldering gaze. "Very impressive, Mr. Cole."

"If you like the way it looks, you'll really be impressed when you see what it can do."

"Show me." I pull his pants all the way down until they're completely off. While kissing, we continue to move in unison toward the bed. I struggle to catch my breath as his fingers roam seductively up and down my spine, causing a wave of heat to wash over me.

"You are overdressed." Wrapping his arms around me so we're tightly pressed together, he unzips the zipper on the back of my sundress before letting it fall to the floor. Turning me around, he peruses every inch of me, from my black lace bra to the matching panties. Thank God, I picked up new undies on the way here.

"You're as beautiful as I imagined."

His voice, rich with desire, is turning me on even more.

"I've been wanting you since the day you stormed into my office."

"Really?" I shake my head as my fingers circle round to massage his perfect backside. "I never would have guessed." Is there no part of his anatomy that doesn't have muscles? I could get used to this. I don't know about *then*, but I want him now. "I thought I was being a colossal pain in the ass?"

"You were." He hovers over me, nibbling on my earlobe as we make our way to the bed. "But I liked it."

"I'll have to be a pain in the ass more often." I squirm with pleasure.

He laughs. "I'm sure that won't be a problem for you."

I'm too breathless, too lost in his touch to say anything else as his skilled hands tenderly and slowly caress every inch of my body. Those perfect lips trail kisses from the arch of my foot, to the back of my knee, and even farther, beyond my hips and thighs. My body arches up to meet him as he continues sucking, nipping, and tantalizing me until I am a mass of tingling sensations, ready for him to take me completely.

But he stops and lingers, pulling me closer until I am on the brink of screaming out in ecstasy.

I can't touch him enough. My hands caress his shoulders, his chest, and thighs until I hear him moan. His mouth is demanding as he explores every inch, caressing my breast and slowly moving down, his tongue circling my navel. As he continues, I clutch the sheets and writhe with ecstasy, knowing that I am ready for him to take me completely, but his lips move back up my torso and his fingers replace his tongue until I can't take it anymore.

"David…" I barely catch my breath as his fingers explore me and I run my tongue across his arm. "What are you waiting for?" I manage to whisper.

"You. I'm waiting for you to say that you want this—want *me*—right now."

I caress him and hear his gasp before he rips open the condom package and slips it on.

"Yes, I want you now," I pant, guiding him to the entrance of my deepest desires. Our bodies connect as one and we ride a wave of ecstasy until we scream out together. I'm totally satiated, nerve endings that I didn't know I had have been pleasured until I now lay completely, ecstatically satisfied.

"Wow." I can't stop beaming. "That was really fantastic." Not sure if I should have said that out loud, but it's too late. The words are already out there. Is he always this good with everyone? If he is, he's probably used to getting compliments on his sexual prowess.

"It was." He rolls off me, tucks me under his arm, then trails his fingers down my waist and over my hip. "I have to agree with you." Leaning up on one elbow, he tenderly gazes down at me. He kisses my collarbone, then up my neck and along my eyebrows. "In a few minutes, I'm going to want a repeat and then probably another, and, after that, probably another."

"Don't go getting crazy." I playfully swat his hands away while taking his words as a sign that he enjoyed himself as much as me. "A girl can take only so much.

Plus, it's not as if you don't have family members right next door."

"I thought about that." He lifts me on top of him. "That's why you are going to have to control your screaming out my name this time."

"What? Did I really? I am so embarrassed." I swear I don't know if he's teasing me or not. Still, now that I'm on top, it's only fair that I should torture *him* with desire and make him scream out my name.

I start by kissing his chest and making my way down to his hard abs and flat belly. I continue thoroughly pleasuring him with my hands and mouth until he clutches my waist.

"What are you doing to me?"

"Me?" I look at him innocently before I take my time moving back up his beautiful body until I'm clasping him between my thighs and he's holding on to my hips and yelling my name.

"Damn woman, have some mercy on a man." He flips me over and kisses my breast and caresses every inch of my skin until I can't take it anymore. I don't know how much time elapses before, completely exhausted and spent, we collapse on the bed. I'm nestled against his chest when he leans down and pulls the blanket up to cover my shoulders. He tenderly kisses my neck and, with his arms wrapped around me, we finally fall asleep.

I don't know how much time passes, but when I open my eyes, the sun is brightly shining in David's room. The sheets are halfway on the floor and numerous condom wrappers are on the nightstand. I roll over, expecting to see David sprawled out beside me, but he's not there. Did he leave already? Normally, I'm not a deep sleeper, but last night was probably the best night's sleep I've had in a long time. I close my eyes and savor the aroma of the sheets, a mixture of his scent and mine.

"Hey, what are you doing over there?" David comes into the room, looking at me suspiciously. "Are you smelling the sheets?"

"Of course not." There's no reason for him to know what I was doing. He's already showered and dressed, while I know my hair is sticking up all over my head and my eyes aren't completely opened.

"How are you feeling this morning?" He smiles at me, brushing a strand of hair away from my cheek.

"Honestly?" My body is still humming with pleasure, but I'm not about to tell him that. "I feel wonderful."

He raises his eyebrows and picks up my hand, gently kissing the knuckles. "Good to know that I'm not alone in that sentiment. I'd love to have an instant replay, but everyone will be meeting downstairs in the patio in about twenty minutes."

David straightens his room, throws away the condom wrappers and makes the bed while I gather my toiletries and quickly shower. I put on my powder blue denim skirt and my new purple linen blouse. I do the best I can with my hair and add a touch of make-up before joining David.

When I walk into the room, he tilts his head to the side and eyes me appreciatively. "You look good enough to eat."

"Hmmm." I frown at him. "Don't go getting any ideas. Your family is probably waiting for us to join them."

"You're right." He takes my hand in his as we make our way down the stairs. "I was thinking that, looking at you now, no one would know what a wild woman you were in bed last night."

"Hey." I nudge him in the side with my elbow.

"By the way," he kisses the top of my head. "I mean that as a compliment in every sense of the word."

****

A bouquet of daisies decorates the center of the table. Mrs. Cole has spread out a platter filled with scrambled eggs, hash brown potatoes, and bacon. A bowl of cheese grits is being passed around.

"Elaine, did you enjoy your first Strawberry Festival?" David's mother hands me a bowl of fluffy homemade biscuits.

"I did." I take one. "It was a lot of fun," I say, thinking that the real fun came *after* the festival.

"Did I just hear someone at the door?" Amanda asks. "There it is again—someone's definitely at the door. Can you get that, Stanley?"

Before he has a chance to leave the room, a woman in a pair of white, silver-studded skinny jeans, matching jacket, and stiletto heels enters the patio area, waving her hands and smiling brightly at everyone. She blows kisses to David's parents before bending down and scooping up the twins in a warm embrace.

"Hi, Aunty Courtney," Madison manages between bouts of laughter.

"Hello, my darlings," she says, reaching into her bag and pulling out small gift bags, which she hands to each of them. "I hope I'm not interrupting anything."

She opens her eyes wide and scans the room, pausing for a second when she notices me. She flips her long hair off her perfectly-made-up face. "Sorry for barging in like this. I was going to ring the doorbell when I remembered I still have my key." She dangles a single key off of a gold chain. "So sorry to miss the festival this year, but I still wanted to come by and say hello to everyone." She turns and focuses a laser like beam on me. "Oh, I'm being *so* rude. I haven't introduced myself." She holds out a manicured hand, complete with the largest, sparkling, diamond wedding ring I've ever seen.

"I'm Courtney, David's wife, and you are?" Her voice is syrupy sweet, but her eyes tell a different story.

"I'm… Elaine." I force myself not to stammer. *David is married*? How does someone forget to mention something as significant as a wife? I guess he thought I would believe that he really cared for me. I feel sick to my stomach, thinking about how we made love all night. How he held me, brushed my bangs back from my forehead, and pressed his lips against the scar on my brow. How could something that felt so right be so wrong?

Courtney cocks her head to the side and takes her time looking me over, obviously checking to see if I'm any competition. "So, Elaine, are you the new maid? David is always bringing new people to the house, aren't you, dear?"

I can't look at David right now. *Or* his family. They must have been laughing at me, thinking I was one of David's playthings. "Excuse me." I abruptly stand, clutch the back of my chair, and force my voice to sound normal, as if my world hadn't come crashing down around me because the chance for something real hadn't just disappeared. "I forgot something in my room."

No doubt about it, I've been played—big time. My first impression of David was obviously correct; ice *does* run through his veins. He's so cold, he's a glacier, even if he did make the sweetest and most passionate love to me that I've ever experienced. I never knew a man could be so sizzling hot and tender at the same time. I'm surprised that I'm able to leave the room without stumbling.

I don't know what I feel more: humiliation or anger. Loud, undecipherable voices echo behind me. I hear my name being called, but I keep moving, make my way to the stairs to get to the room where David and I had made passionate love, over and over again, only hours ago. I grab my purse and bag from the dresser, silently make my way to the kitchen, open the back door, and step out of David's life for good.

Chapter 11
The Consolation Prize

Amanda loudly claps her hands. "Bravo! What a performance, Courtney—pretending you and David are still married." Amanda shakes her head in disgust.

My sister never liked Courtney, not even when we first started dating; she felt she wasn't the right one for me. In this case, listening to my twin would have saved me a lot of heartache.

"I *am* still married to David, at least until the paperwork is finalized." Courtney places a proprietary hand on my arm before turning her gaze on me. "Darling, I couldn't bring myself to sign the papers."

"Really, David?" Amanda says. "After all she's done, I'd think you would have made certain that she had followed through."

"David," my mother says, looking at me disapprovingly, "I thought the divorce was done a while ago."

"Those documents *were* supposed to have been signed last week." I hope that Courtney hears the scorn in my voice as I remove her hand from my arm. "I'm going to escort my soon-to-be *ex-wife* out of the house."

The women in the family are obviously not pleased by Courtney's sweeping into the room like a prima donna. Her intention of making Elaine uncomfortable was evident in her petty comments. I've got to clean up the mess before Elaine comes back downstairs.

I firmly place my hand on Courtney's back and escort her to the front door. "I'll need that key back." I hold out my palm.

"Don't be mad at me, sweetie." Batting her eyes as she reluctantly turns over the key, she gives me the once-over. "You're not the type of man a woman would give up on without a good fight." She glances over her shoulder, as if Elaine may have come back in the room. "That woman isn't worthy of you, even *I* could tell that. Her clothes look like she got them at the dollar store." She shakes her head in dismay.

"Elaine is worth *two* of you. The divorce will be finalized on Friday, and that will put an end to any more of your useless attempts to get us back together. I told you months ago that there was no turning back."

"You'll change your mind." She places a manicured hand on my chest. "You always have. What makes you think this time will be any different?"

"Let's just say that I've finally learned what *real* love feels like and, unfortunately, that's something we never had." I open the front door. "I hope you find satisfaction in your next relationship, Courtney." I give her a gentle nudge and shut the door before she can say anything else.

Silence descends upon the table when I return to the patio.

"I suggest you go check on Elaine," Amanda says, grabbing Madison and Dillon by their hands. "I'm going to clean up my messy kids and you need to clean up the mess left by your wife."

"Ex-wife," I mutter. "I don't need your advice, Mandy." I plop down in the nearest chair, run my fingers through my hair, and curse under my breath.

"After the spectacle Courtney made, I'm not so sure." Amanda shakes her head disapprovingly. "I like Elaine and, with her father just having passed away, she sure didn't deserve the crap that Courtney just dumped on her."

"David." My mother purses her lips, raises her eyebrows. "Elaine looked like she was in a state of shock. I gather she didn't know you had a wife."

I nod my head. "Guilty as charged."

Now, my whole family knows that I've messed up with Elaine. It was amazing how she fit right in with everyone, not to mention how well the two of us fit together. Or, at least, we did. Last night was amazing. I would have said something about Courtney, if I had any idea that she hadn't signed the divorce papers. Everything happening so fast during the last couple of days. One minute Elaine had been stranded on the road, and the next, she was in my bed and I didn't want her to leave. I don't even know how the hell this happened. I had sworn off women for a while, but that was before Elaine Hart had burst into my life like a tornado, leaving nothing the same in her wake.

My father, who usually avoids any discussions of personal matters, sets the newspaper down. "What are you doing here?" he asks sternly. "If she's important to you, you need to do some damage control."

But when I go upstairs, Elaine is gone. She's taken her purse and left, without so much as a goodbye. I didn't plan on Courtney showing up at the house and making a scene. Hell, I didn't plan on any part of this weekend. I hadn't believed my good luck when I saw her car broken down on the side of the road. I did the decent thing, which was to offer her a ride. She had to have somewhere to stay while waiting for Jim to repair her car, didn't she? All the rooms in town were already taken. None of it was planned, especially not the feel of her in my arms, the softness of her skin against mine or how my body ached to hold her again.

"Where's Elaine?" my mother asks after I've come back downstairs.

"I don't know." I sigh, feeling like I've lost something important. "She was gone by the time I got upstairs."

"I see," my mother says. "She must have gone out the back door. Can't say I blame her. That must have felt mortifying."

"Mother, you are not helping."

"Well, it's true. There's no use sugar-coating it. Your father and I just realized why her name sounded familiar. Is she connected to the Hartland account?"

"She's the daughter. Now that her father has passed, she's taken over running the ranch."

"That's a big responsibility and now *this* on top of losing her father." My mother shakes her head, makes a small, undecipherable sound.

"What's happening with their loan?" my father asks. "I know you were concerned that they were delinquent, if I recall correctly."

"They had already been given one extension." A muscle in my jaw twitches as I recall making a series of bad business decisions in the past. "You both have put a lot of faith in Amanda and me, trusting us to keep the business strong. I can't support a business that isn't paying their loan on time."

"Does Elaine have a plan to turn things around?"

my mother asks.

"Yes. She asked for an additional thirty-day extension."

"That sounds reasonable to me," she says. "I'm *assuming* you are willing to allow her that additional time."

"I... I don't know." I rub my jaw. "I want to do the right thing by our business."

"Son," my father says, "you've always been too hard on yourself. Look, I know you're still thinking about the losses we incurred when you first started in the business."

"Dad," I say, "We lost—"

"Stop." He holds up his hand. "Enough beating yourself up about that. It was my fault. It happened ten years ago when you had just graduated from college and were learning the ropes. I gave you too much responsibility. Besides, during the last four years, we have enjoyed record profits under your leadership. The company is thriving, which is why your mother and I are able to retire. Nothing is going to change that, including the Hartland Ranch account."

"I just thought that I can't... that *we* couldn't support a failing business."

Amanda returns to the room, walks over, and places a hand on my arm. "Give it a break, David."

"Your sister is right this time. Give it a break." My dad pats my back. "I've been in the banking and loan business a long time, son. All businesses have their ups and downs. Hartland has been in their family for decades and it will recover. Elaine seems very bright. After all, the father must have left the business to her for a reason."

"I believe she has a degree in horticulture, isn't that what you told me, David?" Amanda pipes in while nibbling on a piece of bacon.

"Yes, but—"

"That's impressive," my mother says, while clearing the table. "I'm sure David will make this right with Hartland and Elaine, won't you, David?"

Ignoring Amanda's smirk, I nod. "Yes, I'm going to get on that right away."

****

There's no time for tears. Anger, yes. Tears, no. I didn't *intentionally* sleep with a married man. My shoulders tense as I squint and try to recall the sequence of events that led to me abandoning all rational thought and making love with David, several times, last night. I can't honestly declare that he seduced me. Thinking back on how I unzipped his pants, I clearly let it be known that I wanted him as much as he wanted me. Now that his wife is there, he probably hasn't even noticed that I've slipped out.

Readjusting my purse and shopping bag, I look up and down the quiet street, as if a taxi will magically appear, which lets me know that I'm not thinking clearly. Only in New York and Washington, D.C. do taxis appear with the snap of a finger. After circling the same quiet block three times, I plop down on a neighborhood park bench and rummage in my handbag for five minutes before I find the receipt from the mechanic. Twelve minutes after I have used my ride share app, a sedan pulls up to the curb. Apparently, I selected the carpool option because there's an older lady in the back seat already.

"Hello, dear. I'm Mrs. Edgeworth." She has a

short, purple natural and neon orange glasses. She's one of those older women whose age is impossible to discern. She could be anywhere from fifty-five to eighty years old. "And you are?"

I scoot closer to the door even though I won't be able to avoid conversing with her without appearing completely rude. "I'm Elaine."

"Nice to meet you." She nods her head. "Here for the Strawberry Festival?" She holds her hands out in an open gesture. Bright glittery rings adorn every finger.

"Kind of." Although, not really. I'm not about to share that I came to see my long-lost mother who abandoned me and had an affair with my uncle, and then, to top it off, I had sex with a married man. Way too much information.

"Did you like it?" She looks at me encouragingly.

"Yes." At first, I think she's talking about the sex but, of course, she knows nothing about that. "The festival was fun."

"I love it." Smiling brightly, she turns toward me. "Sometimes you just have to let loose and enjoy yourself."

"I definitely did that." I shudder as I recall sitting astride David this morning, attempting to provide him with as much pleasure as he had given me. "Maybe a little too much."

"Oh, don't be hard on yourself." Her laughter rings out in the car. "It's so easy to take things too seriously when we're young. If there's one thing that I've learned since I've gotten older, it's to lighten up." She points to her hair. "I'd never have had done this when I was in my twenties," she states while displaying her rings. "Nor would I wear all of these at once, but now I do whatever pleases me and don't beat myself up over little things."

"But how do you do that, just let go of the mistakes?" No sooner are the words out of my mouth when the car stops in front of a bus station.

"This is my stop. Time to head back home." She lifts her paisley overnight bag out of the car. "Nice talking with you dear." She pats my hand. "Remember to lighten up."

Easy for her to say, I think as the driver continues to the car repair shop. What kind of mistakes had she made? It's highly unlikely that she was indulging in wild, wonderful sex last night with a man she thought was single, only to later discover he had a wife—and not just any wife, but a petite, curvy little woman who looked great in her trendy outfit. At some point yesterday, or even when I was at his apartment, would it have taken too much effort for him to mention her?

His wife hadn't hesitated in staking her claim and why should she? Her timing was almost perfect. Too bad I'd already made the mistake of falling hard for David. Didn't plan on it, but there it is. If only she had arrived a day earlier. Everyone in his family, the entire Cole clan, probably thinks I am a complete slut—a homewrecker of the worst kind, a woman of seriously questionable morals. And to think they may have heard me screaming out his name like some sex-starved nymphomaniac… Talk about humiliating. And I actually like Amanda. What must she think of me?

This entire two-day trip has been a living hell. Okay, maybe not last night; I can't lie, that part was unbelievably fantastic. The man has got some serious skills. I close my eyes and wince. Maybe I'm not the first affair he's had. After all, with his virile good looks and position in the bank, I'm sure he meets lots of women who would be more than happy to spend a night in his bed.

I have to drag myself out of the car. All the sleep that I didn't get last night is finally catching up with me. Luckily, Jim's already at the shop and, dropping the keys in my hand, he lets me know that Betsy is ready. I yawn and give him my credit card before loading my stuff into the passenger seat. My stomach growls and I remember that I didn't have a chance to eat breakfast before I rushed out of the house. After fastening my seatbelt and adjusting the rear-view mirror, I'm eager to get home and put this whole weekend behind me. I can always eat later. At least I've satisfied my father's request to meet with my mother.

Unfortunately, after two months of no rain and a week of dry, dusty Santa Ana winds, the rain picks *now* to pour down and practically flood the narrow two-lane highway. Not just a smattering of little drops here and there, but a heavy downpour with flashes of thunder and lightning streaking through the black sky. As grateful as I am for how this will help the groves, it can't lighten the burden of my heavy heart.

I peer through the windshield, straining to see the road ahead as several large clouds block out the sun. I'm numb, overcome with too many thoughts to even want to process everything that happened this weekend with my mother, my uncle, and David. Maybe, if I just concentrate on the road ahead, I can drown out all the jumbled, painful thoughts that keep popping up, making me feel like crap. I've already endured too much with losing my father, possibly the farm, and now this. Is it *me*? Am *I* unlovable? Is there a sign on my forehead that says *she's the one you can use or walk away from or even hate*? Wait a minute. I don't want to think about my life right now and *all* of the betrayals. A little music will block out all the pain, at least for now.

Glancing down, I turn on the radio and push the button to change the station, so that I'm not listening to my usual mellow jazz. I need something more upbeat to distract me—something loud, like rap or rock music. After adjusting the volume, I focus back on the road and see an out of control red cargo truck hydroplaning across his lane and veering to the left, full speed ahead straight toward me.

Desperately honking the horn, I yell, "Stop!" knowing he can't hear me. A quick glance at his face reveals that he's frantically struggling to control his massive vehicle but is obviously not winning the battle. Tightly clutching the steering wheel, I quickly swerve to the side of the road, barely missing landing in a ditch as the truck speeds by.

Shaking and covered with sweat, I inhale deeply, drop my head against the steering wheel, and wait for my heartbeat to return to normal. Talk about seeing your life flash before your eyes. Unbelievable. And just when I thought it couldn't get any worse, I'm almost wiped out coming home from one of the most painful weekends of my life.

I lift my head in time to see a flash of lightning pierce the sky. Should I stay here and wait for the storm to subside or keep going? The rain is still pouring down in heavy torrents, as if it's attempting to make up for the long dry spell of the last year. Better to not be stuck here at nightfall. These roads don't have a lot of light and my car doesn't have a lot of warmth. Time to get going.

With the radio off, I cautiously merge back onto the highway, driving the last twenty-three miles home, keeping my distance from the cars in front of me and vigilantly scanning the road ahead for any oncoming out-of-control vehicles. Two miles from our ranch, I stop at Louie's, the local market, so that I can stock up on a few necessities. I don't plan on leaving the house again for several days—if ever. At least, that's how I feel at this very moment.

Grabbing a shopping cart, I head straight to the snack aisles. This won't take long. I know exactly what I need to tide me over for the next couple of days.

I place four candy bars in the cart and then go back and add two more in case Morgan wants a couple. Next, one bag of kettle corn, two of buttered popcorn, two bags of cheese puffs, a package of chocolate chip cookies, raspberry licorice, oatmeal cookies, and two frozen extra-large pizzas, one pepperoni and one cheese. Halfway to the checkout counter, I pause, realizing that I forgot to pick up root beer soda and vanilla caramel ice cream to make a root beer float. After remedying the situation, I head over to the only open cash register.

"Well, hello there, Elaine. Haven't seen you in a while." Overhead fluorescent lights cast a glow around Myrtle Smith, whose voice echoes loudly in the small grocery store. Living in California for over ten years hasn't diminished her thick, South Carolina drawl.

"Hello, Myrtle." I smile and load my food onto the conveyor belt, eager to be back on the ranch and hoping to avoid running into a lot of familiar faces, which isn't easy considering the size of Santa Lorena.

"Lordy, I reckon you all must be having some kind of a big party at your house with all of this here junk food." Picking up one of the candy bars, she slowly turns it over in her hand, scrutinizing it as closely as a detective would contraband.

"Not really," I mumble, not in any mood for small talk.

"I see." She nods her head, obviously not convinced. "It's just that I know you always eat real healthy, so it can't be for you. I reckon you all must be having some kind of a shindig." Pausing, she peers over her glasses and scans my face. "Maybe some kids are coming by or something. They love this kind of stuff." She points to the frozen pizza.

"No party." A long line of customers forms behind me, including my middle school nemesis, Rick Robertson, who used to follow me around campus and tease me about my frizzy hair. He catches me looking at him and blows me a kiss. That's all the evidence I need to know that he's still as obnoxious as he was when he was thirteen.

"Well." Myrtle scans the ice cream. "In any case, I'm so sorry about your dad passing and all. He was such a lovely man."

"Thank you." Only two more items to ring up and then I'll be out of here.

"And you and Morgan not having your mother and all. That man was a saint if you ask me. Raising two little girls with no woman around to help him." She pauses and purses her thin lips. "I know you all are missing him something terrible. When my daddy died, it just about *killed* me. He weren't nothing like your pa, though; he was kind of a rascal." Chuckling, she bags the last item. "I loved him just the same and miss him every day."

Myrtle's reminiscence is interrupted when someone from the back of the line loudly clears his throat. I'm guessing it's Bob, my postman, who just has one bottle of water and probably needs to get back to his route. Catching me looking at him gratefully, he gives me a quick grin.

"Cool it!" she yells back, all sentiment now gone.

"Thanks for your sympathies." I nod and swipe my ATM card, eager to leave the store.

"I didn't charge you for the bags. You girls have gone through enough, you don't need to worry about paying for grocery bags, especially when we use to give them out for free." She furrows her brow. "Shoot, they can just take it out of my check if they have a problem with it."

After thanking Myrtle, I quickly make my way out of the store with the sound of her voice echoing behind me, "If you all need anything, you just let me know, you hear?"

****

Is it just my imagination or am I stopping and having to wait for every red light as I finally make my way to Hartland? Once inside, I place the ice cream and pizza in the freezer and the soda in the refrigerator. Everything else goes upstairs with me. My brisk steps slow down as I walk past my father's closed bedroom door. I'll always think of it as his room, even if he's no longer here. Setting down the two grocery bags, I stand in front of the door and take down all of the memorabilia that Dad had taped there. First, the report cards, then the handmade cards and everything else.

It feels strange to *not* have to knock first before I slowly open the door. Stranger still to not see him sitting up in bed, eagerly waiting to begin one of our father-daughter chats filled with his words of wisdom.

I run my fingers across the bedspread, wishing he was here for me to talk to about seeing Mom and Uncle Robert and loving David. But my daddy's gone now, and, for the first time, I'll have to keep myself together. No father to lean on. It's just Morgan, the ranch, and me. Who knows how long we'll even have that? With a heavy sigh and a heavier heart, I set the remnants of days long past on his desk right beside the last book he was reading.

Now that I'm in my room, I spread my food across my dresser. The brightly colored packages instantly make me feel better. After turning on the television, I plop on my bed and rip open the jumbo bag of popcorn, prepared to binge-watch nothing but love stories for the next twenty-four hours. Even though I do not get the man—the one I foolishly thought I loved— who has a wife he probably loves (which basically makes me a side piece), I'm still up for watching other people win the prize. *My* prize which is the consolation prize is that I get to eat all the junk food I want over the next couple of days. Yippee.

Just as I'm stuffing my mouth with a handful of popcorn, Morgan walks into the room and sits beside me on the bed.

"Welcome back." She frowns at all the junk food. "What's going on? I know that's not your usual dinner. Was the weekend that bad?"

"Yes." Morgan doesn't have a clue as to how

screwed up our family is. Sure, she knows we didn't have a mother to raise us, but that's all. And there's so much more. Would I be doing her a favor by letting her stay oblivious to the facts? Our father decided to keep us both in the dark, but at what cost? I'm sure he meant well but look what it did to me. I chew on my bottom lip, struggling to decide if I should share more or stay silent.

"Do you want to talk about it?" Morgan asks, as she lies down beside me and grasps my hand.

"No, I'd rather not." I jam my mouth with more popcorn, chewing it slowly, and focus on the television. I point to the screen. "Love stories twenty-four hours a day."

She releases my hand long enough to scoop out a handful of popcorn. "Love stories are good for the soul."

"Except our parents' love story." Sitting up, I click on the mute button and turn toward her. "It was ugly."

"What do you mean?" she asks, not questioning my sudden change of mind.

"I don't know where to begin." I pause, still vacillating between protecting her from the sordid details and just putting it all out there. Will the truth destroy her lighthearted, good-natured disposition? If it does, I'll have that on my conscience forever.

"I always suggest my students start at the beginning. Maybe that's what you should do." She leans against the headboard, pillows propped around her, inquisitive eyes laser-focused on my face.

"Good idea... I think." I slowly get up and peruse my stash. "This will require chocolate and nuts combined, as in this candy bar. There's a lot you don't know—stuff that happened before you were born. It's the cause of all the nightmares—stuff I blamed myself for. Dad never brought it up, so neither did I." I hesitate, thinking that the only way I can get through this is to plunge in and say it all and never have to say it again. And I need to. It's time for no more secrets. She deserves to know the truth, as horrible as it is.

"We—no, *I*—had a baby brother." I smile as I remember his chubby little face, silky black curls, and big round eyes. "His name was Julian and he was born when I was two years old. I tried to be a good big sister. He had asthma and my job was to watch him at night to make sure that he kept breathing. But one night, when I was only three years old, I fell asleep and he had an asthma attack and I couldn't wake him up."

I turn toward Morgan and look deep into her eyes, searching for signs of contempt, or blame for Julian's death. "I couldn't save him."

"And you shouldn't have been expected to. Jesus, Elaine, you were only a child yourself. No one could blame you. That wouldn't make sense."

She's angry now, but not at me, but *for* me, for all the pain I endured all these years. I can see the outrage in the set of her mouth, the flush in her cheeks, and the fisted palms, as if she's ready to fight anyone who would dare blame me.

I put my hands in my hair, slowly push back the bangs, and reveal the scar that I viewed as a constant reminder of my failure, evidence of my incompetence and why my mother had to leave. "I always told you that this was from a bicycle fall." I pause now as my throat constricts, and I visualize that one life-altering early morning series of events in the room I shared with

Julian.

"Julian's breathing was loud, and he was making a wheezing sound. Of course, at the time, I didn't know that he had asthma or what an asthma attack even was. All I knew was that it was my job to keep an 'eye on him' each night." My shoulders tense, as I remember how I'd wanted to help my brother but didn't know what to do. "I ran as fast as I could to our parents' room to tell our mother that something was wrong with Julian. For the longest time, she tried to revive Julian and, when nothing worked, she blamed me for falling asleep, then she hit me." I fold my hands together as if in prayer and shudder as I recount the details of that morning. "My lip was busted and the skin above my eye was ripped. I fell onto the floor, doubled over in pain, trying to protect my head from the onslaught of repeated blows. Honestly, I probably would have been dead, if Dad hadn't pulled her off me right before I blacked out. Our mother never looked at me the same again. She made it abundantly clear that she felt it was *my* fault, so I always tried to be the perfect daughter so she'd love me again. But she never did."

For several seconds, neither of us utters a word, each lost in our own thoughts. Had I said too much? "It's my belief that she felt the wrong child died or maybe she felt like I should join Julian in death." I shudder as I say the words that have stayed buried inside for so long. "I hate to say that, but it's what I felt."

"There's something wrong with that woman, I don't care if she is our mother. You don't put that kind of burden on a three-year-old child. You needed to sleep. Did they think of that?" She wraps her arms around my shoulders and gives me a tight hug. "I'm so sorry that you've had to carry that burden with you all these years."

"It's been a lot." I nod. "But I feel better now that I've told you. I was around some three-year-olds this weekend and it made me realize how young they were and couldn't be responsible for another child, especially one who had special medical needs. It was like I had a long-overdue epiphany."

"Good. I just wish you hadn't felt responsible for Julian's death."

"He was an adorable little boy and I loved my baby brother so much; I would have done anything I could to save his life." I reach down and grab the throw and secure it around my shoulders. "When I was about twelve or so, I made it a point to learn about asthma. He should have had an inhaler, at the very least. The fact that all the adults smoked didn't help either."

"You're right." Morgan tilts her head and looks at me with tears in her eyes. "I'd love to see Julian. I missed out on getting to have a brother. Are there any pictures?"

"Dad probably has some buried in his room." I swipe a tear from her cheek. "I'll check another time."

"I would love to see him and am grateful you're telling me about our family. I had no idea there was another child. Sorry that you're having to even speak about the pain, but I'm glad you decided to not hold it inside anymore."

"I don't want to have any more family secrets. From now on, we've got to share what we know."

"I agree." She squeezes my hand before walking over to the consolation table and picking up the bag of licorice. Sitting back down on the bed, she takes a deep breath and runs a hand through her short curls. She peers at me hesitantly. "That's all, right?"

"I wish it was, but that was the past. I haven't told you about the present." I throw the empty candy bar wrapper into the garbage can, brush the crumbs off the bed, and take a deep breath. "You already know that Betsy broke down and that I had to stay overnight while the car was being fixed. What I didn't tell you is that David gave me a ride to Mom's and that I spent the night with him."

"Whoa." Morgan holds a hand out in front of her, as if to block my words. "What the heck? Are you kidding me? I *knew* there was some electricity flowing between you two. I want to hear all about it."

"I'll give you the details, but, first, let me finish telling you about the visit with our mother. She's not the most loving woman."

"I already know that, what with her just leaving the family and, now, knowing how she treated you, it's evident that she probably shouldn't have had children."

"Fasten your seat belt because you don't know the half of it. Uncle Robert was at Mom's house—or should I say *their* house. They live together."

"What the hell? That's… that's sick and, I don't know, isn't that illegal?" She throws her hands up before jumping up from the bed. "It sounds like some kind of reality television show. Good Lord." Clearly in shock, she holds her hands to her cheeks, her eyes large and her mouth gaping open.

"Calm down. Now you have a clue as to why all this," I point to my junk food table, "is necessary."

"You're right, I do. Uncle Robert is such a sleaze

ball." Her hands on her hips, she looks at me aghast. "Do you think Dad knew?"

"Not sure. Maybe." I shrug. "Let's just say that Uncle Robert and our mother share a lot of personality traits that revolve around anger and resentment."

"Sounds like they deserve each other. Poor Dad— betrayed by both his wife *and* his brother. Some part of me would like to believe he didn't know."

"I guess he had me go there so I could see my mother as the woman she really is and so I could finally stop carrying around the false belief that *I* broke up the family."

"Oh my God Elaine, you didn't really believe that, did you?" She continues, not waiting for a response, "I see that in my students all the time. They blame themselves for their parents' divorce and, of course, it has nothing to do with them."

"Believe me, I don't think that anymore." I walk to the window that looks out on the backyard. The rain has finally stopped and a double rainbow curves across the sky. Two hummingbirds take a quick moment to taste the nectar from the jasmine tree below. Where do they go to survive the storm? They seem so fragile, yet resilient.

"Apparently Dad bought the lockets and said they were from our mother." I turn from the window and, judging by her expression, see that I've stunned Morgan once again. "She knew *nothing* about them." I decide not to mention that she never asked anything about us, such as did we go to college, were we married, did we have children or were we happy? I also won't mention that, once again, she'd raised her hand to me.

"We got raised by the right parent." I sigh and lovingly think of our father. "You're caught up now. You know the whole sordid truth."

"It makes me appreciate Dad even more." She puts her hand to her stomach. "I don't know if it's all this junk food or hearing about our mother that's making me feel sick."

"Probably a combination." I smile faintly. "Why don't you go downstairs and get something healthy to eat? I'm staying here for a while."

"Oh no you don't. You can't get rid of me that easily. What about the night with David? When you called, you just said that your car had broken down and that you'd have to stay overnight to have it repaired. You didn't mention the handsome banker. Spill it."

She plops back onto the bed, looking like an eager puppy about to get a treat.

"No." I shake my head, knowing that I'm not ready to talk about David's betrayal. It's too fresh. "I can't talk about it now. It's… too hard."

"Come on. After everything else you just shared, this has got to be easier to say."

"You'd think so, wouldn't you? But it isn't. Uncle Robert and Mom hadn't been nice to me since, well, forever. They deserve each other, but David…" It had felt so good being in his arms. Making love with him was the most earth-shattering experience I ever had. I *never* knew it could really be that way, where the sensations are so intense that you can't take it anymore, but then you do because it feels so good. More importantly, I had never felt so loved and cherished. No, I can't talk about David. That wound is too raw.

"Okay, I'll give you some time. But at least tell me

that he didn't hurt you." Morgan's voice is soft as she picks up my hand and scrutinizes my face for the truth.

"Only my feelings, and I'll get over them. I'm used to it but losing the ranch… that's another story. I love this place. It means everything to me."

"I had completely forgotten about that what with everything else happening. What are we going to do? I know you probably have a plan."

"No plan." I tap the bedspread. "We own our home, but we don't have the money to pay our delinquent loans, which means the bank can claim our property by default. I'll have to notify the workers and we'll need to find a new home." I shrug. "We'll probably have to put a lot of our belongings in storage."

"I can't believe this is happening. I mean, even though I never loved Hartland the way you do, I would never have imagined it would go down like this." Shaking her head, she slowly rises from the bed and heads toward the door. "I'm going to do something I can control, like grade student papers and prepare us some real food."

When my cell phone rings, I recognize David's number. Is he calling to give me a final move-out date or to inform me that he forgot to mention that there was a curvy and petite Mrs. Cole who'd looked at me with contempt and somehow made me feel less than average. Not that I could blame her. She had the type of body that made grown men drool, while I was more ordinary in every way, neither statuesque nor voluptuous. Somehow, when David had trailed kisses down my thighs and caressed my breasts, I'd felt beautiful and desired, transformed by the tenderness of his touch and the intensity of his desire. Now, all those intoxicatingly delicious feelings have disappeared, and I have only myself to blame. I know a thing or two about the land, but my ability to identify a good man is way off-kilter. First, Jared and now, David. There's no way I'm answering that the phone. I mute the call, knowing I've got nothing more to say to him. He can email me the exact date that my home becomes his.

First, he steals my heart, and now, he's about to take my land. But the truth is, I freely gave him my heart and surrendered to his charm, his touch, and all the delicious heat they ignited in me. How can I regret experiencing, for the first time, what it feels like to have someone's every caress set me on fire, making me breathless and tingle with ecstasy? Now I know what it feels like to abandon myself to full sensual pleasure and, for that, I'll always be grateful.

After he calls four more times, I finally block his number and get back to torturing myself by watching television movies where other couples effortlessly live out their dreams. Just as my sugar high is wearing off and I'm about to doze off, there's a knock on my door.

"I'm asleep... almost," I mumble while squeezing my eyes shut and pulling the covers over my face. And no, I haven't taken off my clothes, washed my face or bothered brushing my teeth. I'm too tired to care.

Morgan enters the room. "Obviously, *almost* asleep is not all-the-way asleep. I'm just saying—"

"Morgan," I interrupt. "I don't need a lecture right now. I'm exhausted and I want to sleep."

"I get it, but there's someone downstairs who wants to see you." Her voice is hesitant. "You may want to see him, too."

"Does that someone have a name?" I mumble, still

under the covers. "Because there is absolutely no one I can think of who I want to see."

"Are you going to remove the covers from your face, because I can hardly hear you?"

"No." She's trying to trick me because she knows, once the covers are off, I might as well get up and see who is downstairs. "I'm very tired. It was a rough ride back from your mother's town."

"Oh, thanks a lot. She's now *my* mother and I don't even remember the woman. Look, don't try to distract me. David is downstairs."

"What?" I toss the covers off of my head and sit up straight in the bed. My heart pounds with a mixture of anger and excitement.

"You'll see him, right?" Morgan's voice is hopeful as she flicks on the lights. "I mean, he *is* our banker, so you do need to speak to him."

"I can't—at least not now." I make a shooing motion with my hands. "You'll need to make him go away."

"I don't know if I can. He seems very determined." She straightens out my snack bar, closing bags and picking up spilled popcorn.

"You're a teacher. I'm sure you've handled all kinds of persistent students who couldn't have their way. I'd greatly appreciate you sending him away. Siberia would be great, but downtown Santa Lorena will have to do." I lie back down and pull the covers back over my head.

"You are not being very mature about this," she says sternly.

"Not trying to be. I'll see Mr. Cole when I'm ready, but, for now, I want to eat my snacks and be left alone. He owes me that much at least, considering all that he's gotten from me." I angrily toss my blanket onto the floor while my body burns hot as a furnace as I recall, in vivid detail, the night I spent in David's bed. "I didn't even know I wasn't having orgasms until we made love, and then I knew that this was what everyone had been going on about. The big O. No mistaking that. I guess it was all just foreplay before. Now, I know I'm going to want even more. Yep, definitely will want a lot more, but not from him—Mr. Married Man who forgot to mention that he happened to have a sexy and beautiful wife. Please feel free to tell him exactly what I said and send him away."

Morgan is strangely quiet. She's standing there looking like she saw a ghost, with her mouth agape and her eyes practically popping out of her head.

"What's wrong with you?" I'm not accustomed to her not responding with one of her quick retorts.

"I… I don't know where to begin. That was quite a bit of info you just dumped." She comes over and gives me a high-five. "Girl, we have got to talk."

"You have a point. But I'm not up to it now." I can't help the quiver in my voice, but I refuse to cry because of David's betrayal. "Please do me a favor and send him away."

"Okay, I got it." She nods, but doesn't move, a mischievous expression on her face.

"What is it, Morgan?" I'm growing impatient. "I'm not done wallowing in my misery and it needs to be done alone."

"Well, it's just that considering the orgasm—or perhaps I should say *orgasms*—I'm wondering if I should give him one of the stars I give my students when they do a really good job of something. 'Cause, it sounds like he had a stellar performance in this one area." She dramatically bows.

"You better not." I can't help laughing as I toss a pillow in her direction. "Now, *please* get rid of him. No stars, no ribbons, nothing. Just make him go away. Teachers are good at that; you all expel or suspend students or whatever you have to do to make them disappear."

"Technically, this is not the same." She holds up a finger.

"Morgan, stop." I get up out of bed and turn her around to face the door. "What's the problem?"

"It's just that he looks so sad and desperate to see you. I hate to send him away."

"Really? I'm your sister and I assure you I am much more sad and desperate than he is right now, well, except for the orgasms. Everything else…" I point my thumbs down, "is not good. He's the bad guy. Seriously, he's taking away Hartland. Need I say more?"

"Okay, you don't have to push me out the door." She shakes off my hands. "You're right. My loyalty is to you, of course. No doubt about that. It's just that… well, he is *so* good looking…"

"Morgan, stop." I do not need a reminder of David's appearance. "I know what David looks like, thank you very much."

"Of course, you do." She places a hand to her forehead. "What was I thinking? It's just that I get distracted when I see a really good-looking man. It's a weakness of mine. Deplorable really. I'm so sorry. I'll let him know right now."

Chapter 12
The Intervention

"I'm considering enrolling the twins in a driver's education class."

It's our weekly management meeting and Amanda, dressed in one of her usual designer outfits, sits across from me.

"That's great." I study the excel spreadsheets on my desk.

"Pink elephants are falling from the sky."

"Nice." Finished with the first document, I move on to the next page. "We've got to finish going over these by this afternoon."

Amanda makes a clicking sound with her mouth, before throwing her hands in the air. "This is impossible."

"What's impossible?" She's got my attention now. Maybe something is going on with her and Stanley. Hmmm. You never know, even marriages that appear perfect on the outside have their ups and downs. "What's got you so riled up?"

"You've got to be kidding me." She abruptly stands and leans against my desk. "You've got to know what I'm talking about."

"Nope." I push aside one of the spreadsheets. "What's wrong? Something going on with you and Stanley?"

"Stanley and I are fine." She folds her hands and tilts her head to the side.

"It's not the twins, is it?" I wish she'd just get to the point. She can take forever to say something.

She shakes her head so vehemently that one of her dangling earrings falls off. Picking it up, she says, "No, it's not Madison or Dillon."

"Well, what are you so up in arms about then? As long as the family's good, I'd think you'd be happy." I dismissively shrug before picking up a financial report. "We're in the middle of a meeting; enough with the twenty questions already."

"It's you." She looks at me as if I'm the one acting crazy. "You are useless these days."

"What are you talking about?" She's really lost me now.

"I just told you that I'm going to enroll the kids in driving lessons, and you didn't bat an eye." She jabs a finger in my chest.

"So, I'm a little distracted." I can't stop thinking about how much I need to see Elaine, but Mandy doesn't know anything about that.

"A little distracted? I told you that pink elephants were falling from the sky and got no reaction from you. Since when have you passed up on an opportunity to tell me what I'm saying doesn't make sense. Now, I've just said two outlandish statements and you don't even know it."

"I don't know what you're talking about." I'm not about to go into anything personal with Amanda. I'm going to make everything right with Elaine, even if I don't have a clue how to go about it, especially since she's refusing to talk to me at the moment. I mean, how long can she ignore my calls?

"Okay." She folds her hands. "If you won't say it, I will. You haven't been able to focus on work since you came back from the weekend at our parents' house."

"I'm fine." I rub the back of my neck. "I have the situation under control. Everything is being sorted out." I'm not about to tell Amanda that Elaine has blocked my calls and hasn't seen me the three times I've gone by the ranch.

"Hallelujah, I'm so relieved." She claps her hands, while deeply exhaling. "Truth be told, you have been some kind of a mess."

"You exaggerate. Always have." I chuckle, hoping that we can move on to another *work*-related topic.

"Oh, do I?" She laughs before coming over and straightening my tie. "It's turned the wrong way."

"What the heck?" I ask, glancing down and seeing that she has a point. The inside seam is turned to the front. Damn. "Has it been like that all morning? You could have said something sooner."

"I could have, but then I would have missed out on the fun of seeing you not be Mr. Perfect for a change. Elaine must have really gotten to you."

Before I have a chance to respond, my intercom goes off. Although, really, what could I say? The truth is the truth. Elaine *has* really gotten to me and I miss her like hell.

"Yes, Linda, what is it?"

"Your parents are here to see you, Mr. Cole."

"Send them right in."

I'm always glad to see my parents. I only hope that I can be as fit and as active as they are when I'm their age. I'd be lucky to have the woman of my dreams by my side as I move through life, but, first, I have to get her to see me.

"Mom, Dad." I walk over and give my mother a kiss on the cheek and my dad an affectionate pat on the back. "This is a surprise, but I'm always happy to see you both."

Amanda warmly greets them, and I notice that she doesn't look at all surprised to see them. I could be imagining it, but it seems like she gave my mother a quick wink.

"I needed to run some errands in town, so your father and I decided that we might as well try that new French restaurant everyone is raving about. It's gotten excellent reviews."

Before I can stop myself, I make a loud grunting sound as I vividly recall the image of Elaine and Jared kissing in front of the restaurant.

I unclench my fists and try not to frown. "I don't know if it's all that."

"Oh, you've tried it?" my mother asks while setting her purse on the corner of my desk. "It wasn't to your liking?"

"French food is an acquired taste," my dad adds while shoving his hands into his pockets. "Look, we better head over to the restaurant now. I want to finish eating and be back home before the traffic picks up."

"There's not that much traffic out here, Dad," Amanda says. "It's not like San Francisco."

"You're right about that." He smiles. "That's part of the reason for the move."

"Well, even if you didn't have a good experience there, I've made reservations for the four of us, so you can give it another try." My mother looks pleased with herself. She loves trying exotic foods.

"I haven't been there. I just…" I can't say I don't want to go because I'm in no mood to run into Jared. Obviously, he likes the place, which means I hate it.

"Good, you can check it out for yourself." My father is already half-way out the door and my mother is close behind him.

"See, told ya you weren't making sense." Smiling mischievously, Amanda tugs on my tie. "This should be fun."

****

I don't have much choice but to go along since the reservations are already made and I don't have enough time to come up with a logical excuse to get out of eating at Elaine's and Jared's restaurant. I know I'm being unreasonable, but there it is. That's how I feel. I saw them about to dine there and the image is forever branded in my brain. If he kissed her like that outside the restaurant, I can only imagine what he did later.

It takes a minute for my eyes to adjust to the dim lighting. How are we supposed to see our food with just a flicker of a candle on our table? The deep burgundy curtains and a large fireplace with glowing electric logs create a romantic atmosphere which is great if you like that sort of artificial environment. I have *real* logs that you light with a match, for the fireplace at my condo—that don't need to be plugged in. Wonder where they sat when they were here—probably in that corner over there, where the seats are partially obscured behind a tall potted plant. They'd be able to have all the privacy they wanted sitting at that table for two.

"Son, what's going on?" My father pulls out a chair for my mother and then Amanda before taking a seat himself. "Have a seat." He points to the remaining seat.

"What do you mean?" I need to focus on what they're saying, but, thanks to Elaine, my thoughts are all jumbled. Why hadn't I told Elaine Courtney and I were separated and had been for over a year? What they say is true; everything is clear in hindsight. When I drove out to my parents' home, I wasn't planning to see Elaine stranded on the side of the road. And I never would have predicted that we'd end up making love all night long.

The waiter promptly arrives and brings us a basket of French rolls and hands us menus. "*Bonjour, Madame et Monsieur*. Welcome to *Le Petit Bistro*. Today's special includes poached salmon with a creamy hollandaise sauce, asparagus tips, and potatoes au gratin."

"Thank you." Opening the wine menu, my mother selects one of the recommended beverages. "We'll need a few minutes to decide on what we'll be eating for lunch. However, we will have a bottle of this Bordeaux."

Although nothing appeals to me, everyone else seems excited as they discuss the entrée options.

"The Salad Niçoise sounds good." Amanda closes her menu with a flourish. "What about you, Mom?"

"I'm going to have the Quiche Lorraine." My mother places the menu on the table before scanning my face. "What are you thinking of having?"

"Maybe I'll order the same thing," I answer absently.

"Nonsense." Concern clouds her eyes. "You've always hated quiche. When you were a little boy, you called it scrambled egg pie and made it clear that you wouldn't have anything to do with it."

"See what I mean?" Amanda nods her head in my direction. "This is a *perfect* example of how he hasn't been making any sense lately."

"Amanda doesn't know what she's talking about," I reply, even though there is some validity to what she's saying. I *do* hate quiche. "I'll have the steak and fries."

"Good choice." My father takes his glasses off and rubs the bridge of his nose. "I'll have the same."

The waiter returns with the Bordeaux and, after my mother approves, our glasses are filled and the waiter proceeds to take our orders.

After the waiter departs, my father raises his glass in a toast. "Cheers, everyone."

I'll be darned if I know what we're toasting, but sometimes it's easier to go along with the program, especially when I have other things on my mind.

After we've all tasted the wine, my father loudly clears his throat and my mother turns her chair toward me.

"Amanda tells us that you haven't been yourself lately." She folds her hands and intently scans my face.

Usually, I appreciate my mother's directness. Today… I'm not so sure. I can't hide anything from her.

"Is this some sort of ambush?" I squash the French roll I was about to butter, and suspiciously look at my family.

"Of course not." My mother takes the crumbled roll from my hand and sets it onto a bread plate. "But your father and I can see for ourselves that you aren't yourself and we think we know the reason why."

"Why does everyone keep saying I'm distracted? I'm fine." Brushing the crumbs from my hands, I pick up another roll. This time, I slowly butter it before taking a bite.

"His tie was on backwards this morning," Amanda chimes in gleefully.

"Was it really necessary for you to share that bit of information?" Irritated, I glare at her. "Everyone makes little mistakes sometimes. It's no big deal."

"That's true for other people, but not you," Amanda says. "You are—or should I say, were—always impeccably dressed."

"Son, I wasn't going to say anything, but the ladies may have a point." Glancing under the table, he points down and I wonder what now? "One of your socks is navy blue and the other one is black." He scratches his head. "That's not like you."

Sighing, I look down and see that my socks aren't matching. Damn, maybe I am a wreck. "Well, I don't like being ambushed like this... or maybe this is an intervention? In any case, I'll admit that Elaine has been on my mind."

"Aha!" Amanda pumps a fist in the air and yells triumphantly. A few patrons, eyebrows raised, look in our direction. Amanda continues in a much lower voice, "Just as I expected."

"Don't gloat, dear," my mother chastises her. "It's unbecoming."

"When your mother and I first began dating, we went through a couple rough spots." My father strokes my mother's hand. "I don't mind telling you that it was rough going for a while, but if she's worth it, *you* have to make it right. After all, you *are* the one who's still married."

The waiter brings the food and we eat in silence until my father continues. "Courtney could not have popped up at a more inopportune time. However, I trust that you've made things right with Elaine—"

"Doesn't look like it." Amanda rolls her eyes and speaks loud enough for everyone to hear.

"I've tried, but the woman won't answer my phone calls."

"Have you gone to the ranch?" my mother adds between bites of her quiche. "This, by the way, is the best quiche I've ever tasted."

"I've been by the house and she won't see me." I cut a piece of my steak. "The steak is so-so. I've had better."

"Well, my food is delicious. So, she won't see you or take your calls and you have a problem with the restaurant. Why?" my mother asks.

"Oh, I know," Amanda says while popping up in her seat like a jack-in-the-box. "I remember now—he told me that he saw Elaine *here* with another man." She claps her hands triumphantly while ignoring my seething glare.

"Oh, I see." Putting down her fork, my always-practical mother adds, "Well, in that case, you need to get a move on."

"I didn't realize you had competition." My dad takes a sip of his wine. "There are two things at risk here. First, does she know that she's not going to lose the ranch? Second, it's obvious you love her, and she needs to know that, too."

I rub my jawline and feel the stubble. Hmmm, it's not like me to forget to shave. And now, look at me. I can barely eat or sleep, that's how much I miss Elaine. So, this is love, huh? I need to get this woman back in my life before I really fall apart. No wonder my family staged this lunch. "I haven't had a chance to tell her anything."

"But you do have a plan, right?" My dad looks at me hopefully.

With all eyes on me, I suddenly think of a strategy—a fail-proof one, that will have Elaine back in my arms in no time at all.

****

After lunch, I notify my secretary that I won't be returning to the office. Instead, I take the elevator to the parking lot where I get my car and head back to my condominium. Excitement mounts in me as I reflect on my plan to see Elaine again. I'm overdue. It feels like three weeks, not three days since she decided to give me the silent treatment and it's been hell. I'd rather have her yelling at me than not saying anything at all. It's time for me to finally sort out the mess I've made of things with her. Even when Courtney betrayed me, I never experienced this sense of loss. Sure, my pride was bruised, but that was it. But this feeling is new, and it has nothing to do with pride or my ego. I miss seeing Elaine's smile and feeling her in my arms with her head of tangled curls nestled against my chest.

As I let myself into the condo, Roscoe immediately greets me at the door with a two-paw shove against my legs. Rubbing his head and kneeling down on one knee, I peer into his big, brown eyes.

"Look Roscoe, I need you now more than ever. I know you're up to the task. She likes you—probably more than me at this point. So, man, you've got to help me out. It's time for you to earn your keep."

Roscoe barks twice before licking my face. "I'll take that as a *yes*."

Getting up, I head to the cabinet where I keep his doggy treats. "I get it; you want to know what's in it for you." I hold up the bag of bacon-flavored snacks and shake it. "Here's one for now, and I'm saving this one for later." I hold one snack in my hand for him to take and the other one is placed in my back pocket. "You'll get it *after* your mission has been accomplished."

Elaine had immediately taken to Roscoe and the feeling was mutual. Smiling, I recall how he had followed her around and finally dropped onto the bed, resting half-way on her feet while she snoozed. He wasn't the only one who wanted to get into that bed with her.

I remove his leash from the hook in the back room and, after a quick walk around the block, we head to the garage and my car where I secure him in the back seat. As soon as the window is down, Roscoe pokes his head out and enjoys the wind blowing against his face. Ten minutes later, the sky turns dark gray with heavy clouds and a rush of cold air fills the car as a sprinkling of rain splatters against the windshield.

"Roscoe, head back inside."

He's a smart dog and turns away, stretching out on the seat as I quickly put the window up.

I hesitate when a new, disturbing thought takes root. What if Elaine isn't thinking of me the way I can't stop obsessing about her? Maybe I'm the only one whose heart is aching. Maybe she really is over it and has moved on.

No, I can't believe that. It's too soon and what we

experienced together was too intense for a passing fling. Not that Elaine is the type of woman who would indulge in a casual fling. She couldn't make love to me the way she did and not feel something.

Roscoe starts whining, letting me know he's eager to hop out of the car.

"Okay. Here I come. Hold on a minute." Opening the back door, I unstrap Roscoe and let him out. Always ready to take a walk or play in the grass, he pulls on his leash.

"I know how you feel. I'm excited about seeing her again, too." I walk him to the front door. "But can you at least play it cool?" I ring the doorbell. "We're males. We don't want to look as desperate as we feel."

Roscoe sits, as if he understands exactly what I'm saying.

"Good boy."

A few minutes later, he's restless again, probably tired of standing on the porch with the rain drizzling down on us. I don't hear any noise inside and the lights aren't on—at least not that I can see from here. Looks like I've missed them both since there is no sign of Morgan either. Could be that they're somewhere together. I shove down a wave of disappointment as I flex my fingers and fight the urge to pound my fist against the door, as if that will do some good. Still, I don't want to leave, so I ring the doorbell again.

"Hey, wait a minute, boy," I say as Roscoe tugs on the leash and takes off toward the back of the house.

I'm jogging to keep up, until he stops by the side of the house in front of a large window that reveals a spacious living room. A brown sofa and matching chairs face a large brick fireplace. There aren't any paintings on the wall, but a large silver picture frame is on the mantel. It's obviously a photograph of a young Elaine, Morgan, and their parents. But what really captures my attention are the large cardboard boxes scattered across the gray carpet. My heart sinks. This is not what I was expecting to find. Have they already packed up to make the big move? Would she really leave that quickly? I run my fingers through my damp hair. This is my fault. I'm the one who insisted she repay their loan.

I've got to stop her before she's gone permanently. How can Roscoe steal her heart and win her back if she's not even here? Her car may still be here because she finally replaced it with a more reliable vehicle and she's loading things into her new apartment at this very moment. I've waited too long and now she's gone and I'm stuck feeling like all kinds of an idiot. When I lift my hand to rub the heaviness that's settled in my chest, the leash falls to the soggy ground and Roscoe leaps into action like a newly freed man, sprinting across the yard and running ahead at full force.

With a loud moan, I shake my head, figuring that at least *he's* enjoying this rainy day. "Roscoe!" I raise my voice, but he's moving so fast that I'm not sure he hears me. I squint, barely able to make him out as he dashes down a long narrow road.

Good thing I work out because I have to run fast to keep up with him as he eventually reaches the orange groves. When I finally catch up with him, I don't know who's breathing more heavily, him or me.

He halts in front of a row of orange trees full with fruit that looks ripe enough to be picked. The scent of fresh citrus surrounds me and fills me with an almost painful longing for Elaine. This scent of nature and earth and all that's pure and good is her scent.

I follow Roscoe as he lets out a bark and sprints deeper into the groves until the oranges have completely disappeared and we are surrounded by another type of tree. Frowning, I look more closely and see that these are the avocado groves Elaine had attempted to tell me about, but I'd been in too much of a rush that day and hadn't been interested. The pear-shaped, deep green fruit hang heavily on the trees. As I'm about to pick one, Roscoe begins to dance around in circles and yelps at the top of his lungs.

"Hey, boy, what have you got there?" Thinking he's probably caught a squirrel, I finally catch up to him. "Let's see what you dragged me all the way out here for."

Curious and eager to see what he's chasing, I glance down and spot Elaine, eyes closed and lying face up in the grass. Dropping to my knees, panic sets in as I wonder if she's okay and why she's lying here with nothing on but a soaked cotton t-shirt and jeans.

Tail wagging, Roscoe pounces on her, licking her face until she bolts up and sees us hovering over her.

"Hey, Roscoe." She laughs while stroking his fur. "You are such a handsome boy." She pauses long enough to acknowledge me. "What are you doing here?" It's an accusation more than a question. Suddenly serious, the sadness in her eyes tells me that she's not happy to see me and that rain may have been on her face, but tears are in her eyes. Roscoe settles comfortably in her lap.

"Isn't it obvious?" I give in to the urge to touch the softness of her hair as it fans out around her head.

"Looking for you."

"I don't want to be found." She holds her arms out wide. "I'm having a moment here."

"I need to talk to you." I take off my jacket and wrap it around her shoulders. "You're going to get sick out here, lying in the wet grass."

"What if I do?" She shrugs the jacket off and hands it back to me. "I can take care of myself. I don't need you to rescue me today."

"You're being unreasonable." I point to the sky. "In case you haven't noticed, it's raining."

"You can tell your wife what to do, but you don't control me." She jumps to her feet and folds her arms tightly against her shivering body. "I'm just your side piece or, at least, I *was* for one night."

"Jesus, Elaine, you know that's not true." I feel like crap. Is that what she really thinks, that I only wanted her for a one-night stand? "You know that you mean more than that."

"I don't know anything at all." She throws her shoulders back defiantly before shrugging. "I didn't even know you had a wife. You never told me. You just let me fall for you and feel things I haven't felt before." Turning from me, she puts her head in her hands. "And, on top of that, you made me look like a strumpet in front of your parents and the rest of your family."

"The hell I did." I step toward her. "I don't even know what a strumpet is, so how could I have made you out to be one?"

"David." She glares at me like a lawyer who knows she has a guilty client in front of her. "Do you or do you not have a wife?"

"Well, technically, yes, but only until tomorrow.

That's part of what I came out here to tell you. If you hadn't been ignoring my calls, I would have told you sooner." So much for my plans of us having a calm, rational conversation. Instead, I feel like I'm the one who just got ambushed.

"If I give you a chance to say something—oh, that's rich." She places her hands on her hips. "You had plenty of time to talk before you got me in bed."

"It's not like I forced you or anything." I rub my brow and try to think of a way to get back on course since the conversation has obviously derailed badly.

"No, no you didn't." Pausing, she tilts her head to the side. "As a matter of fact, I made it very clear that I wanted you. And, the truth is, I enjoyed every single moment. You were not a disappointment."

"Well, thank you, at least, for that." I smile, feeling relieved to know that the feelings were mutual and that we were both equally affected by the same burning, crazy passion. She had enjoyed every tantalizing moment as much as I had.

"But that's not the point. I never would have made love with you if I had known you belonged to another woman. I would never sleep with someone's husband." Throwing her hands up and raising her voice, she says, "I don't do that sort of thing."

"Elaine, I'm sorry. I should have said something. Courtney and I have been separated for over a year and she was supposed to have signed the papers." I take her hands in mine. Her fingers are icy cold. "As of tomorrow, the divorce is finalized."

"Good for you." She yanks her hands away. "But that's not enough. There are several reasons why I could never be with you. Not long ago, I made a promise to myself to never mix business with pleasure. I can't believe that I allowed this to happen. For that, I blame myself." Turning away from me, she peers up at the clouds, before biting down on her bottom lip. "I came out here to say goodbye to the beautiful land that has been in my family for decades. Plus, even if you are divorced, I could never have a relationship with the man who took away our family legacy, so this is goodbye. Best of luck with your new single life." With those dismissive words, she brushes past me and stomps off down the road.

Roscoe starts barking like crazy and nudges my leg to get my attention. He looks at me as if to say, *You're not just going to let it end like that, are you*? Or maybe that's just what I'm thinking. In any case, I take a few quick strides and go after her, taking her by her upper arm and gently turning her so that she faces me.

"You can't just walk away from me like that." Even as I say the words, I know it's not true. As much as it pains me, I will respect her right to not want to be with me. I had my chance and if I've blown it, I'll have to respect her wishes.

"Really?" She frowns at me and takes a step back. "Because I just did."

"There's something you should know."

I take her other arm so I'm holding her close to me, feeling her body barely touching mine. Before I can change my mind or she has time to pull away again, I bring my lips to hers as if in slow motion. I search her eyes, pausing a fraction of an inch before I finally pull her completely against me. I'd stand in the rain for hours just to have this woman in my arms again. It's magical when her full lips open and our tongues mingle. There's a hunger and a longing here that we are powerless to deny. I feel victorious as she lets out a long moan. Finally, I force myself to pull away, aware that we are both trying to steady our breathing.

"I don't have the perfect words to undo how crummy I made you feel, but what I *can* say is that I'm genuinely sorry." I caress her cheek. "What we experienced was as real as it gets."

Chapter 13
Here Comes the Rain

My thoughts are jumbled, and my teeth are chattering as I trudge back to the house. The nerve of David to show up here without giving me a call first. Not that I would have answered when I saw his name, which is, no doubt, why he took a chance and came looking for me. The man looked damned good with that shirt clinging to his broad chest. The way his clothes mold to his physique is practically sinful. He might as well be naked. Now *that* I wouldn't have been able to resist. The touch of his hand ignited all kinds of sexy memories from that one unforgettable night. And that is exactly why I can't succumb to his charms. But dang, he looked good, with that puppy dog expression on his chiseled face.

Speaking of dogs, I have to give him credit for bringing Roscoe. Good move. I love that dog, and I could tell he was happy to see me, too, what with the way his tail was wagging. I miss him already. I don't suppose it would be right for me to drop by to see Roscoe every once in a while.

As a shiver passes through me, I try to clear my head of any potential excuses to see David again—to have him hold me and his lips kiss my entire body, even my feet. I stomp in the dirt, causing mud to splash up on my pants. Who knew feet could be such an erogenous zone? No use recalling, in vivid detail, the earth-shattering orgasms that had me raking my nails against his back and writhing with pleasure. I shake my head and attempt to clear it of all the decadent memories.

Once this land transition is over, there will be no reason to ever see him again. I'm going to be more like Morgan. She finds plenty of men on dating apps. Swipe right or left. She'll let me know which one means yes and which one means no. Shouldn't there be a direction for maybe? In any case, I'll be in complete control. Why hadn't I been doing this anyway? I'm done dating men who have any connection to Hartland.

Then it hits me like an earthquake: there won't be any more Hartland. *I'm sorry Dad and Grandpa. I failed you. I tried everything I could, but I didn't succeed.*

I sink to my knees, drop my head into my hands, and sob. I don't hold anything back. Tears, snot, and loud anguished sobs... It all comes out until I don't have anything left. I wipe my nose on my sleeve. Gross, I know, but I don't have a lot of options, kneeling out here in a puddle. *I'm sorry Dad. You suffered the loss of your wife, Julian, and now I'm unable to keep Hartland in the family. I've made a mess of my life and disappointed you.*

I slowly rise and make my way home. After rummaging in my soggy pockets, I pull out the keys. Realizing that my days here are numbered, I choke back another sob before opening the door. Enough already. Crap happens and this is definitely crappy.

I splatter water and mud with every step I take on the way to the bathroom. Shivering, I peel off my clothes and finally step into the warmth of a hot shower. I take my time washing my hair and liberally lather on my lavender shower gel and, later, my lotion. After securing my wet hair in a towel, I put on my favorite kimono-style, red silk robe, the one my father bought me for my twentieth birthday. I've worn it so much that the fabric is beginning to fray. In the living room, I kneel down, ignite a fire in the fireplace, and sit on the sofa with a glass of chardonnay.

As I'm propping my feet up on the ottoman, the doorbell rings. My heartbeat quickens as I wonder if that's David returning to try to persuade me to give him another chance. If we had kissed one minute longer, I would have been tempted to take him back, even knowing we could never make it with him owning my family's land.

Without remembering to look through the peephole, I open the door and see Jared standing outside. This time, though, I'm not nervous. He followed through on my father's last wishes, no matter that it may have threatened his relationship with my uncle.

"Good evening, Jared. What are you doing here?"

"Sorry for showing up unannounced." He looks at me sheepishly. "Your uncle contacted me on my cell as I was leaving the office."

"Come in." I lead him into the living room, not looking forward to any message he may have from my uncle. The thought of his betrayal of his only brother disgusts me.

"I'm still his attorney and I told him that I had to drop something off at your house and he asked me to pick up a file that he left here." He holds his hands out apologetically. "Sorry, it's so late. I hate to interrupt your evening. He says it's the Remington File. If you don't know where it is right now, I can always pick it up another time."

"My uncle left a lot of folders that I've already packed and was going to mail to his house." What I don't add is that I'm talking about the house he shares with my mother. I walk over to a stack of boxes and find the one labeled with my uncle's name and address before setting it on the coffee table. "This is everything of his."

He hesitates before picking up the box. "I'm about to leave without giving you this envelope from your father. I meant to give it to you after the will was read, but things got a little chaotic and it must have gotten overlooked." He reaches into his jacket and pulls out a manila envelope. "My apologies."

"Thanks for bringing it by." Taking it from him, I fold it and place it in my robe pocket.

"Let me know if you have any questions after you read it." He grins and I think how much he seems like a more relaxed person now than the man I had dated. "By the way, I'll be sending you an invitation soon."

"What for?"

"My wedding. I met someone online and it hasn't been long but we are together every day. Most importantly, the feeling is mutual. Neither of us wants to waste time now that we've found each other."

"Good for you." Wow, that was fast. But if anyone knows that Jared was ready for a wife, it would be me. Maybe he was eager to create the family he never had. "Is it anyone I know?"

"Probably. Her name is Linda, and she works for

David."

"Oh." My eyes open wide in shock as I struggle to think of how to respond. "Congratulations." David's secretary and Jared found each other through an app, so obviously online dating can work. I pat his arm. "That's great."

"She makes me happy." A bright smile spreads across his face. "She's waiting for me in the car. I better get going. She wasn't too thrilled about the idea of me dropping by my ex-girlfriend's house even though she knows it's about business."

"Well, maybe it will help if I walk you to the car." I open the door, but before I can step outside, he places his hand on my arm.

"Probably not a good idea." His eyes quickly glance down, no doubt taking in my robe. "She can be a little jealous. I even told her what an ass I was back then with you." His eyes cloud over, and he takes a deep breath. "I'm sorry for ever laying my hands on you. Growing up in foster care, I got rejected so much that I would get into this fight-or-flight mode when I got hurt." He shakes his head and runs a hand across his light brown hair. "But there's no excuse. I was wrong." He searches my eyes. "I don't want you to be afraid that I'm going to ever do that again. Have you truly forgiven me?"

I don't know. It's such a big word and an even larger concept to grasp. Forgiveness for him taking his anger and frustration out on me is one thing. It's a totally different matter to have to deal with the flashbacks his actions caused—painful, buried images from my early childhood memories of living with a mother who was always angry and volatile.

I sigh, already knowing that, in order to claim my own happiness, I need to forgive both of them—and probably my deplorable uncle, too. But it's going to take time to get there with my family. But, as for Jared, I've already put that period of my life in the past.

"Yes. It's behind us now. You don't want to keep Linda waiting too long." I wave in the direction of the car. "Please tell her congratulations for me. I'm looking forward to attending the wedding. We could use some good news around here."

"Thank you." He gives me a quick hug. "Everything will work out," he says mysteriously before joining his fiancée.

****

When Morgan comes home, her arms are loaded with take-out cartons of what smells like Mediterranean food.

"Please tell me we're having falafels and hummus." I peek inside a white bag she sets down. "It's been a hell of a day and I could use something to make me feel better."

"Hmmm." Morgan takes the wine glass from my hand and takes a sip. "Girl, you don't know what tough is until you've had to deal with a classroom of adolescent boys and girls whose moods change every five minutes. Follow me to the kitchen and we can exchange war stories while we chow down."

"Sounds like a plan. I've got a couple of updates for you, too."

"Does one of them have anything to do with why I saw Jared's car pass by about a quarter mile down the road?" She sets the cartons on the table while I get the paper plates and silverware. "Don't tell me you two are back together."

"What? Absolutely not." I fill my pita bread with the crispy falafel balls, hummus, a squeeze of lemon, and cilantro. "Why would you even think that?"

"Because you're half-naked, sipping on wine, and he just left the house." She bites into her lamb kabob. "It doesn't take a rocket scientist to figure out what's probably been happening around here in my absence."

"You are completely wrong." Maybe one day I'll tell her more about my past relationship with Jared. "Jared came by to pick up some documents for Uncle Robert and... drum roll please... to invite me to his wedding."

"I guess it's safe to say he's over you now." She laughs. "Finally."

"Thank God, yes." I have to laugh, too. "It's so nice to have that chapter of my life closed. Here's the weird part though. He's engaged to David's secretary, Linda."

"Why weird?" she asks as she cuts her falafel with a fork. No pita bread for her. She's watching her carbs.

"I'm not sure. Maybe because I just saw David earlier today."

"I thought you weren't speaking to him." She drops her fork. "Did you change your mind about him? It's so obvious that you're in—"

"Don't," I interrupt her. "Don't say the words, even though we both know it's true. If you say it, it makes it all the more real. He's a closed chapter, too. I need to move on to someone who doesn't lie about having a wife. I really know how to pick them, don't I?"

Morgan squeezes my hand. "Still, it's got to be hard. The way you described it, it seemed like you got to experience that special kind of joy that doesn't come along every day."

"Enough about my day." I take another bite of my messy sandwich.

"Wait a minute. Why was David here? Did he say the 'l' word?"

"No, he did not say the 'l' word. Nothing like that." I pause while reflecting back over our conversation. "He said we both *felt* something." I shrug. That much can't be denied.

When I was younger, I thought my girlfriends were exaggerating when they raved about how hot they got making out with their boyfriends. Wasn't sure I believed in true love or even an intense, all-consuming type of passion that set your body on fire from the inside out. That was before I met David and made the mistake of abandoning all caution and logic. Without any reservations, I had lowered my defenses and allowed myself to just *feel*. I shudder as a sudden wave of sadness washes over me and squeezes my heart until it feels dry and lifeless. I have no expectations that I'll experience that type of exhilaration again. A lot of good it did me to allow him in—to be that vulnerable with someone I didn't know. Someone who, as it turns out, has a wife, even if they are separated.

"Talk about vague. Maybe he didn't know how to put his emotions into words. A lot of men are like that," Morgan adds while she puts the lid on the hummus before placing it in the refrigerator.

"Please don't try to give him an excuse. He knows how to get a message across, and he never said the word one time. He told me his divorce is going to be finalized tomorrow."

"Why didn't you say that sooner?" Morgan grins. "Now we're getting somewhere. He needed to tell you that first."

"Telling me first would have been *before* I slept with him, not days later," I say irritably.

"You have a point. Don't bite my head off." She gets up from the table. "But at least he's available now."

"I'm sorry, sis. No need to take it out on you." I wave my hands. "One day soon, David will own all of this." I twist my lips, feeling the frown crease my forehead as I run a finger across the large oak table where Morgan and I have spent countless hours doing our homework and chatting. "It would be impossible to be with him under those circumstances. So that's that. Now, tell me about your day."

"The kids were impossible as usual, but I know a lot of them have problems at home. For example, there's Ashley. I've told you about her situation before. I noticed some marks on her arm. I asked her to stay after class and she told me she had started cutting herself as a way to cope." She purses her lips and looks reflective. "I just wish I could do more to help them."

"Don't you have a school social worker?"

"Thank God." She nods her head. "She has her hands full. Still, I spoke to her about Ashley. She'll talk to her first thing tomorrow morning."

"I'm glad Ashley trusted you enough to tell you the truth." I finish the last of my falafel. "I don't know why you act like you aren't fond of children. You obviously care deeply for all of your students."

"I don't think I could do it full time. You know, as a parent." Her eyebrows come together in a frown.

"More importantly, I know it's hard for you to leave our home, but I'm excited. I love the new townhouse we're moving into and it's going to be fun living in town."

"Could be." I shrug. I'd like to be more enthusiastic, but I'm no good at faking it. Better change the topic before I get overly emotional—again. One crying fit is more than enough for one day. "I was surprised when you came back after graduation. Happy, but surprised."

"Okay, seems like you are going to make me say it." She rolls her eyes and purses her lips. "I came back because I missed you and Dad."

"We missed you, too. It wasn't the same without you." I nudge her arm. "You really *are* a softy at heart."

"Maybe." She nibbles on a fingernail—a leftover childhood habit that's a sure sign she's feeling stressed, too. "I hadn't planned on sticking around for *so* long."

"I'm grateful you came back home and the three of us had this time together."

"I am, too." She gives me a side hug. "There's nothing like family. But I did not miss our uncle."

"Understandable. If you did, I'd be worried about you. He's not the type of uncle that lights up a room."

"Amen to that, sister." Morgan glances at me and we both start laughing. "He can be a lot to handle."

"Understatement," I mutter, not wanting to think about his betrayal of my father.

Lost in our own thoughts, we're silent as we place leftovers in the refrigerator and clean up the kitchen.

"Maybe the change will do us good." I'm aiming for optimism, but my heart is heavy as the reality of leaving settles uncomfortably in my chest. I'll miss my morning walks along the groves and the scent of orange blossoms in the air.

"What's this?" Morgan asks as she picks up the envelope that's fallen from my pocket. "You dropped something."

"I forgot about that." In no hurry to read about any potentially negative surprises, I sigh and reluctantly take the envelope. "Jared gave this to me. It somehow got lost in the shuffle of papers during the reading of the will. I suppose I should read it."

Morgan watches as I take my time slicing the corner of the envelope open with a butter knife. As I silently scan the first lines, my hand trembles and my legs feel wobbly, as if they might collapse at any minute. I grab a seat while shaking my head in disbelief.

"What is it?" Morgan pulls the letter from my hand. "Since Jared brought it, it must have something to do with Uncle Robert." She scowls in anticipation of Uncle Robert's antics. "What's that man up to now?"

"This has nothing to do with him." My voice cracks. "Hurry up and read it."

"Okay." She speeds through the letter, her head moving from side to side before she tosses the paper from our father's insurance company so high into the air that it hits the ceiling fan. "Thank God!" She grabs my hands and starts swirling me around in circles, all the while laughing and singing. "Now you don't have to leave."

"You mean *we* don't have to leave." I stop dancing as a huge smile spreads across my face and happiness lifts my spirit. "This insurance money is more than enough to cover our loan payments. We can finally own the land outright." All the tightness in my chest dissipates and a sense of relief takes over, leaving me light-headed with joy.

"Hallelujah!" Morgan shouts while pumping her fist in the air. "I'm so happy for you. Now you can stay at Hartland and grow oranges, avocados, mangos, and whatever else suits your fancy." She gives me a big hug, squeezing me so tightly that I have to push her away.

"Very funny. It's only oranges and avocados. But you don't need to leave now either. Dad was always thinking of us. So now we can stay in our home." It's as if our father is looking down on us from Heaven, making sure we're good.

"Sis, I don't want to live here, but I *am* thrilled you can fulfill your dream," Morgan says. "I want to live in town, remember?" She takes my shoulders in her hands and seeks out my eyes.

"Of course, I do. Now you can have your dream, too." The thought of not living with Morgan takes some of the joy out of the moment, but I know I'm being selfish. She has the right to have her own dream. "Maybe you can take a trip to one of those exotic places you're always talking about."

"Maybe?" She clasps her hands together. "There's no maybe about it. Girl, I will not be spending my summer vacations in Santa Lorena." She paces excitedly from one end of the room to the other. "Exotic adventures, here I come."

"Good for you." Peering out the window at the bright full moon shining a light on the lush magenta flower petals and the deep green foliage surrounding the backyard, visions of my own dreams becoming a reality begin to surface. "So, this is what financial freedom feels like."

Spinning around, I face Morgan. "I can't wait to see the look on David's face when I pop into his office and hand him the money to pay off our loan."

Chapter 14
The Hug

"Yes, Linda?" What part of the DO NOT DISTURB sign on the door did the woman not understand? Hell, work is the only thing that makes sense so that's what I'm giving my full attention. Not that it's helped me erase the image of Elaine and Jared wrapped in each other's arms. Reluctantly, I look up from the stack of documents needing to be reviewed. "What is it?"

"Ms. Elaine Hart is here to see you." She fidgets with a pen in her hand before adding, "She doesn't have an appointment. Should I ask her to come back another time?"

"No, have her come in." Some of the tension in my shoulders eases at the thought of seeing her—which doesn't make any sense considering she's been totally unpredictable since that first time she came storming into my office, all fight and fury, ready to do battle. Even then, with her beauty, passion, and fierce loyalty to everything that was important to her, I knew she'd be trouble, but I never knew it would become personal. That she'd somehow find a way past all the barriers I had erected since the day I walked in on my wife making love with my best friend.

And now, as Elaine walks into the office, I wonder how my judgment could have been so off. Have I again been deceived, blinded by my own desire for this woman who appears so wholesome, so good—the type of woman any sane man would want by his side?

"I'm surprised to see you here this morning." Pushing my chair back from the desk, I move closer to her. She'd looked beautiful yesterday as she'd stood, soaking wet, in the pouring rain and now, as she sits here in a simple blue skirt and white blouse. She crosses her legs, and, not for the first time, I notice how good they look, but I need to concentrate on what she has to say, not how she looks. The last thing I need to think about is how she felt, all soft and yielding in my arms, or the way she cried out my name just as she was about to climax. Now is *not* the time to notice how she's nervously biting her bottom lip and remember how good it felt when she bit *my* bottom lip. If I keep thinking like this, I'll have to return to my seat so she won't see the evidence of how much I want her. Damn. "What with getting caught in the rain and then having a late night and all." Okay. I could have worded that better, but I'm sure she gets the gist, even though she doesn't know I saw her standing in the doorway with her ex.

"What?" She looks at me questioningly. "I didn't have a particularly late night." She shrugs. "In any case, I'm here because we didn't finish our conversation yesterday." Her fingers curl around the handbag on her lap.

"Not my fault." I clear my throat. "You ran away in the middle of our discussion."

"It was raining hard and I was wet." She tilts her head to the side, looking at me as if I've done something wrong. "I needed to get inside and dry off."

"Yes, I realized that later. You had someplace else

to go—someone else to be with besides me." One, two. There I go again, popping my knuckles. I hate that we are having this discussion. Hate that she rejected me but found solace in the arms of another man—a man who I find inferior to me. Hell, yeah, that's right—a man who's a freaking coward.

"What are you talking about?" She stands up now, indignation in her voice. She could win an Academy Award with how innocent she looks.

I clap my hands. "That's good. You almost have me convinced you really don't know what I'm talking about." My voice involuntarily gets louder.

"I don't." She looks at me like I'm not making sense. "I had my favorite Mediterranean food last night—"

"How thoughtful of him, French food one night, Mediterranean the next." I'm pacing now, my voice rising with each step, blood pounding in my head. "Excuse me for being a regular old-fashioned type of guy who doesn't try to impress women with foreign food and Lord knows what else."

"You have totally lost me." She doesn't back down. "You have a very vivid imagination. I don't know what story you have made up, but, as you recall, I was shivering when I left you. I went home, dried off, and then had the dinner *Morgan* brought home." She shakes her head. "What's going on here?"

"Is that the story that you're sticking to?" I'm incredulous that she can stand here and deny what I so clearly saw with my own eyes.

"It's true. What do you want me to say—a lie?" She appears baffled.

I'd believe her if I didn't know better. "I came by

to bring you some chicken noodle soup and I saw you standing in your doorway in just a robe with probably nothing on underneath and you were in that attorney's arms." I hadn't slept much last night because I'd kept seeing the two of them together, silhouetted in the doorframe. I thought I'd feel victorious when I let her know what I saw, but, instead, I feel defeated and tired.

"Really, David?" She glares at me. "That's what you thought? That we were wrapped in each other's arms?" She shakes her head and walks over to stand in front of the window, her back to me. "How could you believe that?"

"What was I supposed to think? The evidence was in front of me. It wasn't a damn mirage." I sit back at my desk. "Dammit, woman, were you or were you not with Jared last night?"

"You don't get to interrogate me." Her hands ball into fists as she spins around and grabs her purse from her seat. "If you have to ask that question, you don't know me at all. Go to hell, David Cole." She pauses at the door, rummages in her bag, pulls out what looks like a check, then drops it onto my desk. "I almost forgot the reason I came here this morning was to drop this off."

"Did he give you the money for the loan?" I yell while scrutinizing the check as if expecting to find his name on the front.

"I wouldn't sell myself for money, you idiot." She slams the door so hard it rattles the frame.

"I take that as a no!" I shout back even though she's no longer in the office.

I've got myself in so deep, I don't know how I'm going to climb back out to see the light. While I'm holding my head in my hands and staring down at my desk as if I'll find some answers to my problems there, there's a tap on the door. Relief runs through me as I glance up, happy she's come back, probably to confess all of her sins. I'll forgive her after she admits she was wrong, that she needed one last time with that asshole to be sure. Hell, no, that's not going to work. She shouldn't have needed one last time. I massage my temples in an attempt to clear my muddled thoughts.

There's another light knock on the door before it creeps open. "Sir?" Linda peeks her head inside, looking around as if to see if the coast is clear of any flying projectiles I might hurl across the room. "Umm, sorry to interrupt, but I wonder if I could have a minute?"

"It's not a good time." You'd think the yelling would have tipped her off to the fact that she should go away and come back much later. "What's your question?"

"It's not a question, Mr. Cole." She cautiously steps into the office, gently closing the door behind her. "May I have a seat?"

"It looks like you already have." I frown as she takes a minute to get comfortable, squirming in the chair. "It'd be better if you came back after lunch."

She tosses her blonde hair over her shoulder. "I don't think so." She blinks and stares at me expectantly.

Have all the women I know suddenly gone crazy? She's the second one who's forced her way into my office this morning and then looks at me like she's afraid I'm going to yell at her which, considering my mood, is a definite possibility.

"Since you insist, spit it out. What do you want?" I

think about her salary. "Is it a raise?"

She shakes her head. "Wait. Actually, that would be great. I mean, who wouldn't want a raise, right?" She chuckles before smoothing out her skirt and sitting up straighter in her chair. "If you're offering me a raise, I will most definitely take it. Thank you very much."

What the hell is happening here? I need to go back to bed and start the day over. I had no plans to give her a raise—at least not yet. "What did you want to see me about?"

"Oh yes, right." She flips her hair one more time. Her eyes dart nervously around the office as she taps her foot against the floor. "It's really none of my business."

"Good, then this meeting is over." I clear my throat before abruptly standing. "You get your raise and that's that." My eyes go from her to the door, but she doesn't take the hint. She sits there, smoothing down her skirt some more and flipping her hair like I have all the time in the world.

"As I was saying, it's really none of *my* business, except I could hear everything and not because I was listening at the door, which I most certainly was not. I'm not that type of secretary. It's just that… well, it was *so* loud in here that I think even the people in the hall could hear your voices. It sounded like you were yelling at the top of your lungs."

"Now that we have established that I wasn't whispering…" Christ, now my secretary is chastising me. "I get the point. Sorry about that. Now that you have your raise and you've informed me that it got loud in here, was there anything else or do I have your permission to end this meeting?"

"Oh." Startled, she blinks rapidly before placing a hand on her chest. "You're funny. You're asking *me* for permission to end the meeting."

"Okay, we're done then." I rub my hands together.

"Not quite." Smiling, she indicates that I should retake my seat. "I... I haven't yet told you why I wanted to talk to you."

"You have exactly two minutes to wrap this up." With all the patience I can muster, I sit back down. If she didn't want the raise, why is she wasting my time?

"Understood. As I was saying, I couldn't help overhearing you. Not that I wanted to at all. There's something you should know. You were saying how you thought Ms. Hart was seeing *my* Jared."

"Excuse me, *what* did you say?" And here I thought she was about to ramble on about something inconsequential. "*Your* Jared?"

"That's right, sir—*my* Jared." She beams as if she's announcing that she's won a million-dollar lottery.

I have to give it to the man; he seems to have two women eating out of his hands.

"I was there last night. At her home." She says this last statement as if it explains everything.

"And you don't mind?" Now, I'm really confused. Santa Lorena is obviously not the sleepy little Southern California town I was expecting.

"Not at all. I was in the car with him, except I wasn't comfortable enough to go into the house with him."

"I can understand why that would be uncomfortable for you." I'm leaning forward in my seat now, curious what she'll say next.

"Right, since it was raining and I hadn't brought a

coat," she says while running her hands up and down her arms as if even talking about the weather has caused a chill.

"Makes sense to me." I give her a reassuring look. "Continue."

"Yes, well, it wasn't what you thought. He went there to give her a legal document from her father's estate and to pick up some of the papers her uncle left at the house."

"That sounds all well and good, but I saw otherwise." I fold my hands on my desk and fight the disappointment at discovering Elaine was not the woman I thought she was. "Something *not* so innocent."

"You're so funny." She places a hand over her mouth and laughs until she notices my expression and abruptly stops. "Sorry. It's just that we wanted to keep it a secret until later, but Jared and I are engaged. I know he didn't behave very well before when he used to date Ms. Hart. He told me all about it. But I told him I wouldn't say yes until he got counseling for anger management." Her eyes grow somber. "So, you see, it was just a congratulatory hug. Nothing more. I trust Jared. Maybe you ought to trust her, too."

****

"Hold on!" Mandy calls out from somewhere in the house. "I'm coming."

The laughter from my niece and nephew bounces off the walls before Mandy finally flings open the front door. The sophisticated sister who works beside me at the office has been replaced by a woman whose usually stiff hair is now flattened and plastered against her head and whose face is devoid of any traces of the daring make-up she usually wears.

"Oh." One quick glance at her smudged blouse tells me all I need to know. This is *not* a good time to drop by. "Are you in the middle of painting something?"

"Why would you ask that?" She raises one perfectly arched eyebrow.

"You're obviously covered with paint." I nod in the direction of her stained shirt before squinting to take a closer look. "What else could that be?"

"That, baby brother, is dinner." She shakes her head and indicates that I should follow her into the kitchen.

I dodge the scattered toys littering the floor. It looks like my adorable niece and nephew couldn't decide what to play with, so they flipped over their entire toy box to survey their stash.

"By the way, this is spaghetti sauce, not paint." She chuckles at my stunned expression.

"Okay, I'll take your word for it." I've never seen my sister's home look less than perfect. Usually, every coordinated pillow is upright on the couch, every dish put away, and each child impeccably groomed. But today, they are barely recognizable with the amount of food that's smeared on their round cheeks as they sit at a miniature table, giggling and stuffing their mouths with noodles.

"Hi Uncle David," they say in unison while grinning from ear to ear.

"Hey, you two." Bending down, I hug both of them, knowing that I won't be able to wear this shirt again without taking it to the cleaners.

"Sorry about that." Mandy sighs and runs a finger

through her hair. "Darn. I probably have marinara sauce in my hair now."

"Looks like your day has been as rough as mine." Looking at the chaos of the sink filled with dirty dishes and the pans piled on the stove, I suppress a laugh. "What happened in here? Did a tornado whip through the place?"

"The man's got jokes." She grabs a dishcloth and starts scrubbing a dark red stain on the stove. "Stanley has some doctor appointments today which is why I decided to work from home. Obviously, that's easier said than done." After gritting her teeth and scrubbing hard for a few more seconds, she tosses the dishcloth into the sink. "Oh, forget it. I don't know how people can get anything done at home when they have kids. I sure can't. I not only didn't accomplish anything, I'm exhausted. Stanley is a saint. I'm grateful he's so good around the house or we'd have to hire someone to pick up the slack."

I struggle to come up with words of encouragement, but I'm clearly out of my league here. I know nothing about children or parenting, and after my conversations with Elaine and Linda, everything I thought I knew about women is most likely inaccurate. "At least they look happy."

"That's for sure. Spaghetti is always a crowd-pleaser, probably because it's so messy." She leans down and kisses the tops of her children's heads, before grabbing two beers from the refrigerator. In the living room, she collapses on the sofa. "Obviously, you didn't come here to observe my lack of homemaking skills. We grew up together, so you already know I'm useless in the kitchen." She hands me one of the beers before opening her own and taking a swig. "Frankly, you don't look too great yourself. What's happened?"

Leave it to Amanda to get straight to the point. She's always been able to read my moods, probably one of those weird twin things that creep out non-twins.

"Hell if I know where to begin." I scratch my head, trying to figure out how I created such a mess of my relationship—if it can even be called that—with Elaine. I read the label on the beer, note the words *light*, *designer,* and *gluten free* and place the bottle back on the coffee table. "What is this stuff?"

"Hey, don't knock it until you try it. Some of us are trying to be health conscious. But I'm guessing you've got more important things on your mind than designer beers." She takes a second swig. "Cheers. Now, what's up? You look like you just lost your best friend. This isn't about Roscoe, is it?"

"Well, yes and no, but not really." I decide to live dangerously. I twist off the top and take a small swig of the beer. She's right, it's not half-bad. It's not exactly half-good either, but it will do. "Roscoe was my secret weapon to get Elaine back. They really like each other. So, the two of us went over to her place to straighten out everything."

"Let me get this straight: you and *Roscoe* went over to Elaine's so the *two* of you could straighten out everything?" She raises her eyebrows and looks at me suspiciously. "Just want to make sure I've got this right."

"Correct. And don't look at me like that. It was a good plan, but, between the rain and all the boxes, it threw me off."

"What boxes?" she asks, confused.

"Try to keep up with me, will you? She had already started packing to leave and was outside saying goodbye to the oranges."

"Uh huh, I see," she says, but I can tell by her tone she clearly doesn't.

"She wasn't thrilled to see me. As a matter of fact, she appeared irritated."

"So, what'd you do?" She sets her bottle down, turns, and faces me in my seat.

"I left since she obviously wanted to be alone with her fruit. But then I got to thinking about how cold she was from getting caught in the rain. So, I went and picked up some chicken soup from the deli and brought it back to her." I'm not about to tell her that I kissed her. A man has to keep some details to himself.

Mandy nods. "Of course, makes sense. You brought her soup. Continue."

I decide to ignore her obvious sarcasm. "When I got there, she was practically naked and kissing some asshole."

"Admittedly, I've had a long and exhausting day, however, your efforts to sort out things with Elaine sound like they got totally botched, especially since your actions were followed by her being, um, as you said, practically naked with another man. Maybe you didn't make your feelings for her completely clear."

"That's just it. I'm not sure of anything except that I screwed up." Coupled with now knowing that Jared's engagement with Linda means he really has moved on from Elaine tells me that I'm clueless. And I'd made everything worse by opening my big mouth and accusing her of still being with him. "I have since learned that it was only a friendly hug—nothing more.

The guy is engaged and wasn't making a move on Elaine."

"Let me ask you this—did you tell her you love her? Because that could go a long way." She leans back in her seat and looks at me curiously.

Of course, Amanda's right, but with everything that was going on, I totally forgot to tell Elaine how I felt. "No, but I did tell her that the divorce was going to be finalized."

"You get credit for telling her that you're divorced," she says while giving me a crooked smile, "but without her knowing how you feel about *her*, it doesn't mean a whole heck of a lot." She gets up from the sofa. "I'm going to check on the kids and get them cleaned up." She points a finger at me. "You stay here. I'll be right back."

While she's gone, I fight nodding off to sleep. Since Elaine walked out of my parent's house, I keep imagining how I could have handled things differently—all the lost opportunities when I could have told her about being estranged from my wife. I should have told her before we got in my bed that night and definitely before we made love. I was like a schoolboy, so caught up in the moment and the softness of her skin, the freshness of her scent, the trust in her eyes, that I couldn't think straight. And now, like an idiot, I've made it worse by insulting her integrity and morals. As if I don't know she's one of the finest human beings I've ever met.

"Wake up."

I don't know how much time has elapsed when I open my eyes after Amanda nudges my shoulder.

"Sorry. That took longer than I'd expected, but

they're settled in for the night now. You were telling me that you forgot to let her know you love her."

"I meant to tell her, but everything happened so fast that I couldn't think straight. When I saw her with the attorney, I felt like socking someone." I frown as I recall how I'd acted when she'd come to my office. "I said some stuff I wish I could take back."

"I'm surprised." Squinting, she scans my face. "Obviously, love can make even a practical guy like you wacko." She shakes her head and holds out her hand. "Wait a minute. Maybe I'm presuming too much. You *do* love her, don't you?"

"I love her or I wouldn't be, as you so elegantly put it, wacko. I didn't come here for you to confirm that I've thoroughly messed up with Elaine. I already know *that*. I came so you can help me win her back."

"If only I could." She pats me on the back. "I'm afraid this is something you'll have to straighten out on your own. The only advice I can give you is that, since you appear to have screwed up royally, you'll have to make a grand gesture so she knows, without any doubt, that you love her and want her in your life. How you'll do that is up to you. And since you're one of the three most intelligent men I know, I'll leave it to you to figure out the details." She pauses, and, looking at me with a twinkle in her eye, asks, "Would you like to stay for some spaghetti?"

"Absolutely not." I laugh as I head toward the door. "And you can tell the kids good night for me because I've got a woman to woo."

****

I don't notice anything unusual in front of the house until I kneel down to pick up the newspaper that's been tossed on the lawn that I look up and spot David's vehicle. David's car is covered with a fine mist of dew which lets me know that he's been here for a while. Who knows how long? Bending down, I peer in the passenger side's tinted windows. His head is slumped over the steering wheel and he looks so peaceful that it reminds me of the night we spent together. What a great night it'd been. But that was before everything turned sour—including his marital status and nasty accusations about my character. Just thinking about it has me doing a quick turn away from the car to head back into the house. He can stay out there for days for all I care. I don't need him and his complicated life. My life is complicated enough without him making things worse.

Setting the paper on the table, I prepare a pot of fresh coffee before placing two slices of bread in the toaster. Next, I remove the eggs and bacon from the refrigerator. I start frying the bacon and try hard to not think about David, his neck pressed against the steering wheel at an awkward angle, his body sliding half-way down the seat. He'll be sore when he wakes up.

Oh hell. I turn the heat off under the bacon, rinse my hands, then march outside to the car. Yep, he's in the exact same position, chin tucked against his chest the way resting birds do.

"David!" I yell against the cold window, condensation from my breath melting a circle of dew.

Nothing. The man doesn't budge. It's like he's frozen, not even a flutter of an eyelash. Then it dawns on me, what if he's *not* sleeping? I've left him outside and I don't know if he's even breathing. Maybe he's had a heart attack and I'm all cozy inside making breakfast as if I don't have a care in the world. I bang on the window, frantic now, not sure if I should call 911 or just break into the car and give him CPR. What if he's had a stroke? I mean, I didn't know he had a wife, so maybe he has a heart condition or suffered from a seizure and he needs me to save him. There could be a lot of things I don't know about him.

Pounding my fist against the window with all my strength doesn't get him to budge. My heart thumps in my chest as I make a quick dash into the house, enter the garage through the kitchen, and grab my toolbox. Securing it under my arm, I race back outside, and, kneeling down on the grass, rummage in the metal box before grabbing the heaviest hammer I can find. Lifting it up in the air, I bring it down hard against the glass, which results in the slenderest of cracks.

I can't believe this. Did I actually say I wished he were dead? I may have, but it was only because I was angry. I didn't mean it.

Perspiration trickles down my forehead and sweat moistens the palms of my hands, making it difficult to securely tighten my grasp of the hammer, but I manage to bring it up again and then down as hard as I can before the glass shatters and scatters outward. I crouch down and cover my head to avoid being cut by the flying shards.

"What the hell?" David's voice booms out above me, reverberating in the air.

My hands drop to my sides as I stand up on unsteady legs. "You're alive." I pat his arms, tears springing to my eyes. "It was a close call there for a minute, but you're alive."

He shakes his head in confusion. "What are you

talking about and why did you break my car window?" He doesn't sound remotely grateful. As a matter of fact, he sounds irritated, which is pretty *ungrateful*.

"I didn't know how long you'd been out here—if you'd had a heart attack, a seizure or what, so I had to rescue you."

"By breaking my car window?" He scrunches his face, then frowns at the broken glass.

"It was to *save* you," I say with all the patience I can muster. "You could have been dying in there. You hear about people dying all the time in their locked cars when they can't get out."

"That's when babies get stuck in closed cars in the heat, not a grown man."

"You are so ungrateful." Exasperated, I throw my arms up.

"Did it ever occur to you to open the door? That maybe it wasn't locked?"

A muscle twitches along his unshaven jaw. His eyes are heavy as if he hasn't slept in days. Inhaling deeply, I attempt to clear away a curtain of brain fog. It's the same sensation I used to experience when I had to do algebra in middle school. Everything grew murky, letters and numbers merged together in undecipherable configurations. "What are you saying?"

"The car door isn't locked." He mumbles something unintelligible under his breath. "You're really something else." A slow smile spreads across his face, eventually making its way up to his eyes. "Admit it, you really do care about me."

Embarrassed by the whole broken-window fiasco, I decide to ignore his last statement. "I'm sorry about that." I assess what little is left of the passenger side window. "I'll replace it."

"Don't worry about it." He holds up a hand. "I have my own mistakes to atone for." He glances at the house. "Can we go inside? We need to talk."

Once we're in the kitchen, I pour him a mug of coffee and place it on the table in front of him.

"Thank you," he says, taking a sip. "This coffee is perfect."

The words bring up memories of Uncle Robert's negative comparison of my coffee to my mother's. Of course, it was never *really* about the coffee; I just didn't know it at the time. But that was then—part of my past—and now I've moved on from all that guilt and pain.

I block out the troubling images, glad I won't be eating breakfast alone. I set the food on the table, then place a plate and silverware in front of David before taking my seat across from him. We eat in silence, each of us lost in our own thoughts.

"It all started here." Setting down his fork, he grabs my hand and squeezes it as he glances around the kitchen. "Well, it started at the door, but what I remember most is you standing at that sink over there, water dripping down your blouse and you pretending like it was nothing out of the ordinary."

"I know. Ridiculous, right?" I sigh, tilt my head to the side, and glance up at him. "The truth is, I was so worried about the meeting I had spent hours rehearsing for going well that when Jared showed up, he threw me off my game."

"I get it. I know something about events not turning out the way you plan. When I got married, I thought I would eventually fall in love with my wife."

"What do you mean?" Confused, I place my mug on the table. "Isn't it supposed to be the other way around? First comes love and then marriage?"

"That's the way it should be." He nods. "But, at that time, I didn't believe that people fell in love—at least, not how they do in movies. The way I pictured it, there was a certain order to life." Scoffing at his own words, he shakes his head. "I planned out every detail, thinking that I had a foolproof strategy. First establish your career, then you get married to someone you are compatible with, and then eventually you go on to have two to three children. I thought you grew to love a person, not that it could ever happen spontaneously… or the other way around."

He pauses, his ebony eyes focusing on me for so long that I turn away, uncomfortable with the intensity of his gaze.

"It probably explains why our marriage was doomed from the beginning. It's been over for Courtney and me for years. I escaped into my work and tried to ignore the fact that we were both miserable but pretending to be happily married. I never did fall in love with her. Ultimately, we weren't right for each other. But we kept deceiving ourselves. I worked longer and longer hours and she kept herself busy with other people, no doubt searching for the love and affection that I was unable to provide. We should *never* have gotten married, but we were too young and obstinate to admit it."

"Still, you should have clued me in on your marital status," I say, torn between wanting to hold on to my anger and feeling relieved to know that he wasn't strung out on the woman he'd married. "I was caught off-guard and embarrassed when Courtney came storming into your parents' house. I felt like a fool."

"Everything happened so quickly—you spending the night at my place after being with your dad at the hospital, and then seeing you standing along the side of the road. I hadn't planned any of it." He wraps his hand around mine. "You were like a hurricane that blew me away. I made a ton of mistakes. I'm sorry about not being upfront with you about my ex-wife and saying some asinine things back at the office. I didn't mean what I said. You are the most incredible woman I've ever met."

"I accept your apology." I move my hands out from under his, then fold them in my lap. "We both need time to figure things out. So much has changed during the last month. You don't know half of it." I look down, think of my sweet baby brother Julian and wish he hadn't had an asthma attack that night—that he'd lived long enough to grow up and experience a rich full life. He was the one child my mother truly loved. At least the burden of believing it was my fault is finally gone.

"I don't need to know everything now, but I do know you and that's all that matters."

"You say that now, but you come from a normal family and… well… I don't." I have to be honest with him. Appearances can be deceiving. The grounds are beautiful at the ranch, but my family history is ugly. Who would want to be part of it?

I look out the window, taking comfort, as usual, in nature—the golden grass turning green once again and the lushness of the purple bougainvillea vines spread out along the wire fence. The rain has cleared the sky so that the white clouds look especially bright against the blue horizon.

"You come from good people. No one's family is perfect. I knew your father and he was a fine man. You can't try to deny that you and Morgan are close. I know everything I need to know about you. If you ever want to tell me more, you can. It's up to you. But I'm *not* going anywhere. There's nothing you can say that can ever turn me away from you. You're the best thing that's ever happened to me."

When he looks at me, his eyes brimming with tenderness, I know what it feels like to be cherished.

Blinking away the tears that threaten to fall, I swallow my fears and decide to believe every word he's saying. "Why were you sitting in your car?" I caress the stubble on his face. "Why didn't you come to the front door?"

Clearing his throat, he says, "I needed to talk to you, but I wasn't sure what to say, and while I sat out there, I fell asleep." He rubs his jaw, looking reflective.

"What did you want to tell me?" Knowing he's not an impetuous man, I'm curious about what was so important that he would sit outside in his car all night.

"I knew I had blown it." His eyes cloud over. "What I couldn't figure out was a way to make it right, so I talked to a couple of people."

"Really? What did they say?"

"Before I can reveal that, you have to sit closer to me." He pulls my chair over so I'm sitting beside him.

"Okay." Laughing, I roll my eyes. "I'm listening…" This close, I feel the heat of his body and smell his scent, something between musk and cedar. "But, first, you have to tell me who gave you this advice."

"I wish I could, but I'm kind of sworn to secrecy," he says, somberly.

"What do you mean, *kind of*? You are either sworn to secrecy or not." I eye him suspiciously.

"Okay, then, I can't tell you their names, but I can share their advice."

"You have my full attention." In all honesty, it's a struggle to not be distracted by his nearness, to suppress the longing to be in his arms and feel his lips pressed against mine.

"One told me to trust you." When he brushes back my bangs, it feels good to no longer be self-conscious about my scar. "I think that's good advice, don't you?"

"Yes. You should try it."

"I plan to—starting now." He responds to my smile with a somber expression. "I do trust you. It took me some time to realize it, but I do."

Raising my chin up with his finger, he brings our lips together and I hold onto him, feeling like I've been given a lifeline as I savor the tingling sensations moving through my body.

It's only been a week and I've missed him. How did I let that happen? I place my hands between us, creating some distance so I can think clearly. "You said there were two things?"

"There are. I was told that I needed to make a grand gesture because, well, I forgot to tell you something important."

I don't know if he looks more embarrassed or contrite.

"I love you. You probably know that by now." He furrows his brows. "I'll be damned if I know how that happened, but it did."

"You don't look too happy about it." I'm not sure how to react to his declaration. A part of me is overjoyed. When we made love, I knew that what we had was something special. What I didn't know was if I was the only one whose world had been flipped into a tailspin.

"Happy can't begin to describe how I feel about you. I never thought this kind of love existed and now, I *know* it does. I've been going crazy since you walked out of my life. I want you by my side forever."

He pulls a small white box out of his pocket and opens it. Inside, two square amethysts surround a stunning circular diamond ring. "This is how much I love you. Will you, Elaine Hart, marry me?"

"Wow." I can't stop myself from laughing with joy as I wrap my arms around his neck. "That's some grand gesture, Mr. Cole. Of course, I love you and may even consider marriage since I've paid off my family's debt." I kiss his jawline. "So, it's not like I'd be breaking my rule of never mixing work and pleasure."

"Now that you own your land outright, I don't believe we need to worry about that, do we?" There's a spark in his eyes as his lips trail kisses down my neck.

"No, we don't." Who would have ever thought I'd marry Ol' Man Cole? "You're not at all like what I was expecting. You're much better." I run my fingers through his dark, tightly curled hair.

"Believe me, my love, you are, too." He leans back. The heat in his gaze as he peruses my body sets me on fire. "I'm so glad your father invited me by the house." He slips his hands under my robe and moves them up my thighs.

I gasp in delight as his fingers explore further. "My father was always watching out for me. He may have known exactly what he was doing that day."

Under my breath, I whisper a soft *thank you* to my father, confident that he's looking down on us right now and feeling pleased with the way things turned out.